PUZZLE ME DEAD

KATHY CHILDS

Jamuna
Press

Published in Australia by
Jamuna Press
Postal: PO Box 92, Port Melbourne, Victoria 3207, Australia
Email: kathychildswrites@gmail.com
Website: www.kathychilds.com

First published in Australia 2020
Copyright © Kathy Childs 2020

National Library of Australia Cataloguing in Publication entry

 A catalogue record for this
book is available from the
National Library of Australia

ISBN: 978-0-6489208-0-9 (paperback)
ISBN: 978-0-6489208-3-0 (hardback)
ISBN: 978-0-6489208-2-3 (epub)

Cover design by Evocative
Layout by Sophie White Design
Printed by Ingram Spark

This book is a work of fiction. Names, characters, places and incidents either are the
product of the author's imagination or are used fictitiously, and any resemblance to
actual persons, living or dead, events or locales is entirely coincidental.

For Dad

The light flickers as if it senses his presence. He is out of place here amongst the solid stone office buildings with their empty glass foyers and cold marble floors. He slides his index finger across the company names etched on the plaque and smiles as he reaches "Montage". He runs his thumb back and forth across the name, softly, like a lover's caress. He treads lightly, keeps his head tilted, his face in shadow, as he moves towards the front doors of the building. He tries the door, his gloved hands pulling on the metal handle. It is locked. He knew it would be. She is so pedantic, so careful in everything she does. The door will remain locked until the security staff arrives. It makes her feel safe. His jacket rustles in the quiet of the morning as he draws the envelope from his pocket. He licks his lips, enjoying the taste of the salty sweat, and then raises the card under the mask to his lips but he does not touch them. The red lip-marks that are imprinted where the stamp should be are not his; they are merely a symbol, a reminder of her past. He holds the envelope a minute longer, savouring the moment, pretending to himself that he may walk away and leave her to her ghosts, but he knows he cannot, will not. This can only end one way. He bends down and pushes the envelope under the glass door, watches as it slides on the marble floor and stops where it cannot be missed. It is done. He bows to the security camera as he leaves. He has preparations to make. The game has just begun.

If she had to say when it all began, she'd pinpoint the moment when he took that photo, the click as the camera shutter fell, capturing a manufactured image of accomplishment, confidence and glamour. But she would have been wrong. It all started a long time before that.

ONE

"Now, if you could just stand against the bookshelf. I'll grab a few shots there." The photographer nodded towards the large bookcase to Careen's left. She glanced in her compact mirror to check her foundation still covered her freckles before moving across.

"Is it possible we can have one with your hair down?" he suggested as he peered through the lens, adjusting the focus.

Careen raised her hand and tucked a few wayward strands of honey-blonde hair back into her tight bun. "I'd rather leave it up. It's who I am at work."

"Can you elaborate on that?" Louise, the journalist, who had been sitting quietly on the sofa until now, perked up.

"No reason. I prefer to wear it that way." However, every time she pictured her future self in Italy, walking along the cobblestone streets, drinking espresso at a little café, her hair was either in a ponytail or floating loosely around her shoulders.

The photographer moved Careen to stand by the window. "Just drop your chin a little. Turn towards Louise." She heard the shutter click a few times. "Good. Now one last picture at your desk. I'd like you standing up with your fingers touching the corner. Now face me." A few more clicks. "All done." He started to pack up his equipment.

"Will you continue to wear your hair up after you've

retired?" Louise asked.

Careen pivoted away. How did Louise know about her retirement? It was confidential. No one was meant to know about that clause in the will.

"I'm not sure what you mean." Careen turned back, her face carefully neutral.

"A little bird told me you were handing over the reins to Chris Maxwell. Thirty-nine years old and retiring. Must be a story in that." Louise smiled. Waited. Pen poised.

"I'm not sure what you're talking about."

"Come on Careen, don't be shy about it." Louise wheedled. "I know that John put a clause in his will and the seven years is up. I'm interested as to why."

"Louise, it's been a pleasure working with you on this article but I have a meeting shortly and I need some time to prepare." Careen indicated towards the door. The meeting was over.

"I have so enjoyed our time together too." Louise clasped her hands and grinned, not a friendly grin, more like the expression on a cat's face just before it devours a canary. "I've pitched an idea for a podcast: 'The life and times of Careen Tamley'. I seem to be garnering some interest."

"Why on earth would you want to do that?"

"You've had an interesting life, Careen. So much pain, so much trauma. It would be good for the public to understand how you rose up and remade yourself after the attack. From victim to success story." Louise edged her glasses up her nose. "From what I understand, the Clown Killer was never caught."

"Victim." Careen spat. "I detest that word." She strode to her office door. "That is a long time in the past and it's over."

"Leaving that aside, you have climbed the corporate ladder extremely fast. You have talent, Careen," Louise added with a smile that didn't reach her eyes, "and an extraordinary amount of luck."

"As John used to say, 'Luck is when hard work meets opportunity.'"

"Well you have definitely had a few opportunities come your way. I'd like to spend some time with you over the next few weeks. Get to know the real Careen Tamley, the woman behind the corporate mask."

Careen coughed, raising her hand to her mouth to hide her discomfort. "I'm sorry, Louise. I'm not interested." She turned and opened the door. "If you'll excuse me, I have a meeting to prepare for."

Louise paused next to Careen. "I've done a draft of the first episode – quite enthralling. I'd love your input. Your side of the story, so to speak." Louise's smile held no warmth. "In particular, your insight on Tony Fisher. Suicide wasn't it?" Louise smirked, turned on her pointed heels and strode out before Careen could respond.

Careen closed the solid oak door and leaned against it. Her retirement was not public knowledge, she hadn't even told Chris yet. She needed to find out where the leak was coming from. And why was Louise interested in Tony?

"I have brought you a fresh coffee." Lei pushed the door open with her shoulder. She had her notebook tucked under one arm and a steaming black coffee balanced carefully on a silver tray along with a small jug of milk. Being only five foot two Lei wore lofty heels, invariably black patent leather and buffed to a high gloss. She was dressed in what Careen joked was her uniform, a navy-blue skirt and long-sleeved white shirt that offset her dark skin and, Careen had lately suspected, hid the bruises inflicted by Lei's partner Gary. Careen had asked Lei about the bruises a few months ago but Lei had dismissed her concerns and said she'd fallen.

"Here is your mail." Lei spoke in what Careen considered "proper Queen's English". Lei had been taught English by an elderly neighbour after she'd arrived from China and had never been introduced to contractions or idioms. "There is an envelope marked personal. I have put that on top. I will have the other mail responded to and ready for you to sign after lunch. Is there anything else?"

Careen took a sip of the coffee and leaned back in her chair. "Yes. I need you to follow something up for me."

"It is about your last appointment?"

"Louise Mears, while researching the article she is writing on my Business Woman of the Year Award, has come across some confidential information. I need you to get in touch with McNaughton & McEwan Investigations. I want them to do a preliminary search on Miss Mears. Who she is, who she sees, what makes her tick. But most importantly I want to know where she is getting her information from."

"I will give them the initial brief and set up a meeting for next week so that you can give them the details." Lei made a note on her pad.

"Can you also set up a lunch with Ben for Tuesday? And I'll need to meet with Chris on Wednesday when he's back from Sydney." She didn't need Chris hearing about her retirement from Louise, and she'd like Ben's advice on what to do about the podcast. After Louise had left, Careen had googled "Louise Mears" and "podcast" and was horrified to discover Louise was a regular guest on the *True Lives and Lies*, a series high on sensationalism and light on truth. The last thing Careen needed was anyone digging into her past.

Careen was about to pick up the top envelope, when her mobile rang. She glanced at the screen and smiled, nodding to Lei that she could go.

"Hey, gorgeous." Warmth infused her. Her best friend Mel may live on the other side of the world these days but after twenty-two years of friendship, so much laughter and more than a few tears, a mere ocean couldn't separate them. "How was the tour?"

As Mel updated her on her latest whirlwind tour Careen settled back into her chair, laughing along with her, gasping with Mel's audacity and shaking her head in disbelief, even though Mel couldn't see her. She'd love to be more like Mel – so confident, so carefree, so exuberant.

"Enough about me, tell me the latest on your trip," Mel said.

"It's going to be so good, Mel. No deadlines, no meetings." It was easy to tell the lie over the phone; hell, it was easy enough to lie face to face if you had enough practise. "Imagine me, footloose and fancy-free. Now there's a shift. It'll be great."

If she repeated it often enough maybe she'd believe it. Perhaps then she could begin to tamp down the fear of filling in all those blank hours; the dark, lonely nights. She could set up a schedule, with walks, sights to see, perhaps book some tours? Careen snickered.

"What?" Mel asked.

"I was just thinking about how I could put together a calendar of activities."

Mel barked out a laugh. "Yep. That sounds like the Careen I know."

"I've always wanted this, Mel. To travel. To spend time in Italy."

Her voice was wistful. Hope mixed with fear. She wondered if she had the courage. Could she do this? Leave everything behind. She wasn't even sure who she was anymore. When she was no longer Careen Tamley, CEO of Montage, who would be left? She wanted to tell Mel that this wasn't just a holiday; that she was resigning from the hotel chain, but she was still struggling with the enormity of it all. It wasn't as if it was her idea.

"Careen, you need this break."

"I know. But why does it feel so scary?"

"It doesn't need to be. You know your limitations. Just stay within them."

And there it was. Stay in well-lit places. Never park in a high-rise car park. Only stay out after dark if you're with others. A circus was to be avoided at all costs and never ever stray to a sideshow at a fair. She'd been following the rules for twenty years now. How much longer before the nightmares stopped? Before she felt safe.

"Tell me about the place you've chosen." Mel interrupted Careen's thoughts.

"There's an Airbnb apartment in Amalfi, right on the coast. I'll send you a link." Her voice projected an enthusiasm she didn't feel.

"No, tell me about it. That way I can get excited about visiting you."

"It's a tiny one-bedroom apartment in this windy narrow street. The houses appear to be all tangled together. The host actually lives in the one next door." She especially loved the photo of the stairway up to the front door – each step was neatly edged with a blue tile and had a red or golden flower in the centre. Careen scanned the screen in front of her. "There's a piazza nearby. The apartment gets the morning sun and the listing says the kitchen is small but functional."

"Like you'll be cooking anyway." Mel countered. Careen had never mastered the art of cooking. A basic salad or a boiled egg was about her limit. "I bet there are plenty of those wonderful trattorias in that piazza of yours."

"Absolutely. I'll be the size of a house in no time on a diet of pizza and pasta."

Careen was tall and slim; the stress of her job seemed to keep the weight off.

"Yeah, right. I'd kill for your metabolism."

Mel had always had to work hard to stay in shape. She was a

naturally curvy brunette who had a predilection for chocolate and desserts.

"You could try staying off the sugar."

"Cut out your tongue, girl. You know how that worked out last time."

Careen laughed as she recalled how bitchy Mel had become after two weeks on a sugar-free diet. In the end Careen had been buying the chocolate éclairs for her. They'd been through a lot together, both before and after that night.

"Back on track. More info please." Mel had always refused to let Careen dwell.

"The apartment has a tiled balcony that's just big enough for a chair and table. Imagine me sitting in the sun, sipping coffee, while watching hot fishermen bringing in the daily catch. Hey, perhaps I can take up fishing?"

The laughter that came down the line was free and unfettered. Mel loved to laugh and did it often. "Really, Careen. You. Fishing?"

"I'd get someone else to clean them."

"Of course you would."

"I can't wait to see you. It feels like forever." Mel was due to fly to Melbourne for an overnight stay next week. Careen wondered how she'd go with the lies face to face. Should she tell Mel everything? 'Full disclosure' they used to say. But that was before.

It was late and Careen was tired. She started putting her desk in order when she noticed the square faux-linen envelope that Lei had left on her desk before she'd left for the day. It was embossed and clearly expensive. Where the stamp should be was an imprint of red lips. She smiled – a secret admirer perhaps. She raised it to her nose, breathing in. Nothing. Turning it over she noticed a single word where the return address should be – "Pagliaccio". Strange. She'd never heard of the place. A restaurant, perhaps, or a club. Promotional material most likely, a new marketing stunt. The envelope, however, appeared to be empty. She turned it upside down and a small piece of dark-grey jigsaw fell on her desk – an edge piece. Perplexed she picked it up and turned it over. On the back, written in black ballpoint pen, was the number twelve. She picked up the envelope again. Pagliaccio. She typed it into Google. *Pagliaccio – the clown*. Careen dropped the envelope. Kicked it away from her. Scooted back, her feet pushing her wheeled office chair away from her desk, away from the clown images on the computer screen. Her chair hit the bookshelf and she lurched to a stop, her breathing ragged.

It was meant to be over. It was twenty years ago. Was this some sort of joke? Who would do this? She stood up, smoothed down her skirt, wheeled her chair back to her desk, and stood behind it staring at the screen. Breathe. In and out. In and out. In. And. Out. Other than the word "Pagliaccio" there was nothing to tie it to *him*. It was a jigsaw piece with a number on it. Nothing more. She couldn't even distinguish what the jigsaw picture was. The number twelve could mean anything.

She picked up the envelope and dropped it in the bin along with the jigsaw piece. She felt her face flush, embarrassed by her overreaction. If Louise hadn't mentioned the Clown Killer today she probably wouldn't have even made the connection. It's just a word. It would be some newfangled marketing technique. The latest gimmick thought up by some young go-getter. She'd likely get a few more before they decided to let her know what the product was – provoke some interest then swoop in. Maybe it would work for them, whatever they were selling with an Italian name and a clown, but from now on she'd have Lei open all mail, marked personal or not.

Careen forced herself to walk out to the executive kitchen to make a cup of tea. She ran her hands up and down her arms, rubbing to brush away the chill. She heated the teapot, swirling around the boiling water. She added two level spoons of fresh tea leaves to the pot then more hot water, breathing in the steam and herbal aroma. Careen picked her favourite cup and saucer from the drying rack and set them on a tray alongside the teapot and strainer. When everything was in place she carried the tray back to her office, ignoring the rattling china from her still shaking hands.

The tea had calmed her, and the thirty minutes of budgeting spreadsheets had ensured her focus was elsewhere. She'd left a message for Chris, her chief operating officer, earlier on in the day and wanted to speak with him before signing off the numbers.

"Ciao." Careen answered her phone as it rang as if on cue. Chris was aware that she was planning a trip to Italy and had been coaching her in the language. But instead of a "Ciao, signora capo" there was silence. Careen gripped the receiver, her knuckles white. She swallowed several times, trying to ease the sudden dryness in her throat. She should have told Chris to ring her mobile.

"I take it you're not fluent in Italian then?" Careen heard the tremor in her voice. Hated herself for it. "Hola? Bonjour? Yassas perhaps?" There was only the breathing. Even breaths. Calm. She could be calm too. "Okay we'll go with 'hello' shall we?" Her tone was stronger, firmer. It was only because of the envelope and the conversation with Louise that she was rattled. There was no need to be. None of these things was related. One was a marketing stunt, the calls were – well, she wasn't sure what they were. And Louise, she was just playing games. The humming started up. "You are consistent, I must say. And even quite persistent, but I'm tired of this game." The humming increased in volume. "Enough," she barked.

Careen knew the tune, just couldn't place it. Every time she thought she was close it was as if her mind shut down, pushed it back out of reach and buried the answer deep inside. She slowly replaced the receiver. Three times each week, the same call, the same tune. Intermittent calls at random times, but always on her private office line. She started humming the tune. It was catchy she had to admit. A memory stirred. The words to the tune began to surface.

"Send in the clowns ... No!" Her voice was shrill and echoed in the empty office. "No. No. No. No. No." She propelled herself away from her desk, the wheels of her chair catching on the carpet. She shot up out of the chair, rubbing her arms, suddenly feeling cold again. Glanced out the window. She could see herself reflected in the glass, backlit against her office. Exposed. Alone. Could he see her? The building opposite was dark. She searched the black for movement as she backed up against the door, her hand feeling for the dimmer switch. She turned down the lights, leaving a soft glow. She couldn't handle the dark. She moved her hand towards the doorknob, then froze. What if he was outside the door? She clicked the lock, slid down to the floor, wrapped her arms around her knees and dropped her head, closing her eyes.

She saw it again then, the image ingrained in her memory. The scarred white clown mask with blood red tears and sharp teeth. She shook her head to make it disappear, to delete the image. It remained. She slid across to the bookshelf keeping the door and the wall at her back. Grabbing a heavy statue, she dropped back to the floor, knees pulled up against her chest, tears streaming down her face. Weighing and balancing the solid marble bust in her hand, she breathed deeply to calm herself. It couldn't be him. That was twenty years ago. She had been a different person then. Only a girl. A frivolous girl. But what if it was him? Why now? When she'd almost got up the courage to walk down a street in the dark; could, with a little help, sleep through most nights without the nightmares. She wasn't a scatterbrained teenager anymore. She was organised, controlled. He couldn't scare her. She stood up on shaky legs, replaced the statue and reached for a tissue. She blew her nose and wiped the running mascara from under her eyes.

Pagliaccio – "the clown" in Italian. Italy, so far away at the opposite side of the world. A place that should be safe. Would be safe. The phone calls, the tune, the jigsaw – they were here, in Melbourne. But why now? She didn't want to live like that again. She wouldn't live like that again. She reached for her mobile and called her brother Logan.

"Logan, it's Careen." Her voice shook as she left a message. "Logan, call me as soon as you get this. It's important. I'm in my office. I need to see you. Now." He was often quite blasé about things but he would understand. He knew what had happened all those years ago and had held her hand through countless nights when she was too afraid to sleep.

Her office line shrilled. She reached out. Hesitated. It could be Logan phoning back. Using the office line out of habit. She hit the speakerphone button and pushed record on her mobile just in case.

"Logan?"

"No, Princess. Not Logan." A whisper; full of menace.

"Who is this?"

"Don't you remember me? We were close once." She could almost feel his hot breath on the back of her neck, feel the wiry arm that circled her waist and pulled her to him. She whimpered with the memory.

"Ah, it seems you do remember me. How nice."

"What do you want?" Her voice was feeble.

"Just checking you got my little gift?" A harsh laugh echoed down the line.

Careen almost cried out; bit her lip to stop herself. I am not that girl. I am Careen Tamley. I am a strong and successful businesswoman. I am not that stupid naive girl. She sat up straight, placed her feet firmly on the floor. He would not turn back the clock.

"There is no gift and you are not doing this to me." Careen's voice was strong and commanding, a skill she'd perfected over many years in the boardroom. "This is my life and you will not interfere with it again." She jabbed the cancel button and sat, hunched over, shutting her eyes against the memory of his last words. Three words she'd never forget. 'We're not done.'

TWO

The next morning Careen rang the local police station and asked to speak with the detective who had been in charge of her case all those years ago. He'd long since retired and she was shunted around until reaching a Sergeant Lawson who, after a short conversation, agreed to get a copy of the old file and call her back. He'd left her a message earlier in the afternoon, but she'd waited until Lei had left for the day before she called him back.

"Miss Tamley. I've reviewed the case and checked the system. You're correct. No one was ever charged." He clicked his pen. "From what you explained earlier there appears to be a number of inconsistencies with the original case."

"Yes, I know." Careen had had plenty of time to think. "The jigsaw doesn't fit with what he did last time and he never spoke when he phoned. I'm not sure why he would call me 'Princess', either."

"I checked the media releases. The articles did mention the phone calls and the card each year on your birthday. Postcards, according to the file, but this detail wasn't made public – perhaps this person thinks the mail came in envelopes. There is also a mention here of the small cards left on site at the murders and the numbers on them – that did leak to the press, unfortunately. Not sure where the jigsaw fits in."

"He attacked twelve girls. I was the first. I got away. The

other eleven didn't. He killed them. The number twelve on the jigsaw. Pagliaccio. It has to tie in somehow." Careen took a breath to calm down. "Can you trace the calls?"

Sergeant Lawson agreed to try and trace the calls but didn't hold out much hope. There was no point in testing the envelope or jigsaw piece for fingerprints until they had someone to compare them with, but he asked her to put them in a plastic bag and keep it safe.

"So, what happens now?" Careen asked.

"Not much I can do. I've made a note in the file." His pen clicked off and on again. "Given what you have told me, my guess is someone is trying to stir up your past but doesn't quite have all the facts."

"I was sort of hoping that was the case. But could he be back? Perhaps he's just got out of prison after being caught for something else. Can you check if there are any other recent unsolved cases that are similar?"

"I can look. Tell me about the original attack."

Her body went icy cold. *Tell him about it.* Did he have no idea at all? She'd spent the last twenty years trying to forget and he wanted her to go through it again. She closed her eyes, bit her bottom lip hard. How could Sergeant Lawson, a man who feels safe in his world, understand what it's like to wake up at night terrified, with the memory of the killer's breath on the back of her neck, or how it feels to walk down a darkened street always imaging that raspy voice taunting her from the shadows? How could he grasp what it feels like when a guy you are dating puts his arms around you from behind and you freeze, remembering the Clown Killer pulling you to him? How could he ever comprehend how many ways that night affected her life? Like when a friend invites you to her child's birthday party and you are too afraid to go because seeing a clown could send you into meltdown. Just tell him about it, he says.

She sat in her office chair, rocking back and forth, her fingers caressing the aquamarine stone that hung from the chain at her neck, seeking comfort.

"Miss Tamley. Are you still there?"

"Yes." Her voice was croaky.

"If I am to help, I need some further information."

So, she told him about that night, about the five years that followed when the killer sent her a birthday card every year, about the fifteen years of silence, about the fear that he was back.

And when she'd hung up the phone, she put her head on her desk and wept.

She was drained. She so seldom cried. She blew her nose then opened a packet of cleansing towelettes and cleaned her face, reapplied her lipstick. The mirror showed her green eyes were circled in red. There wasn't much she could do about that. She'd put a cold face washer over them when she got home. She tidied up her desk, put everything in its proper place in her desk drawers and, after a last glance to ensure all was where it should be, she locked the office door behind her. It was seven o'clock; early for her to leave the office. She was hesitant as she walked down the dimly lit corridor, staring into the shadows seeking movement, cautiously peering around corners as she walked to the lift. Telling Sergeant Lawson had brought it all back.

Careen stepped out of the brightly lit foyer onto the darkened city street, careful to stay in the middle of the pavement where the most light fell. She breathed deeply, wanting to taste the fresh night air, but it tasted old, like stale petrol fumes trapped in an underground car park. She lifted her pendant and clutched the aquamarine stone. She'd put it on this morning, a talisman for courage, fortitude and peace. She kissed the stone lightly and let it fall back between her breasts. It was all in the past. It couldn't be him, there were inconsistencies, as Sergeant Lawson had pointed out. She consciously unclenched her jaw, tucked a few stray hairs behind her ears and looked around. During the day the commercial district was a bustling hive but as a layer of darkness crept over the city, it became vast expanse of empty streets, unlit alcoves and deserted alleys. Careen scanned the street for anyone watching, then satisfied she was alone, walked briskly down to Collins Street and got into the lone cab sitting at the rank.

This is his favourite part of the day. Observing her is delicious. Like ice cream on a burning-hot afternoon. He watches as she strides down the darkened street, her countenance one of a woman in control, but her furtive glances betray her. He longs to call out to her, to taunt her, but he remains hidden for now.

Careen pulled her apartment door shut behind her, securing it with the safety chain. She dropped her briefcase at her feet and leant heavily against the door. She had spent the whole trip home glancing out the rear window of the cab to see if anyone was following. She didn't want to be that person again. She would not be that person again.

"Princess". John had called her that. She couldn't remember when he started to, or why for that matter, but it had always been a term of endearment and his alone. He'd never used that name when they were in public, only with family. Why use John's pet name? It had no place in that part of her life.

Placing her briefcase under the hall table and her keys in the marble bowl on it, Careen reached for the photo of her, Logan, John and his son Ben. It had been taken after a night of too much wine and plenty of laughter. One of many. How she missed John. It had been seven years since he died and she still thought about him every day. She removed her shoes, placed them neatly on the shoe rack by the door and curled up on the couch, still holding the photo. She had first met John at Logan and Ben's scruffy old single-fronted weatherboard in Essendon. The rented two-bedroom house had a lean-to that served as Ben's art studio. With the exception of the studio, the house was dimly lit for the most part and badly in need of repair. The furniture was third or fourth hand and no one would have defined it as pre-loved. She adored the place. When her parents had died, she'd moved in with Logan and Ben, sleeping on the couch in the lounge, trying each night to find a comfortable position amid the rusted springs.

On the rare occasions John visited he talked almost non-stop about his hotel business, hoping to get Ben enthused. It never happened. Ben wanted to paint. Careen, however, was fascinated, and during these visits she'd caught John's enthusiasm. They started to meet, just her and John, playing chess into the small hours, strolling in the public gardens, talking constantly as they brainstormed answers to all the problems of the world. Her first job had been as a receptionist in one of John's hotels. John became the father she wished she'd had.

No one had been more surprised than her to find she had inherited Montage, the hotel chain John owned. After the shock had worn off, she realised it made sense. John knew she'd take care of it, run it well and make it her own. Ben's passion was painting, and he had repeatedly spurned John's offers to become involved in Montage. He did not want his inheritance. She wondered where she would be today if Tony Fisher had lived – then stopped herself. Remembering another death wasn't going to help her settle tonight.

Feeling melancholy, she rose and poured herself a glass of chilled Pinot Gris, hit play on Spotify and strolled through the apartment as Vivaldi serenaded her. When she'd decided to move into one of the company's hotel apartments, she'd chosen this one specifically for the view – out front was Port Phillip Bay and facing north she could see the city lights in the distance. She'd never intended to stay long term, always meaning to buy a place. It still felt like a temporary abode. It wasn't a home; it was a place to sleep and eat between workdays. She had added a few personal items over the years, mainly gifts from John, Ben or Logan. Her favourite, the sword which hung over the hall table; was ancient, passed down from generation to generation in John's family. He had left it to her in his will. The note that accompanied the gift had explained that the sword represented protection, strength and courage. She ran her finger lightly across the indent in the side of the blade. Did she need protection?

She opened the balcony door, stepped out and stood listening to the wind as it whistled around the corner of the apartment.

"You always said I was too focused and needed to stop and smell the roses occasionally or I'd end up a crotchety old bloke like you." She spoke softly as she always did when talking to John's ghost. "Well time's up, so I suppose I'm going to have to make the best of it." Careen placed both her hands on the balcony rail; leaning out and scanning the dark sky wondering again what the hell she was going to do to fill up her days without Montage.

She moved back inside and was heading to the bedroom to get changed when she spotted her reflection in the mirror. She stopped and stared. The end of a long day and still immaculately groomed. Well, almost. She tucked the stray hairs behind her ears again and then changed her mind and pulled out the pins and bands that held her bun in place. Her hair tumbled past her shoulders and she shook her head to feel the freedom. She smiled at her reflection, the softer Careen.

When I'm in Italy I'll wear it down every day. She bunched her hair up and tested out the ponytail then dropped it, letting it flow loose again. She looked younger – felt younger – with her hair down, more like the teenage Careen who had spent her nights cutting out pictures of exotic places from travel magazines and pasting them in her scrapbooks.

She took a sip of her wine, placed the glass on a coaster on the coffee table and was heading to the bedroom to change when her mobile rang. She reached into her bag, checked the number. Blocked. She pushed the decline button and threw the phone onto the coffee table nearly knocking over the wine. She sank down on the nearest sofa and picked up the glass, the ripples in the liquid emphasising how much her hands were shaking. She set it back down carefully on the coaster and stared at the phone. She didn't want to be alone tonight with her thoughts, her memories. Mel was in New York and waking her up seemed selfish. She'd understand Careen's fear and offer to fly back to Melbourne. She was not going to drag Mel all the way here just because some sick bastard was playing games. Then she realised Logan hadn't called her back yesterday. She grabbed her phone and texted him to call her then sat sipping her wine as she stared at her phone, willing it to ring. She smiled as Logan's picture came up on the screen as it rang.

"What's up, sis? Better be important, I was ... otherwise occupied." Careen could imagine Logan winking at his latest girlfriend. His neatly trimmed ginger beard would hide his dimples but his wicked smile always shone through.

"I—" Careen started but Logan interrupted her.

"Hang on." Careen heard a soft laugh and a whisper. "I'm back. You've got five minutes then I need to jump in the shower. It's Sam's birthday tonight and we're having a quick bite at Naked in the Sky, then partying on."

"You didn't return my call."

"Sorry, wall-to-wall meetings. You're the one who sent me off to Adelaide to charm and entertain. Which, I must admit, I did with aplomb."

"Logan, we need to talk. It's important."

"Isn't it always with you, sis? So serious all the time. Work hours are over for the day. Hey, how about coming out with us tonight. There'll be quite a crowd. You might get lucky and meet Mister Right. In fact maybe I could be the one to introduce you two."

"Logan ..."

"Sam's brother's single. Tall, dark, lawyer type. Serious. Works long hours. Should suit you to a tee." Given the slurring Careen was beginning to wonder how long Logan had already been celebrating.

"Logan." She tried to keep the exasperation out of her voice.

"Or her cousin. Short and stocky. Plays football, I think. Runs his own business too. Probably too lowly though, only a plumber. Or a friend of mine who's here from out of town. Now there's a match."

"Oh, Logan, why can't you just listen for a change? Think about someone other than yourself."

"Ouch. Here I am trying to help you to get a social life, which, I might add, you are in serious need of, and you say I'm only thinking of myself. Hardly fair."

Careen sighed. She should have known better. Logan spent his life caught up in the moment, *his* moment. She needed him to come over, to be with her, to be a supportive brother. It wasn't going to happen.

"So what did you ring for?" Finally it seemed to dawn on him that there might be a reason for the call.

"There's some weird stuff happening at work and I'm a bit freaked." How much to tell him? "I wondered if you wouldn't mind staying over here tonight."

"Actually, we're about to head out. How about you join us? Then you can camp on our couch tonight."

Just what she needed, a night out lurching from pub to club, walking down dark streets with endless shadowy corners. She'd be safer here.

"Don't worry about it, Logan. Let's talk tomorrow."

"If you change your mind about coming, check my Instagram, it'll have where we are."

Careen hung up the phone and wandered back over to the window. She wished Ben was in town. Calling him when he was overseas would only worry him. He'd be back on Monday night and Lei had booked lunch for Tuesday; she'd talk to him then.

She sipped her wine, surprised to find it was no longer chilled. She'd get security to change her private office number in the morning and they could monitor the old line and perhaps get a trace on it. And letting the few people who had her personal mobile number know it had changed wasn't going to be too hard. She felt herself relax as common sense overrode her fears. With her logic firmly in place Careen settled into the sofa with a fresh glass of wine.

She'd just picked up the latest Jack Reacher novel, when the intercom buzzed. She froze, the menacing voice on the phone yesterday echoing in her head.

"Jesus, girl. Stop panicking," she admonished herself out loud. She'd chosen an apartment in the hotel over a residential complex because of the tight security, and the video monitor would show her who was calling. She peered into the fuzzy grey screen and saw Phillip, the delivery boy from Manzi's Satay Bar. Perplexed, she pushed the speak button.

"Yes?"

"Takeaway for you, Miss Tamley."

"You must have it wrong. I didn't order any takeaway tonight."

"Miss Tamley, this is your order. Like you get every week."

"But I didn't order any takeaway tonight."

"Perhaps someone else ordered it for you? I can check. It's chicken satay, Gado Gado with extra chilli, just like you ask for."

It was her regular order.

"Hang on, there's a note." She saw him pull a small slip of paper out of his pocket. "Dinner's on me tonight." He gave her a winning smile.

Logan. It was obviously a peace offering for being so preoccupied on the phone. He'd done this before when he felt he'd offended her; always sure he could buy her off, as if one thoughtful gesture would outweigh any number of selfish ones. Careen buzzed the security release and opened her door.

THREE

Careen massaged her temples as she waited for the head waiter. She was tired from a combination of a lack of sleep and the unsettling dreams when she finally fell asleep. The cramped light-rail trip to the office this morning hadn't helped. She'd slept through her alarm and didn't have time to walk as she usually would so had jumped on the light rail, along with the disembarking cruise-ship passengers and all their luggage. She'd ended up hot and out of sorts and this morning's meetings hadn't improved her mood. Where was that damn waiter? Didn't he know she'd been standing here forever?

"Yes miss?" The head waiter finally deemed to speak with her.

"I have a reservation for Tamley. For two."

"Yes. Booth seven over by the window."

Ben was running late as usual, so after being shown her table, Careen detoured to the ladies'. Entering the mirror-laden room she rolled her shoulders hoping to release some of the tension. She checked her appearance in the mirror. Her hair was tied back in a severe bun, but it inevitably seemed to escape its confines. She tucked the stray strands behind her ears, then decided it was more flattering loose. A few freckles were starting to show beneath the foundation and she powdered them out. She stood with her shoulders back admiring herself. The heels she wore highlighted the shape of her legs and the pencil skirt showed off her slim figure. She smiled. Not bad. Hope he notices.

Careen spotted Ben as he entered the restaurant. His hair had a streak of purple today. Ben had a habit of pushing back his shoulder-length hair with his hands when painting, which meant there was often a colourful addition to its sandy blond strands.

Careen stood up and gave Ben a generous hug, holding herself against his warm chest and breathing in his scent. "I've missed you."

Ben's return hug was just as warm, but instead of releasing her he took her shoulders in his slender hands and pushed her away. Holding her at arms-length he scrutinised her.

"You're looking tired. What's up?"

So much for the pep talk in the ladies' room.

"Actually I was feeling fine until you ruined it." She laughed to soften the comment, to hide the hurt.

"Oops sorry." Ben dropped a kiss on her nose. "Let's grab a seat and a drink then we can catch up properly." He slid into the booth. "So what's up?"

"What makes you think something's up? Can't I just catch up for lunch with an old friend?"

Ben laughed. "I don't even think you know you do it."

"Do what?"

"Get Lei to call when it's business."

"Sorry. I don't get you."

"If you want to catch up with me because we're friends you text or call me. If you need to discuss something about business, you get Lei to set up lunch or dinner."

Careen thought for a minute. "That transparent?"

"Clear as day and all that." Ben signalled to the waitress. "Let's order before we talk, I'm starving."

Watching him across the table while he ordered her favourite dishes, she wondered for the hundredth time why she and Ben had never been more than friends.

"Looking very serious there, my girl."

"Why have I never been just that, Ben – your girl?" Careen blurted out.

Ben hooted. "There's a big question. What brought this on?"

"You're not allowed to answer a question with a question, you know." A rule they had made way back when she was staying with Logan and Ben after the death of her parents. Before John. Long before she had inherited the Montage hotel chain.

"Does that still apply?" Ben raised his left eyebrow.

"Today it does." Careen tilted her head and looked into Ben's hazel eyes. "Ben. Seriously. Why?"

"I've often wondered that myself. I remember when Logan first introduced us." He closed his eyes as if to conjure up the picture. "You were in cut-off jeans and a negligible top. You had bare feet and your toenails were painted cobalt blue." He opened his eyes and grinned cheekily. "I could have sworn your legs went all the way up to your armpits. You and Logan must have been mucking around and your eyes were alight, the green sparkling with mischief. I remember standing there thinking, "Wow", with a capital W." He smiled at the memory. "Logan was having none of it and told me to keep my hands to myself. And we both know, crossing Logan isn't the smartest of ideas."

"So I've Logan to blame then?" Careen barely remembered being that girl, that naive guileless girl.

"Yeah. That and we risk mucking up a good friendship if things go south." Taking a sip of his cold beer he grinned. "In hindsight I should have asked you out years ago; would have pleased Dad no end. The daughter he never had becoming the daughter-in-law."

"Hey slow down. I was trying for a date not a proposal." He'd date her to please his father, but that was about it. Why did she bother? "So how are things going with Cherie?"

"Cherie? Oh she's long gone. It's Margot now."

"God, Ben. I can't keep up." And she didn't want to. Ben flirted with her but that was it. There was always a Cherie or Margot around, almost as if Ben kept them as a buffer between him and Careen. She had to let go and move on. Maybe a tall, hunky Italian would be just the ticket.

"So tell me, how did it go in Florence?" Ben had been interviewing for a commission with a well-to-do family.

"They have shortlisted me and one other – an American I haven't come across before. It's for seventeen portraits, the whole extended family. They're an interesting bunch with, I gather, somewhat 'diverse' interests so it could be quite challenging."

"And what do you think your chances are?"

"Quite good, actually. They loved the review by Bortolotti, apparently he's Italian too, which is how I came to their attention in the first place."

"Which review was that?"

Ben put on a decidedly bad Italian accent. "Looking at Ben Seymour's paintings is like gazing deep into the essence of a person. His talent in portraits is unmatched, as is his ability to infuse the canvas with a person's intrinsic nature." The hand gestures he improvised did not help the imitation at all.

Careen laughed. "If so, when will you start?" She'd had always been one of Ben's greatest advocates.

"As soon as I get the go ahead. There'll be a bit of travelling as the family are spread across five different countries, but luckily there are a few of them here in Melbourne so I won't be constantly away."

"Maybe we'll cross paths. If you make it to Amalfi that is."

"Amalfi now, is it?"

"I found this amazing little place ..."

Careen filled him in on the apartment she'd seen the week before. Their lunch arrived and they settled in to eat.

"So what's the real reason for lunch?" Ben asked between mouthfuls.

"We have a problem."

Ben sipped his beer. "What sort of problem?"

"Her name is Louise Mears."

"Isn't she the chick who's writing that article on you? I had a message from her the other day on my voicemail."

"Please tell me you didn't call her back."

"Me? You know I'm hopeless with that sort of thing. So what's this Louise Mears done to you?"

"She's decided that one article is not enough and I'm getting a podcast too. *True Lives and Lies.*"

She sat quietly while Ben digested this information. She had learnt long ago that he would always think before he responded.

"Haven't heard of that one. The title doesn't sound promising though."

"I did some research; it's high on sensationalism, low on facts. They do interviews with friends and family of the subject and then edit them for best effect. She seems to have a particular interest in the attack and how I rebuilt myself afterwards." Careen took a sip of wine. "She's also chasing down the story about Tony." Careen had decided on the way over not to worry Ben about the jigsaw or calls. She would handle that on her own for now.

"Remind me not to call her back."

"Ben. I'm not sure what to do. The lawyers say there's very little I can do to stop her doing this. Redress for defamation is hard and Louise undoubtedly knows the line to walk on this.

And she will also know that I can only go court after the fact. The damage is done by then." She picked up her wine glass and was surprised to find it empty. Careen put her hand over the top as the waitress leant over to refill it. She didn't like to have more than one at lunch. "She also seems to know that I'm handing over Montage to Chris to run. She has someone feeding her information."

"Shit. I didn't think you had told Chris yet."

"I haven't. He's away in Sydney so I'll talk to him tomorrow morning."

"And Logan? You have to hope she doesn't get to Logan before you do."

"You think I don't know that, Ben. This was meant to be a smooth transition. I'm finding it hard enough as it is." She picked up her empty wine glass again and wished she'd let the waitress refill it.

"You need this, Careen. Dad knew it too, that's why the seven years." He paused, sipped his beer. "As long as you get to Chris first, does it matter?"

"Ben what if she digs into the Tony affair?" Careen wanted him to understand how serious this was. "Seven years in the will. Seven years till someone is legally declared dead. What if she connects the dots?"

"Careen." He grabbed her hand, squeezed it. "I don't think there's any link with the seven years. We've been over this. Dad wouldn't do that."

"You don't see it, but what if Louise does?"

"It's old news now. No one's interested."

"It rather depends on how she spins it. Doesn't it?"

"Mr de Paul, please take a seat." Careen indicated the black sofas to the man who appeared to be more like a prize-fighter than a private investigator. He handed her his business card. Gordon de Paul, Senior Investigator, McNaughton & McEwan Investigations. His enormous hand engulfed hers and his handshake was firm, but not overpowering. A man with nothing to prove. "I was expecting Jill McEwan."

"She's busy. You got me."

"I see. Will you and Miss McEwan be working together?"

"We both work there. We both do a good job. I'm not as pretty as her, but I'm just as competent." Not as pretty was an understatement. Careen wondered if she'd ever seen a nose that large and pointed before. Unlikely. She reconsidered the prize-fighter opinion – that nose would have been the first thing to go.

"I understand my PA, Lei, has filled you in on a few basics, Mr de Paul." Careen walked over to the second sofa.

"Name's Gordon. Mr de Paul's my father." His voice was firm, like his handshake. "Now let's get the facts down." Careen watched Gordon as he sat, opened his notebook and then glanced up, obviously surprised to find her still standing. "Are you going to sit, or not?"

Careen smiled and sat.

"My understanding is that you are seeking to dig up some dirt on Louise Mears. Am I correct?"

"That's not quite how I would put it."

"How would you put it then?" His eyes were sharp and he was studying her.

"What I am after is some background on Louise Mears. Who she is, who her contacts are and how she's getting hold of confidential information from within this organisation."

"Which is?" He was a man short on words, it appeared.

"I've been CEO of Montage since I inherited the company from John Seymour. I'm retiring now that it has been seven years since I took over and handing over the role of CEO to Chris Maxwell, my second in charge. Louise has somehow got hold of this information, which has not yet been made public."

"Why seven years?"

"As part of the agreement for me inheriting the Montage hotel chain I was granted the role of CEO for seven years." Careen stood. She hated discussing this part of her agreement, the ties that bound her and then forced her to leave. "After seven years I'm required to retire and appoint someone to replace me as CEO. If I chose to remain as CEO the will is void."

"Void? Everything in the will, or just your shares in the company?"

"I get to keep the personal effects John left me and the cash endowment, but I lose Montage."

"And the other beneficiaries. How do your actions affect them?"

"It doesn't impact them at all. Only me."

"And if the timeline changes?"

"If I stay a minimum of five years, I get to retain Montage. If I delay beyond the seven years, I forfeit my rights to it."

She moved to the window and stared down to the streets below, watched tiny people scurrying to and fro. Seven years. That number had always haunted her. Ben might dismiss it, but Careen couldn't. It takes seven years for a person to be legally declared dead. And it was a death that had changed so much. John had been quite insistent in telling her it wasn't her fault, but she wondered if subconsciously he had still held her to blame.

"Are we still having a conversation or are you happy just to enjoy the view?" Gordon, it seemed, lacked a few social skills.

"Just getting it straight in my head."

"Should have done that before I arrived." He muttered under his breath. "Who other than yourself was aware of this codicil?"

"The executor of the will, the legal team who drew it up, Ben and myself."

"And Ben is?"

"John's son."

"And is there a reason you inherited rather than him?"

"Ben didn't want Montage. He's a portrait artist and has little interest in business. He receives a share of the profits, but I hold the controlling interest."

"So he says," Gordon murmured. "I'll need the name of the executor and the firm that handled the will." Gordon paused and glanced at his notes. "You didn't mention Chris Maxwell as one of the people who knows."

"I have a meeting with Chris tomorrow. The actual time frame for this wasn't for a few months, but now that Louise Mears has this information I have to make sure he hears it from me and not someone else."

"Any chance this Maxwell chap decided to move the schedule up?"

"No. Chris is one of the most straightforward people you are likely to meet. If he'd heard something he would have come straight to me."

"Who else could have an interest?"

The meeting with Gordon had taken up most of the rest of her afternoon, but he assured her she would have a preliminary report by the end of the week. He seemed gruff, but for some reason Careen quite liked him. She'd responded to an email from Louise declining an interview and told Lei not to forward any more of Louise's calls. That woman was certainly persistent.

Careen picked up the fresh tea Lei had delivered, cupped it between her hands, rose and stood to gaze out of the plate-glass window. The Yarra River glistened with reflections, a shimmering ribbon of life winding its way through Melbourne. She'd miss this view. Chris, she knew, would be happy when she told him about her retirement from Montage. She was sure he would select Murray to fill his old role, and she thought it the right decision. But whichever way the puzzle fitted together, there didn't seem to be a place for Logan.

FOUR

Chris knocked, casually leaning on the doorframe. He filled the doorway. It wasn't just his stocky frame or the fact that he topped out at six foot, four inches; it was his presence. He commanded attention and spoke only when he had something worth saying; and when you were speaking, he gave you his undivided attention. With his arresting blue eyes and focused manner he was an exceptional and charismatic leader. Careen knew how lucky she was that he was there to take charge of the Montage Group.

Careen returned his smile warmly. "How was dinner last night?" Chris and his partner Edward had celebrated their ten-year anniversary last night and Careen had managed to secure them a booking at Dinner by Heston.

"Wonderful. I'd thought that it was all hype, but it lived up to its reputation. Edward was over the moon and said to make sure I gave you a big hug from him."

"I'm glad. So, what did you get him as a present?"

"A single stone tanzanite ring set in white gold. You know how he is about jewellery. I'm most definitely partner of the year at the moment."

Careen chuckled. "Make the most of it." She gestured towards the lounge chairs. "Thanks for coming in so early."

Chris settled into the plush armchair, his long legs crossed in front of him.

"I know you were offered the top job at Accord and turned it down." Careen watched for Chris's reaction to her statement.

"News travels fast." His expression showed some surprise, probably due to the confidential nature of the offer. But it was a small industry.

"Can I ask why?"

"I was seriously considering it ..." Chris paused. "You've always given me a lot of latitude here, Careen. If I have an idea, a suggestion, a possible change of direction, you always sit down with me, listen and, more often than not, let me run with it. Before I made my decision I met with each member of the Accord board and put a few ideas forward just to gauge their reaction. They weren't receptive at all. After that the decision was easy."

"I hope this decision will be an easy one too. I'm stepping down as CEO. I'd like you to take over."

She saw the tension seep out of his shoulders. "You know, Edward gave me a hard time for turning Accord down. He said you'd never hand over Montage and I'd always have to settle for second best. We had one hell of a row. It'll be nice to tell him I backed the right horse."

"Thanks, Chris. I take it that means the answer is yes?"

"Definitely yes." He smiled. "I'll take care of Montage for you Careen. You know that."

"I wouldn't be handing it over if I had any doubts at all."

A thought clouded Chris's face and he sat up straight and looked directly at Careen. "Do I get to choose my 2IC?"

"What you mean is do you get Logan?"

"And?" Chris's eyes never left hers.

"No, Chris. Logan may be my brother but he is not 2IC material, we both know that."

Chris relaxed back into his chair. "Have you told him yet?"

"No." And, she added silently, I am not looking forward to

that at all. Careen leaned back into her chair with a sigh.

"I'd like Murray to take over as vice president." Chris had clearly given some thought to his future career at Montage.

"I agree with you. But let me break it to Logan first."

"He'll understand."

No, he wouldn't. Shaking her head Careen felt a sadness well up inside. Logan took everything personally – he always had. She remembered him not being chosen to play centre half-forward for the school football team. The fact that the other guy was faster, better and bothered to show up at training was irrelevant. He'd wanted that position on the team. He'd sabotaged the training sessions for weeks after that, deflating all the balls, locking them out of the change rooms and stacking all of their towels in the shower with the water on. No one had been able to prove anything but she knew he'd done it. Logan always paid back those who ousted him. So far, she'd never put brotherly love to the test. She was about to find out if family was different.

After Chris left, Careen sat sipping her tea, her gaze drifting around her office. She'd thought about John a lot last night and was feeling melancholy this morning. This had been his office. Sleek would be a good way to describe it. She ran her hand over the highly polished ebony surface. "Ah, John, this is still very much your office, isn't it?" The bookshelves held an eclectic mixture of reading material, interspersed with collectables from all over the world – none of them belonging to her. The huge black desk dwarfed Careen, but John had said the size of the desk reflects the size of the job, so she had stuck with that too. Two plush sofas with a dark coffee table filled the rest of the space, but plenty of carpet showed. In a perverse moment John had ordered maroon carpet with the hotel monogram as a repeating pattern. She smiled to herself as she recalled his horrified expression when it was laid and he saw the result. Admitting he was wrong was never John's strong point, so the carpet stayed.

Careen turned to admire the view and sat staring out, enjoying the play of the sun as it glinted off the other high-rise buildings, turning the city into a giant jewellery box. A hesitant knock at the door from Lei signalled the start to another day.

"Come in." She turned to greet Lei. Lei gave Careen a summary of her day, filled her in on any correspondence that required action and updated her on potential diary changes. She hated when people changed the set meeting times on the day. Peter should know better.

"Please change the two p.m. with Peter back to three when it was initially set or move it until tomorrow at the same time if something more urgent has arisen. I'd allocated that hour to go through the papers before I saw him." Careen reached into the side pocket of her handbag. "Can you drop my car in for a service? I don't plan on driving it for a while so it's a good chance to get a tune up." She passed Lei the keys. "Please ensure they detail it properly after the service."

"Of course." Lei stood as Logan knocked on the doorframe and entered the office. "If you need anything else let me know."

Careen stood up and embraced Logan as he entered her office – a reminder that he was family, not just an employee. He towered over her, his slim frame belying his strength as he picked her up and spun her round.

"Morning, sis."

"Hi, Logan. You look remarkably well for a man who was out until all hours."

"Checking up on me now?"

"No just a guess." Not a hard one either. Logan was out most nights.

"Still be in bed if it wasn't for your important meeting.

Head hurts like hell." He rubbed at his beard then paused, glancing around, taking in the empty armchairs. "Where is everyone then?"

"We're it today."

"What trouble am I in now?" He absently ran his finger along the book spines on Careen's shelf before turning back to her. "Forgot my monthly report? Chased the secretary round the desk too many times? Or perhaps this time it's good news." He grinned. "You're giving me a bonus to show your appreciation for the overwhelming success of our new social media strategy."

"You did a great job there. I don't quite understand all the ins and outs, but the sales team have reported that brand awareness has made a considerable difference to their ability to get company bookings across the line."

"What would you do without me?"

Careen groaned. This was not going to be easy. She gestured towards the chairs.

"Logan, how about—"

"Speaking of getting things out there. Didn't see you at the bar the other night. Decided to stay single then?" He absently picked up the crystal paperweight from her desk replacing it carelessly.

"Logan, please, sit down."

"So where were you then?"

"I stayed home," she answered carefully, keeping the exasperation out of her voice. She could feel her fists clenching and she made a conscious effort to release them.

"Surprise, surprise."

Logan picked up her framed photo of John and turned it over and over in his hands. Why must he fiddle with everything? Every time Logan left her office she had to put everything back in its place.

"Thanks for the dinner. It was a nice thought."

"Pardon?" The photo frame stopped turning.

"Dinner. The takeaway. All my favourites too."

"Yeah, right. No problem, sis. Hope you enjoyed it." He paused, looking perplexed. "How did you know it was me?"

"The note."

"Oh yes, the note. They got it right then." He was staring out the window, avoiding Careen's gaze. The photo frame had resumed its rotation.

"You did order the food, didn't you?" A cold sensation was creeping up on her. He'd been known to take the credit for a good deed whether it was due or not and she didn't want to think of the alternative if it hadn't been him.

"Of course I did." He turned with a big smile and promptly changed the subject. "So what's so important that I had to be here at nine sharp?"

Careen walked over to Logan and removed John's picture from his hands. She set it down on the desk and placed the paperweight back where it belonged.

"Logan, take a seat."

"This sounds serious." He threw himself into the lounge chair. "Could do with a coffee."

Careen sighed. He'd never change. She decided the best approach was straight to the point. "Logan, I've decided to hand over the reins of Montage to Chris. He's been my 2IC for four years and is ready to manage Montage. I'll be stepping back and taking on a more consultative role."

"About time." Logan smiled and sat forward, hope flaring in his eyes.

"Logan, Murray will be taking over Chris's old role." She blurted it out, watching as his face darkened and he looked at her with incredulity.

"Murray?" he spluttered. "Murray has only been here five minutes."

"Two years, Logan. And prior to that he was in a similar position with Ascott. You know that."

"And me? What do I get?" He stood up, deliberately towering over her. "Another four years as head of marketing and PR as they laugh at me. Passed over for promotion by my own sister." His voice was bitter.

"Logan it's not like that." But it was. She'd spent hours trying to find a soft landing for Logan, a way to cushion the blow, to make it easier for him, to enable him to keep his pride, but ultimately every option she could think of was disruptive to the business.

Logan turned and paced up and down, his face red and his eyes glowing dangerously. The paperweight was in his hands again – this time, however, it resembled not so much an abstract object as a weapon. "How can you do this to me after all we have been through? If it wasn't for me you wouldn't even have your damn hotels." He turned to her with bewilderment in his eyes. "You've strung me along all these years, letting me believe I'd have a key role, and now ..." Shaking his head with disbelief he continued, "Now you hand it over to Murray." He paused, a sneer developing on his face. "Sleeping with you, is he? Keeping you from being the lonely old spinster."

"Logan!" She pushed herself out of her chair and rose to her full height.

"Well, is he? Probably a good match. Both all business and outcomes. No fun."

Careen closed her eyes, trying to block out the bitterness. "You know me better than that. My business is my life and I'm ..."

"My business is my life," he mimicked her. "And what about your brother? Isn't he worth something to you too?" He slammed the paperweight onto the desk with a crash.

Careen opened her mouth to reply but knew nothing she

said would make any difference. Perhaps she should have invented a new role, a promotion of sorts for him, but he'd have seen through that eventually and then would have been even more resentful.

The jealousy had been there for a long time, simmering just below the surface. After their parents died Logan had played the role of the capable and wise older brother – for a while at least. He'd been very supportive in the initial stages of building her dream, but as her accomplishments grew, so had his resentment. She had the success he wanted so badly. The fact was, however, that he wasn't prepared to work for it.

"Logan. You know ..." Her voice was soft, a reflection of the pain and sadness welling inside.

"Don't *Logan* me!" he spat. "You and your millions. You and your success. You can keep it. I don't want anything more to do with you or your damn hotels." He turned, pain in his eyes. His arm swept in a deliberate arc over her desk, sending the paperweight crashing to the floor. "If I'm not good enough to be 2IC, then I'm probably not good enough to be your brother either." The door slammed behind him.

FIVE

"I do not mean to intrude." Lei stuck her head around the door tentatively. "I was concerned. Is there anything I can do?"

"I'm okay. Just hold all calls for a while." Careen bent down and picked up the paperweight, caressing its smooth surfaces, only to stop when her fingers felt a small chip. She ran her finger over the sharp edge. She'd had this paperweight for twenty-two years, it was the last thing Dad had given her before the accident and now it was cracked. Logan knew its importance, its link to family. Is that why he had chosen to damage it?

"When I am unsettled I find if I go for a walk I feel better." Lei had approached her quietly.

Careen's head was throbbing. "Yes, perhaps that's what I need." She replaced the paperweight on her desk, running her fingers around the edge of the work surface to ensure it too hadn't suffered from Logan's tantrum. John's stout desk had weathered the storm; sturdy like its previous owner.

"When do I need to be back?"

"Your meeting with Peter is at three o'clock."

She was walking across the tiled floor to the lifts when Murray waved and called out to her.

"Careen, I wondered if we could touch base regarding the financials. There are a number of items I wish to discuss in more detail."

"Financials?" Careen stopped. "What's wrong with the financials?" Her highly polished nails were digging into her palms. "Is there a problem?" Her words came out slowly, deliberately. After all these years she still cringed when anyone mentioned the figures. It always reminded her of Tony.

"No, not at all," Murray replied. "I just have a few ideas I wanted to run past you." His voice was sharp and his lips pursed.

Chris was more qualified than she was in matters relating to the numbers in the business, and she knew Murray was aware of this. He didn't hide his irritation at her insistence on keeping control of all financials. He'd be pleased to learn that would all be changing soon.

"Ah. Of course." Careen made a conscious effort to unclench her fists and stabbed at the lift button. "Just check with Lei for a time."

She stopped at the security desk to discuss the calls to her private line then headed outside. The sunshine warmed her back and she took deep breaths as she headed towards Flagstaff Gardens. The hustle and bustle of the street invigorated her. Lei was right, this was what she needed.

What was she going to do about Logan? They had been close growing up. He was all the family she had now. How did people cope with more than one family member? She imagined the stress of a whole tribe of brothers and sisters could kill you. Maybe that's where parents came in; they taught you how to deal with that sort of thing. Maybe other people's parents anyhow. Dad was what Careen termed 'son-centric', so focused on making a success of Logan that she'd felt she didn't exist. He'd celebrated every success Logan had and minimised hers. She'd tried so hard to be the perfect child, but when it came down to it, she didn't have the required anatomy and therefore didn't stand a chance.

Her mother was the complete opposite of her father – flighty, the life of the party. Logan got frustrated that Dad was trying to mould him into the ideal son, and Mum was off doing charity work and taking long liquid lunches, so she wasn't around to act as a buffer. Careen used to joke with Logan that they got the sexes muddled up – she was too much like Dad and Logan was too much like Mum.

Careen took a seat in the gardens under a large oak. She hadn't thought of her parents in months. The fear of handing over Montage and what she was going to do now had eclipsed everything. Mum and Dad. The accident. Logan. She'd had a row with her father that night. It was the last time she spoke with him. Harsh, angry words that couldn't be taken back.

Two police officers had come to the house. She'd been home alone – Logan had moved out a few months before and was living in the share house with Ben.

"What has Logan done now?" she'd asked the taller of the two policemen. The week before Careen had bailed out Logan after an arrest for drunk and disorderly. He hadn't wanted their father to know. She'd had to use some of her savings that night and she was frustrated that he thought she could do it again. That was her escape money, her travel fund, and be damned if she was bailing him out again when he hadn't repaid her for the last time.

"Careen Tamley?" The way the officer had said it sent shivers cascading through her. Too serious. She'd wondered what would happen if she said no. "Can we please come in?"

"Do you have to?" She'd stayed where she was, blocking the door, delaying.

"If we can come in."

She'd moved to one side.

"Are you here alone?"

"Yes."

"Please take a seat."

She'd moved to the dining table, pulled out a straight-backed chair and plonked herself in it. The officer who'd spoken removed a chair from the end of the table and sat facing her. She'd hung her head tracing patterns on the carpet with her bare toes.

"Miss Tamley, I am sorry to inform you that there has been an accident."

"Is Logan okay?" She'd refused to look up.

"It's not Logan. In fact we've been trying to locate him. It's your parents."

Careen had stared blankly at the policeman, rubbed absently at her arms. "Mum and Dad?"

"Yes. There was an accident, the car they were travelling in hit a tree." He'd reached out and taken her hand. "Miss Tamley. I am very sorry, but neither of them survived the crash."

"You're wrong." She'd pulled her hand away from him and rubbed her arms again. She had felt cold, very cold.

"A colleague who was following identified them. I'm sorry, there's no mistake."

She'd shaken her head. "I want to see them."

"I think that can wait until tomorrow. Is there someone who I can call, someone who can stay with you tonight?"

"Logan. Where's Logan?"

"We've been trying to contact Logan, but he's not answering his phone."

Careen had pushed away from the table, scrambled in her handbag for her mobile, dialled with shaking hands. "Come on, answer. Logan, please answer." She'd sunk to the floor, her back leaning against the cold leather of the sofa. "Logan. Please."

And he had answered. He had been there when she needed him. He'd come straight home, had held her close and told her he would always be there for her. He'd been her rock through her grieving, had held her as she cried, and had accepted her need to slam doors and cupboards as they packed up their home, angry at how little time it had taken for her father's employers to come calling to request the return of the house; a company perk that they no longer had any right to.

She had packed her clothes into a suitcase and filled two cartons with books. That was all she took when she moved into Logan and Ben's place. The rest they'd packed into cardboard boxes, identical in size and shape, stacked to the cage roof in a storage warehouse to minimise the cost.

She hadn't thought about that storage cage in years – maybe it was time to go back, to clean up and sort out those boxes; to read through her old dairies, flick through her travel scrapbooks. Before her life had been turned upside down, Careen had wanted to travel. She'd had a different book for each country she wanted to visit – fourteen in all. Pictures, articles, snippets of the language, all in one place so she could pick it up and take it with her when she went. Only she hadn't gone. After the accident she and Logan discovered that her parents didn't own the house and all the travelling they'd done was on credit. Careen and Logan spent years paying off what their parents owed. Logan had helped her pack up the scrapbooks – telling her that she was young, there was still plenty of time for travel.

That was before the attack.

Ah, Logan. She needed to mend the rift with him – she owed him that. The decision she made for Montage was the right one and Logan would have to accept that. She'd invite him over for dinner – they would get past this.

Careen rode the empty lift to the executive floor and opened the glass door that separated the suites from the corridor.

"He was cute." Missy was smiling. "Seriously cute – for an old dude that is. Tall, dark, handsome."

Careen smiled at Missy as she entered. Chris's secretary, Missy, often came in for a chat with Lei. Missy didn't have Lei's reticence; she was all curves and bubbles and had a unique dress sense. The bright-pink tailored jacket with flowered lapels must be one of her latest purchases. Her curly shoulder-length locks were jet black with a touch of blue today – a change from last month's white-fringed wonder.

"Who was cute?"

"The guy from BMW, tall, crinkly eyes, piercing blue. Cute moustache. You just missed him. Why can't my mechanic look like that?" Missy expounded with a wide grin and Lei smiled self-consciously.

Careen realised it was the first time in ages she'd seen Lei smile.

"What was he doing here?"

"One of the mechanics dropped the keys into the oil pit. He said they will replace the set but could not get one until tomorrow. As he was coming in to the city on another job, he came to the office to get the spare. I gave him the key from your top drawer," Lei explained. "I hope that was acceptable?"

"That's fine. When will the car be ready?"

"They will ring when it is finished. Peter Steiner is in your office waiting. He seems agitated," Lei added.

"Did you suggest a walk in the sunshine?"

Careen chuckled at Lei's horrified look.

After two gruelling hours Peter left, taking his problems and their solutions with him. Maybe there was something in handing it all over to Chris. Her head ached. Logan and Peter in one day was what she would term overload. For the first time in memory she considered going home early. Pouring herself a glass of water from the crystal jug on her desk, Careen reached into the drawer and pulled out some aspirin. Swallowing two, she leaned back in her chair.

"Excuse me," Lei was standing in the doorway. "The car is ready." Lei handed Careen the keys.

"And was the cute guy there?"

Lei blushed. "He was not."

"Did you ask when the replacement set would be ready?" Careen asked, glancing down at the keys.

"I am sorry. I forgot to ask." Lei appeared upset, she had been forgetting a lot lately, which was out of character. "I will call them in the morning. Is that okay? They were closing when I got the car."

"That's fine. Don't stress. One set is all I need for now."

"Is it all right if I leave now?"

"Yes, go. There's nothing that's urgent tonight. Anyway I'll be off soon myself, I just need to finish up my emails." Careen stopped. She hated prying into other people's lives, just like she hated others asking too many questions about hers, but Lei had not been herself lately. "Lei, is everything all right at home?"

"Yes. Yes, everything is good." The words came but they didn't sound convincing. Lei's mobile phone shrilled. "Gary. He is downstairs. Can I go?"

"Lei. Are you okay? Can I help?"

"I have to go." Lei turned and ran out of the office.

Careen sighed. Tomorrow she would make time to talk to her. She was sure that Lei needed to get away from Gary.

SIX

While she was thinking about Lei, another email dropped into her inbox. The subject line was: Once Upon a Time.

> You've been avoiding me Careen and I am not happy. I wanted to work with you on this, but if you insist on ignoring my calls and emails I may just have to write it on my own. I've been doing a bit of research. What do you think of the opening lines?
>
> Once upon a time there was a girl called Careen Tamley. She was a shy girl, no trouble at all. But we all know what they say about the quiet ones – they are the ones you need to keep an eye on. Sadly, in the past no one did, but it's time someone sat up and took notice and that someone is me. My name is Louise Mears and I am going to let you in on a secret worth dying for.
>
> Do you think it'll get them interested?
> Call me.
> Love, Louise

"Fuck." Careen seldom swore but if there ever was a time, now was it.

Her mobile rang, showing a blocked number. Careen snatched it up. "What the hell are you playing at, Louise? This isn't some sort of game."

"Ah, but a game is just what it is my princess." He chuckled. "And who is this Louise who has you so riled up? This is my game, you see, and I don't like others playing on my turf."

"What the hell are you talking about? I'm no one's turf."

"Ah, Princess. How little you know. We'll have plenty of time to talk later. I just wanted to find out if you enjoyed your dinner the other night?"

"The dinner Logan ordered?"

What did that have to do with anything?

"Is that what he said?" He chuckled again. "It was a present from me to you, Princess. Logan had nothing to do with it."

"What are you—?"

But he'd hung up. Careen threw the mobile onto the carpet in frustration. She moved to the window, a place that usually calmed her, but she was furious. What the hell was he on about with "my turf"? None of it made sense. She paced around her office like a caged tiger. A tiger with a blinding headache. She slumped back into her chair and put her head in her hands, massaging her temples. She reached for the Excedrin to quell the migraine she knew was on its way.

Her door opened and Chris strode in. "You still here?" He looked at her for a moment. "You okay?"

"Not particularly. Headache from hell."

"I take it things didn't go well with Logan?" He paused. "Do you want to talk about it?"

"Not really." She rubbed her temples. "God, I'm tired. What with Logan this morning, the prank calls and now Louise's email."

"What's this about calls and emails?"

She must be tired; she hadn't meant to blurt that out. She shook her head and then wished she hadn't as pain ricocheted through. "Nothing to worry about. I've already spoken to security about it." She brushed it off.

"And the emails?"

"Long story, Chris. Can we talk about it tomorrow?"

"If you're sure it can wait." Chris appeared concerned. He moved out of the doorway towards her desk. "Are you sure you don't want to cover it off tonight rather than sleep on it? You seem quite shaken up."

"I'm not sure how much is annoyance and how much is headache, actually." She stood up. "I think I'll go home and get a good night's sleep. But do remind me in the morning, I need to get you up to speed on Louise Mears and her meddling."

"I've had a couple of messages from a Louise Mears, but I haven't called her back. She refuses to give Missy a reason for the call."

"Do me a favour and don't call her until we've spoken. And let Missy know that she shouldn't speak with her either."

"Now I'm intrigued."

"You'll have to wait until morning when I'm feeling coherent." She groaned. "God, my head hurts."

"Come on, pack up. I'll walk you to your car."

She'd been avoiding going down to the car park, but the thought of having to make conversation with a taxi driver was more than she could bear. She'd be safe with Chris.

Careen was uneasy as she pushed the remote button that raised the underground car-park door at her hotel. Her headache made her sluggish and that was the last thing she needed. She reversed back up the ramp and parked on the street. She'd deal with the parking ticket tomorrow.

She rubbed her temples as she rode the lift to her apartment. She'd need something stronger than Excedrin to fix this. Careen had suffered from migraines ever since the attack. She had a veritable pharmacy of preventative drugs and painkillers lined up in her bathroom cabinet.

The lift opened to the seventeenth floor and she trudged along the carpeted hallway and stopped short. Her door was open. Her head felt like it was trapped in a vice, her thoughts squashed out of shape without the ability to reshape themselves into a logical pattern. Before she had time to panic, a bushy red head poked around the door.

"Hi, sis. Thought I heard the lift." Logan was smiling.

"Logan, what are you doing here?"

And why are you grinning like an idiot?

"I was feeling bad about our row earlier and thought I'd come over and make peace." He held out his hand and attempted to draw her into a hug.

Careen's scepticism must have showed on her face because, after a brief pause, he moved back to allow her though the door and continued. "I mean if you think that Murray's the best person, who am I to question it? I mean you've been successful by making a lot of tough calls." Logan's words were starting to run together as they rushed out. "And I mean, we are family and blood *is* thicker than water, or a job for that matter, so I thought ..."

"Logan what is all this about?" The room was fading in and out of focus and Careen put her hand on the wall for support.

"I'm trying to say sorry for what I said."

She shook her head to clear the fog, which turned out to be a mistake as the migraine hit her with a fresh wave of pain. "Shit. Why now?"

"What do you mean why?"

"You never apologise and you never admit you're wrong." The migraine seemed to be working like a truth serum. Not necessarily a good approach with Logan.

"You don't think much of me, do you?"

"I think the world of you, Logan. It's just that I also know you better than anyone else and this isn't you."

"A friend of mine suggested I'd been unfair."

"And this friend is?" She sunk into the sofa.

"A guy I met at a conference last year. He's staying with me at the moment." Logan looked a little sheepish. "He suggested I'd overreacted and reminded me that family's important."

"I see." Careen sighed. She was too damn tired and her head hurt way too much to deal with this. "Okay, Logan. Let's call a truce and be friends again."

"Hugs?"

She stood up, gave Logan a quick hug. The pain was getting too intense and Logan's behaviour was too hard to figure out. "Now, can you go home so I can go to bed? My head's pounding and I'm too tired to deal with anything more today."

"Want me to run you a bath, give you a scalp massage?"

Careen laughed in spite of herself. "Don't push it. Goodnight, Logan."

He leaned across and gave her a quick peck on the cheek. "Great to be friends again, sis. Love you." She could hear him whistling as he waited in the hallway for the lift.

SEVEN

The sunlight woke her. Careen started to rise, but the pain in her head exploded and she lay her head back on the pillow. She shut her eyes and pulled the duvet over her head to block out the light. The stars bursting behind her eyelids were too bright, triggering another wave of pain, so she opened them again. This was not going away by itself. Throwing back the duvet she hauled herself off the bed and made a direct line to the bathroom cabinet.

"Come on, come on." The childproof lid on the migraine-tablet bottle was fighting her. Twisting it off with force she swallowed two tablets and washed them down with water. She stood up, glancing at herself in the mirror. Not good. She stumbled back into the bedroom, pulled down the blinds and curled up under the covers, pulling the blankets over her head to block out the residual light.

Her silky hair is fanned out over the pillow, her eyelashes fluttering as she dreams. He runs a finger down her cheek, tracks his thumb nail across her exposed throat. She stirs then settles. She looks peaceful as she sleeps. Not for much longer.

Careen awoke much later to the smell of freshly brewed coffee. Still groggy from the after effects of the tablets, she stood up shakily, pulled on her green silk robe and, running her fingers through her hair, headed for the kitchen.

"Logan?"

"No, it is I. Lei. How are you feeling?" Lei was standing in the kitchen. "I have made you some coffee."

"Wonderful. When did you get here?"

"I have been here a while. I did not want to wake you. You started getting restless, so I thought I would make coffee."

"Thanks." Careen took a sip of the coffee. "Lei, what are you doing here?"

"I was worried. You did not come to the office today. You did not answer your phones. Chris said you had not been in. Logan said you had a headache last night and would have slept in. You do not ever sleep in. You always call if you are not coming in. I was worried. I got your apartment swipe from Logan and came to see if you were all right." She offered Careen a biscuit. "Your door was open when I arrived. I checked the apartment. Everything seems okay."

Careen stared at Lei through the drug-induced stupor, her mind slow to register. Her door was open. She felt the hair lift on her arms and nape of her neck. The mystery caller? No. Not possible. You need a swipe to get in the front door and an access pass for the floor, which he couldn't have.

"Logan mustn't have pulled it shut last night when he left." Her mum, who had been fond of idioms, always used to say that Logan was born in a tent. He had a habit of wandering off and leaving the doors unlocked. At the Essendon house, Ben, who was worried about his paints and canvasses, had ended up installing a spring catch so the front door locked behind you when you left. The problem with that, of course, was that Logan inevitably had to be let in when he returned home as he hadn't taken his keys with him.

"You are lucky. My place would have been robbed if I had left it unlocked."

Careen lifted her hands to scrub at her face and yawned. She squinted against the bright sunlight beaming in.

"You have got a migraine?" Lei was tidying up from making the coffee.

"And it's not going away. Although the coffee is helping."

"I have cancelled all of your appointments for today so there is no need to come in. Is there anything else I can do?"

Careen's nails bit into her palms as she clenched her fists. She never cancelled appointments. Ever.

Lei must have seen her reaction and quickly added, "I have rescheduled every appointment for early next week so that tomorrow has no meetings as I was not sure if you were unwell. They are all in your calendar."

Careen made a concerted effort to unclench her fists. "Thanks, Lei."

Lei headed for the door, opened it and turned around. "If you need anything, anything at all, you can call me."

"I will. I appreciate you coming to check up on me."

And as soon as I can get past this damn headache I'm going to return the favour.

"You are welcome." Lei left, closing the door behind her.

Careen stood still for a moment drinking her coffee; the warm sun radiating into the room was comforting on her back. She yawned. It was going to take more than coffee to keep her awake. Careen checked the door was locked before she headed back to bed. She wondered why Lei hadn't used her own swipe, but the thought faded away as she drifted off to sleep.

Careen stretched as she stepped out of the shower. She'd spent the last two days in bed and still felt tired. She slipped into her robe, padded into the lounge and opened the wooden venetians to let in the late afternoon sun. At the edge of her mind there was a question about the blinds but it was elusive, caught up in the after-effects of the painkillers. Her phone rang, interrupting her thoughts. Ben's number flashed up.

"Hey."

"Hey yourself."

"You've heard?" Her face broke into a smile as she moved to the sofa to nestle amongst the cushions.

"I got it Careen. They chose me."

"Congratulations, Ben. I knew they would." She kept her voice light. She was pleased for him but she was going to miss him.

"Anyway, just a quick call to see if you and Logan might like to come over for a feed tomorrow night?"

"Sounds great." She hesitated. "Have you spoken to Logan yet?"

"No. He was next on the list."

Her sigh of relief was almost audible. She had to talk to Ben before Logan did, she needed him to understand. "Please don't. Logan and I had a bit of a run-in at work and he was, well, weird, the other night. I'd like to talk to you about it if that's okay?"

"That's cool. My place, tomorrow at eight?"

"I'll be there." Still smiling, Careen hung up the phone. She stood up and, putting the phone on the hall table, reached for her favourite photo – her, Ben, John and Logan, at Ben's flat. It wasn't there. Strange, she remembered putting it back. Careen scanned the room but she couldn't find it anywhere.

She glanced at the front door. No. What would someone want with that photo? It must have been Logan. He was acting very odd yesterday. She'd call him later and ask why he took it.

Perplexed by the missing photo but still cheerful following Ben's call, Careen decided to get takeaway gyoza and settle in and watch a movie. After two days in bed she thought she should make an effort to get some fresh air, so rather than order via Uber Eats, she dressed and headed to the lifts. It was still light and there were plenty of people around at this time of day.

"Excuse me, Miss Tamley." The concierge beckoned her over. "A package arrived for you earlier today. I called you but you must have been out." He handed her a small parcel. Intrigued, she turned it over. It was about the size of a matchbox and wrapped in holographic silver paper, tied up with a deep-blue silk ribbon.

"Thanks, Jim." Careen tucked the parcel in her bag, much to Jim's obvious disappointment. Jim was known for his curiosity about the guests' lives and Careen was not going to share this with him. She would open it later when she was alone. Logan, it appeared, was taking his apology to the extreme.

She was halfway through the movie, *Decoy Bride*, when she remembered the parcel. The movie had David Tennant in it but that wasn't enough to redeem it. She rummaged through her bag and found the gift. Intrigued, she ran her fingers along the edge of the wrapped box, watched as the light caught on the silver patterns and danced around the apartment. Logan was always good with gifts and surprises. She untied the ribbon and peeled off the sticky tape. It was a matchbox. Careen pushed the cardboard drawer open – and gasped. Inside, on a bed of deep-blue velvet, was a piece of jigsaw. A pink tongue against blood red lips, a white background. Clown makeup. She dropped the box and recoiled, pulled her feet up on the sofa as it landed on the floor near her toes. She used the back of her hand to flick the wrappings to the floor, covering the box completely. She drew her knees up and hugged them to her chest. A whimper escaped involuntarily and she bit her lip to stop a moan from escaping. She thought about Lei's comment this morning, how lucky she was to have such good security.

She stared at the wrappings for a long time, then made a decision. She walked to the balcony, slid open the doors and threw the box and the jigsaw piece out; watched as it fell seventeen floors to the traffic below. She was not that scared girl anymore. She was Careen Tamley. Strong and successful. She turned and, leaving the balcony door wide open, went and made herself a cup of liquorice tea. She was not going to let this get to her. She pressed play on the remote and watched the movie resolutely to the end.

Her dreams that night were fragmented. Her father driving the car in a clown mask. Her mother sitting beside him, a silly smile on her face. The crash as they hit the tree was silent and they both just sat there, grins on their faces as the car caught fire. She tossed and turned as they burnt, calling out to them, but they couldn't hear her. She turned away from the car and watching her from the trees was the Clown Killer, silent and still, holding a takeaway bag.

She jerked awake. The takeaway. She leapt out of bed and almost ran to the rubbish bin. She pulled on a pair of kitchen gloves but still cringed as she rifled through the greasy empty takeaway containers she'd stacked in the bin. The paper bag was soggy as was the jigsaw piece sitting in the bottom. It was there. A piece of jigsaw. Number 11. She stood still, staring at the red smudge across what was presumably the cheek of the mask. She sunk to the floor, moaning softly. She'd not checked if there was a number on the back of the one she'd thrown out over the balcony. This was happening too fast. She glanced up, comforted to find the security latch still on the door. "He can't get in. He can't get in," she repeated the mantra. "I'm safe up here. Safe." But it didn't feel that way. Too much glass. So very alone.

EIGHT

Careen's feet ached and she was starving. Shopping had seemed like such a good idea this morning. She'd bought herself a pair of cut-off denim shorts and a gypsy skirt. Clothes for her new life in Italy. She needed to keep the dream alive. She'd laughed to herself as she purchased the most ridiculous sun hat, but having a pale complexion she burnt easily and she'd need cover for her ambling walks along the Amalfi coastline.

Her most precious purchase was the soft red silk dress that she was planning to wear to Ben's tonight. It fit every curve, had a deliciously low neckline and a sensuously high split up the side. It was time to break the mould and be more like the Careen of old – the one with the "wow factor". She must get her legs waxed. She almost laughed out loud at the thought. She'd been keen on Ben for so long and although, from time to time, he'd seemed interested, they never had got past a friendly peck on the cheek or a cuddle on the couch while watching a movie. She'd decided to make an effort tonight, not so much for him but for her, for her future. For the Careen that was going to wow the local men in Amalfi. Perhaps a new perfume, something girly rather than the mature Coco Chanel she wore at the office. Coffee, then chemist.

He loves that she has so many habits and routines. He knows where she shops, how she likes her coffee, her favourite perfume and even where she gets her nails done. She is always so predictable. Except today. She'd surprised him. That dress, so sassy. He likes that it is red. Red - the colour of blood, of danger, of wrath.

Careen sat at a café table and ordered a black coffee and a blueberry muffin.

"'Scuse me. You Careen Tamley?" The waitress's nasal twang irritated Careen immediately.

"Yes. I am."

"A bloke gave me this. 'E said to give it to you." Careen took the parcel and turned it over several times. It was larger and heavier than the last one, but it was wrapped in the same holographic paper. "Is 'e your fella like? Kinda cute. Not my type though. I like 'em chubby, meat on ..." She paused to take a breath. "So what's in it? Thought the message was a bit strange, like. I mean, you aren't even wearing a red dress." Careen opened the attached card. Black ink. Bold writing. "The sexy red dress suits you." Careen jerked her head back, looked frantically around. An elderly lady on her own, a mum with two young kids and a couple of teenagers texting furiously. She couldn't see him but he was here. She could feel him, his warm breath on the back of her neck. She turned, knowing even as she did, he wasn't there. She shivered, rubbed her arms to get warm.

"... I did ask him, you know. If you'd be wearing a red dress, like. He laughed and went all crinkly around the eyes. How is it eye crinkles look good on blokes but us girls have to hide 'em?"

"Sorry." Careen couldn't focus. He'd followed her here. Watched her shop.

"Not that you 'ave wrinkles, mind. Not like me. Well past my prime and—"

"What did he look like?" Careen's tone was harsh.

"Kinda cute. Already said that, didn't I?"

"Was he tall?"

"Everyone's tall when you're five foot nothin'."

Careen sighed, exhaustion replacing her fear. "Dark or blond hair?"

"Mavis!" A voice boomed from the kitchen.

"Gotta fly. Lovely talking with ya." With that she turned and scurried towards the kitchen entrance.

"Wait." Careen stretched out to grab Mavis, but she was out of reach.

Biting her lip, Careen pulled off the wrapping and started to fold it neatly before realising what she was doing. She brushed the back of her hand across the table and sent the wrapping skittering to the floor. A blue velvet box. She opened the lid. Inside was another piece of jigsaw – the picture this time was a red clown nose. She turned it over – number nine was scrawled on the back. Careen took a deep breath, raised her head and scanned the coffee shop, peering beyond the doorway out into the busy mall. He was here somewhere, had been watching her all day; otherwise, how would he know about the dress? She threw twenty dollars on the table and picked up her handbag. She reached for her shopping bags and changed her mind. She wouldn't wear any of them now; they felt soiled, dirty. She left the parcel on the table next to her half-eaten muffin and strode out of the café.

Careen hailed the first taxi she saw and climbed in the back seat, glad that she hadn't driven into the city. She certainly wasn't going near an underground car park anytime soon.

"Beach St, Port Melbourne," she directed the driver. As the taxi pulled away Careen peered out the window. Maybe he was still following her. But what did he look like? Tall, crinkly eyes, cute. Not the sort of description you could go to the police with and expect them to identify him. Also, what did she have as evidence? An envelope with the first piece of jigsaw, a slightly greasy second piece in the ziplock bag in the kitchen drawer.

The box with the third piece she'd hurled off her seventeenth-floor balcony and the fourth she'd just left behind. She knew she should go back for it. It was evidence. She also knew she wasn't going anywhere near that coffee shop again.

When she reached Port Melbourne she scanned her street for anybody lurking about, cars driving past, people jumping out of taxis. She swiped the front-door access and entered the foyer, hastened to the lift, feeling safer as she passed each level of security. Careen closed her apartment door, sliding the security chain across. She strode to the window, unlatched the balcony door and stepped out. She leaned over the glass railing and looked down. No one was standing there staring up. Everyone she could see was walking, cycling, rollerblading or sunbaking. No one was watching. She stood staring for a moment and then pulling out one of the chairs slumped into it, running her hands through her hair. How long had he watched her shop, select clothes and try them on? Had he been following her all day or just come across her when she was in Saba buying the dress? She shuddered.

A shower had calmed her. She sat on the balcony with a cup of tea and chided herself. She'd let him win. If he'd seen her reaction at the coffee shop, he'd know he had upset her. He would have seen her leave both the parcel and her shopping behind. She glanced at the clock. Three p.m. She was going to spoil herself this afternoon; put some music on and spend time getting ready for tonight. After all, she now had to decide what to wear. She glanced at her nails – not good. The nail salon on Bay Street would fit her in – they always did. She also needed to call Gordon to widen his brief – or did she? Perhaps Louise was part of all of this. Not so much researching the past as writing herself a few new episodes.

Careen swiped the lock on her apartment door, grinning to herself. Purple toenails. She hadn't done that in a while. Her fingernails were more muted but she kept glancing down at her toes. More like the old Careen. She dropped the swipe card into the white marble bowl on the hall table and decided another cup of tea was in order – green with a touch of ginger sounded good.

She was smiling to herself as she reached the kitchen bench; that was until her newly painted toes hit a shopping bag. The bags. How were the bags here? She reached into the closest bag and pulled out the denim shorts, then throwing them aside reached in and grabbed the next item – the red dress. She picked up the bag, turned it upside down. Careen screamed as a piece of jigsaw fell from the bottom of the bag. She put her hand over her mouth to stifle the sound. She stood up, backed away, her eyes sweeping the apartment, searching for movement. Silence. Stillness. Like the unnerving quiet of a dark empty car park.

A slow drip, drip from the kitchen tap had her grabbing for her handbag. As she reached for her swipe she knocked the marble bowl off the hall table, the crash loud in the silence of her apartment. She groped under the table for the key card, her eyes scanning, seeking movement. Her hand touched the card; she scooped it up. She backed out of the door, slammed it behind her, hit the down button on the lift's control panel, once, twice, three times.

"Come on. Come on." Her eyes never left the door of her apartment. The ding of the elevator sounded and after a quick glance, Careen jumped in and hit the ground-floor button.

"Come on, close. Hurry." She hit the close-door button, but the doors stayed open. "Close dammit." And they did, slowly and sedately. She held her handbag in front of her, her arms clasped around it. Her card was clenched in her fists. The lift shuddered and stopped as it reached the ground floor. The lift doors opened and Careen leapt out, then strode towards the concierge, every stride a conscious effort not to run.

"Jim. Someone's been in my apartment today." Careen heard the tremor in her voice and paused. "How could that happen?"

"Ah, that would be your brother, Logan."

"Logan. Logan dropped off the bags." Careen grabbed the desk for support. How could Logan get the bags without ... She didn't want to think about that. Not yet.

"No. Logan stopped by to tell me he was heading up and I gave him the bags that were dropped off earlier."

"Dropped off earlier? By Logan?"

"No. Sorry. I'm confusing you. The bags were left earlier this afternoon. Logan came past on his way up and I asked him to take them."

"Left earlier. By who?"

"Some scruffy kid. Wouldn't leave his name. Said some guy had paid him twenty dollars to leave the bags for you."

"And you just took them? Didn't that sound just a little suspicious to you? Or do scruffy kids always get paid by strangers to deliver parcels here?" Careen's voice was strident now.

"Did I do something wrong? It was addressed to you."

"It could have been anything."

"I am sorry. Is there a problem?"

"Yes, there is. In fact there are two problems," Careen snapped. "Problem one is you don't find anything odd about people paying kids to drop off parcels." She held up her fingers to count on. "Problem two is you then give them to my brother to put in my apartment. There could have been anything in them, there could have been a bomb." Her panic was turning to anger now.

"They were shopping bags. That's all. I don't understand ..."

"And that's the problem. You don't understand anything about security at all." She stepped towards him. "We obviously have some issues with the training here." She paused to ensure she had his full attention. "In future, no one is to go into my apartment unless I personally buzz them in. No one and nothing, no parcels, no deliveries and most of all no people, and that includes Logan. Have I made myself clear?"

"Perfectly." Jim slipped his hands into his pockets, swallowing hard.

"Good. And make sure Bill and any relief staff are aware of this too." Careen turned on her heels and strode back to the lift.

That explained how the bags got in her apartment, but what was Logan doing here? Since the strange visit the other day why would he just go on up? But didn't he always? He seemed to think buzzing in was for visitors and he was family after all.

Careen opened her apartment door and stood for a moment surveying the room. The floor was strewn with the clothes from the bags and the jigsaw piece with the blood red tear sat there as if trying to intimidate her. What now? She picked up the piece of jigsaw and placed it in the ziplock bag with the other piece, slamming the drawer in her haste to get it out of sight. She scooped up all the clothes and shoved them into the bags. She strode out to the garbage chute, dropped the bags in and listened as they clunked and clattered down eighteen floors to the basement bins. It wasn't until she shut the apartment door behind her again that she realised whoever had dropped off the parcels had kept the sunhat.

Careen, needing a distraction, did what she always did when wanting to ignore everything else. She worked. She had three proposals from small businesses wanting support, either mentoring or financially. Three proposals each of thirty pages, each detailing the reasons why she should work with them and in some cases, invest in them. The first two she skimmed and dismissed quickly. They'd not done their homework and there were some major flaws in their logic. The third one would require a closer look. It was a training program for disadvantaged youth and required a work-placement option that would be feasible in some of the Montage hotels. She sat back realising she'd have to run that past Chris – Montage wasn't hers anymore.

NINE

Careen was a bit more settled after working on the proposals for the rest of the afternoon. She'd decided to drive to Ben's, but the problem was that her car was in the car park under the building, she'd moved it there this morning after peeling the parking ticket off the windscreen. She knew there was a concierge shift change at four p.m. so hopefully Jim had gone home and she could ask Bill to walk her to the car. She got lucky, one of the couples on level sixteen got in the lift shortly after her and pushed the basement-level button. She half ran to her car, checked the back seat was empty, jumped in and locked the doors, her finger hovering on the alarm button. Careen took a deep breath, fired up the engine and drove towards the exit. She wanted to be ahead of them leaving the car park. Didn't want to be in there alone. As soon as she was out onto Beach Street she dialled Gordon.

"Yes?"

"Good afternoon to you too, Gordon." She smiled to herself as she imagined his gruff face. "It's Careen. I'm sorry to call you on the weekend."

"Not sorry enough that you avoided calling."

"What have you found out about Louise Mears?"

"Nothing unusual. Worked her way up from gossip columns in the local papers to celebrity news in a couple of magazines. She's had a few jobs writing articles about so-called successful people in *Collections*, but they moved her on as they didn't like her lack of ethics in gathering information. She has a guest slot on that podcast thing we spoke about but mostly she freelances. Gets the bulk of her work through a friend of hers, rather than any business contacts."

"Go back a step. Did *Collections* mention what sort of ethics issues?"

"Met with an ex-colleague of hers who said Louise was happy to offer bribes, threaten and even blackmail people to get the information she wanted. She isn't careful with the truth, either. She's just as happy to write fiction as fact."

"What I don't understand is what she has to gain by stalking me?"

"Stalking. No one mentioned stalking."

Careen ran Gordon through the last few days, giving him as much detail as she could recall.

"Do you have any sort of security system?"

"I never felt I needed one."

"It appears you do now. I'll have my team at your place Monday. Eight a.m. Be there."

"Yes sir." Careen felt like saluting. "What do you have in mind?"

"Change your locks, since I assume you are using the standard hotel security system."

"Actually you're wrong there. I had the lock recoded when I moved in. It's not on the standard hotel master code."

"Wonders will never cease." He muttered. "We'll do it again anyhow. I'll have my guys install a security system and I'll speak with the hotel manager about disabling all the swipes to the floor and re-enabling only those used by current guests. Although that doesn't help much. Why did you decide to live in a hotel for God's sake? It's not normal, and," he added, "hard to secure." Gordon huffed down the phone line. "I want a security camera in the hallway to catch anyone trying to enter."

"That covers the building. What about whoever is following me?"

"I'm getting to that. Where are you now?"

"I'm in my car on Bay Street. I'm heading to Ben's for dinner."

"I see." Gordon paused. "Is that a good idea?"

"Why wouldn't it be?" Careen asked, then it dawned on her why he was asking. "Good grief. No." Careen was horrified. "Ben wouldn't do anything to hurt me."

"You did steal his inheritance."

Careen laughed. "I most certainly did not. Gordon, if you knew Ben you wouldn't even suggest that. He never wanted it. He was relieved when I inherited it. Having to run Montage is his worst nightmare."

"Any other possibilities?"

Careen was reluctant to mention Logan's odd behaviour. Suggesting it might be him was like treason somehow. "No."

"You're holding out on me, Miss Tamley. I wasn't born yesterday you know."

"Let's talk again tomorrow, I'm running late for dinner at Ben's." She indicated to turn left into Graham Street. "It has to be something to do with Louise. I can't think of anything else." *Or am refusing to think about it. Telling Gordon would mean it was a possibility and one she wasn't prepared to deal with yet.*

"She's a disgrace, but no previous stalking charges. Doesn't mean she isn't trying something new. I'll step up the research on her, try and get access to her police record." Gordon paused. "Miss Tamley, if there is anything or anyone else in the picture, I need to know."

"I'll give it some thought. No one springs to mind." She was sure Gordon could hear the lie.

Careen was halfway up Graham Street when the fuel light started flashing. Careen never let the fuel tank fall below half, and she always insisted that the car be filled up with petrol after a service. Lei had been quite absentminded lately; she'd have to speak with her. About that, and about Gary. Careen had a feeling the two issues were related.

Pulling in at the local service station, Careen filled the car with petrol, scanning the forecourt the whole time. Inside, the queue was long and, as she waited, she flicked through the latest *New Idea*, shaking her head at the stupidity of some of the celebrities. Three minutes and she felt she was all caught up on the entertainment news. She had trouble believing that people paid for this trash. Payment made and a Mars Bar secured, she headed back to the car – her mind already plotting the best route to Ben's to avoid the football traffic.

She clicked the car remote to unlock the door. Nothing. She clicked it again. No sound, no lights. She was sure she'd locked it. She knew she locked it. Careen clicked the lock button. The sidelights flashed and she heard the pronounced click. She unlocked the car again. Lock. Unlock. Lock. She never left the car unlocked. Ever. Her eyes swept the forecourt for anyone who was acting suspicious but they all seemed to be going about their normal business. Could she have forgotten? She was a bit distracted after all. She unlocked the car again but kept her finger on the alarm button as she slid into the driver's seat, glancing around as she did so. Nothing out of the ordinary. She was about to put the keys in the ignition when a cold feeling crept up on her. She turned to look over her shoulder at the back seat.

TEN

No one was there. Her hands were shaking as she put the key in the ignition and started the engine, locking the doors as a reflex action. She hit the accelerator too hard and the car screeched onto the service station forecourt and out into the road. She drove around the block once, twice, her mind awhirl. He was getting to her. Even simple mistakes seemed to panic her. What she needed was a friendly voice on the phone.

"Yo!"

"Hi, Ben, it's me."

"Not cancelling, I hope."

"On you, never." She paused. "Ben, I need your help."

"Whatever, whenever. You far away?"

"No, I'll be there in fifteen minutes."

"You okay? You sound a bit odd."

"You have no idea." Careen steadied her voice; she'd be there soon, no need to worry Ben unnecessarily. She shouldn't have phoned. "I'll see you soon. Tell you all about it then."

"Sure about that?"

"Absolutely"

"Ciao!"

Careen decided music would keep her mind from overloading. She always kept a Bryan Adams CD in her car. She hit the button to change from audio to CD and was surprised to hear The Hollies "He Ain't Heavy, He's My Brother" playing.

She ejected the CD and dropped it on the passenger seat. They must have put the CD in to listen to while they serviced the car – each to their own. She'd get Lei to return it on Monday. She hit the audio button and keyed Brian Adams into the Spotify search. Much better. She sang along with gusto to "Summer of '69". She wasn't going to think about anything until she got to Ben's. It didn't however stop her checking the rear-vision mirror. Just in case.

She pulled into a car space right outside Ben's apartment block. At least something was going her way tonight. Before unlocking the doors she peered out into the darkness, checking out the streets. She climbed out and looked around before shutting the car door behind her. She triple-clicked her car remote to check that the car was locked and then turned around. She had often heard the phrase "the hairs on the back of your neck standing up" and now she knew what it meant.

Taking a deep breath, Careen turned and bolted to Ben's building. She pulled out her access card, glad that she hadn't returned it after Ben's long trip away last year. She'd moved in while her apartment was being repainted. Ben had been away and she had enjoyed her stay there. She glanced back and smiled – fast access – you can't follow me in here. Once inside she would be safe. Turning quickly, she checked the street again then pulled the entrance door closed behind her.

She feels safe with Ben, trusts him, even fools herself that she loves him. There is so much joy to be had in breaking that bond; in watching as Ben finds out what she is capable of. Of seeing what Careen will do when what matters to her is jeopardised - when she has to choose.

Careen had always loved Ben's place. Inside the glass foyer stood two massive solid-oak warehouse doors set into 100-year-old bluestone. The floor creaked as she walked towards what she termed the dwarf entrance. The smaller openings, cut out of the oak slabs, were not quite high enough to accommodate a person without them bending down to climb through. With one last look behind her she pushed through the smaller doorway and stepped into the vast expanse of restaurant that now filled the space. She leaned against the ancient wood behind her, waiting for the serenity of the place to engulf her. The late-evening sun streamed through the second-storey windows, not blocked by any roof or floor, and it picked up the dust particles dancing in the breeze she had created. The restaurant had been closed for months, the owner taking some time out before deciding what do with the place. The plain wooden tables and bench seats stood to attention in their abandonment, each table hosting a single candle in a wax-coated bottle. The long bar gleamed and lights behind the glass racks – left on all this time – cast an unearthly glow. She picked her way down the length of the bar to the rickety staircase that led to Ben's room. Unnerved, and holding onto the worn banister for support – she'd never been convinced these stairs would hold her – she climbed quickly, breathing in the musky scent of whichever incense Ben had burnt last night to cover the smell of years of stale beer and wine. She reached the balcony and ducked under Ben's washing that, she had been shocked to discover, he left hung over the balcony, even when the restaurant was open. Slightly breathless from the climb, she rapped on Ben's door.

"It's open."

Careen entered the flat as Ben stepped out of the bathroom, a towel wrapped around his waist and a second one briskly drying his hair.

"You're early."

"Actually I'm not."

But hey, if that's the view, I will be next time. She bit her lip to stop herself from moaning out loud. God he was gorgeous.

Ben strode over, threw his hair towel over an already laden chair, and enveloped her in a hug. Careen breathed deeply, inhaling the scent of soap and Ben's musky smell. She felt the tension melting as she stood with her head resting on his still damp chest. She pulled Ben close, holding him to her as if she could somehow block out the day by staying safely in his arms.

"Now there's a welcome." Ben kissed the top of her head. "I'm still damp. You'll get creased."

Careen realised how long she'd been holding him and decided humour was the best form of defence. She looked up with what she hoped was some approximation of a naughty smile and quipped, "And me all dressed to kill and all." Careen stood back as if to survey the scene. "Mmmm. Not bad. Not bad at all." Her troubles pushed aside for the moment, she grinned lecherously. "After all, what more could a girl want after a hard day at the grindstone than a half-naked man throwing himself at her?"

"A wholly naked man perhaps?" He grinned wickedly, and Careen's heart started racing and the heat rushed to her face. "And I heard you haven't been grinding so much as suffering migraines again." Ben's look changed to one of concern. "What's set this lot off?"

From eligible male to brotherly concern in one sentence. When would she learn? Careen turned away from Ben to hide her disappointment. She picked up the wet towel and started folding it.

"You've got these clothes all damp." She studied the towel she was folding.

"I thought you'd given up on tidying my apartment."

"Look at this place, someone needs to."

"You could always move in and sort me out."

"I accept the challenge." The expression on his face was one of pure horror; a little overdone she thought. "Now before I get any risqué ideas, I suggest you put some clothes on and cook me some dinner."

He turned and headed towards the bathroom, but stopped short and turned around, grinning. "What sort of risqué ideas did you have in mind?"

"Out."

As the door shut behind him Careen glared at the bathroom door. Why did he do that, flirt with her when he wasn't interested? She guessed he thought he was just being playful, and maybe if she didn't feel the way she did, she'd see it that way too. She stamped down her irritation with logic. They'd been friends a long time, she should know better.

She picked up a couple of dirty wine glasses from the bench to rinse them, stopping as she noticed a bright-red lipstick smear on one. Oh Ben, who is it this time? She felt the tears building and knew she couldn't hold them back. She dropped the glasses in the sink and then looked at them wildly as they smashed against the greasy plates already stacked there. She picked out the broken stems and leant on the edge of the sink to gather up the rest of the broken pieces. The pain as she cut her finger on the glass was all it took to have her tears flowing freely. Look at me, pathetic. I'm stronger than this. She knew this wasn't about Ben and his girlfriends, that it was the culmination of the stress of the last week, but it didn't help.

The noise of the bathroom door opening startled her. He can't see me like this. Turning back towards the bench she grabbed the dirty tea towel and wrapped it around her finger to stop the bleeding. Even in her distress she cringed at the state of the towel. Yeah, like we could live together.

"Got to go." She grabbed her handbag from the bench and bolted towards the front door.

"Whoa, girl! Where do you think you're going?" He grabbed

Careen's arm as she shot past him.

"Away."

"I know my place is a mess, but that's no reason to give up on me."

"Ben, just leave me be. I'm tired and I just want to go home." She paused then, remembering she couldn't go home.

"You've slept for the last two days from what I hear. That won't wash." He steered her towards the sofa, and after moving a pile of canvasses, sat her down gently.

"I need tissues."

"Promise you won't run off on me if I leave you for a minute?"

Careen looked into his eyes, the eyes that had for so long captivated her, and saw how worried he was. Brotherly love or not, he did care. "I promise."

She dabbed at her eyes with the filthy towel and looked around. The place was a mess but it was Ben's mess and it was his home. Everything about it screamed *lived in*. Her apartment seemed so barren. A mirror of her personal life. She turned to look at Ben, who she could see was quite perplexed at how to cope with a crying Careen. Was she in love with him or just in love with the idea of being in love with him? Is it because when he put his arms around her, she felt safe? Was that what she wanted? Safe. Was that enough? She'd dated a number of guys over the years, but they'd all got tired of her pulling away, of her inability to relax in bed, their breath on the back of her neck as they slept a trigger for her nightmares. None of them could ever understand. Her brain was spinning, and she was sure if she looked in a mirror, she would see her temples pulsating.

"Careen." Ben put his hand under her chin and tilted her head up until she was looking at him. "What's wrong?"

"Today, yesterday, and several days before." She stared at the damp tissues scrunched in her hand.

"You need to do better than that." His voice was soft, caring.

"Okay. A summary in fifty words or less." She blew her nose on the tissue and then tucked it into her handbag. "As you know, I have to leave Montage soon. I've offered Chris the CEO job. That's all good. Logan is pissed off because I gave Chris's job to Murray and after storming out of the office came to my apartment and apologised to me before stealing my favourite photo. I'm getting prank calls, bitchy emails and pieces of jigsaw. I'm being followed when I shop for clothes and if that isn't enough, I have a blinding headache for the third day in a row. Any more questions?"

"Phew."

"You did ask." She blew her nose again and grabbed a fresh tissue.

"You stay here. I'll open the wine. Seems like it's going to be a long night."

ELEVEN

She'd talked to Ben for hours, or talked at him. He'd listened patiently. She'd cried, he'd hugged her, and somehow with the wine and the comfort she'd fallen asleep in Ben's arms. She awoke in Ben's bed – alone. Even if he had been interested he wouldn't take advantage. More's the pity.

Her dreams last night had been full of clown dolls with bulbous heads, painted red lips and gnashing teeth. She'd woken bleary-eyed and frustrated.

She was still dressed in her jeans and yesterday's top. She spotted her reflection in the mirror and cringed at her crumpled appearance. Ben was painting. Standing behind him she admired his work; enthralled by his serenity and total concentration. He was painting her. Not the calm, perfect façade of corporate Careen, but the frightened vulnerable girl she'd been last night. He closed his eyes, humming softly, opened his eyes then tilted his head and resumed painting. She stood watching for about twenty minutes before her rumbling stomach alerted him to her presence.

"What do you think?"

"It scares me how you do that; find my soul and put it on paper."

He smiled softly. "How are you this morning? Other than hungry," he added as her stomach growled again.

"Better." He was still seated so she rested her chin on his head and slipped her arms around his shoulders. "Thanks, Ben."

"Always here. You know that." He untangled her arms and stood up. "Let's get you some breakfast then."

"I'll cook."

"Nothing personal, my girl, but I'd prefer something edible. You might, however, like to wash up a couple of mugs."

The omelette was delicious. They chatted about Ben's next trip as they ate, Careen deliberately turning her back on the mess in the kitchen. "I'm off again Monday. Only as far as Perth this time to do a couple of preliminary interviews and sketches." He paused. "Will you be okay? I might be able to push it out a few days."

"I'll be fine. I'll meet with Gordon and then I think I'll take the rest of the day off." She had agonised over the decision before getting out of bed, she had never missed a day unless she was bedridden.

"Now I know I should worry."

Careen spent Sunday with Ben. He'd painted, she'd read. They'd ordered takeaway and watched Shaun of the Dead while eating pizza. Ben's theory, that there is nothing like a zombie comedy to take your mind off reality, seemed to be true. For the first time in weeks, Careen relaxed. She'd stayed another night and slept soundly.

"Ready to go?" Ben had offered to meet with her and Gordon before heading to the airport. They walked arm in arm towards her car. Which wasn't there.

"Ben. My car has gone." Careen could feel the blood draining from her face. She gripped his arm.

He peeled her hand off his arm, placed both her hands between his. "Look at me, Careen."

She raised her eyes to his. "Where did you leave it?"

"Here. I parked it here." She pointed at the empty car spot

right next to where they stood. "Right here." Her voice was getting shrill and she hated herself for it.

Ben scanned the street. "It's over there." He pointed across the road to where her dark-blue BMW was standing in a loading zone, a parking ticket affixed to the windscreen.

"In a loading zone." Careen was incensed. "I would never park in a loading zone."

Ben opened his mouth to respond.

"And don't even think about making a smart remark." She turned to him. "Ben, I was thinking yesterday, about my car being unlocked. You know I mentioned that Lei passed over my spare key to the service centre and it wasn't returned. Could he be someone who works there?"

"Or someone who doesn't."

"Sorry?"

"He said he worked with BMW. Lei assumed he did and handed over the key. We only have his word for the fact that he works there."

"But that means Lei has seen him."

"So I suggest we have a chat to Lei."

"Not today. I have a feeling things are bad at home with Gary and I'd like to handle it gently." Careen unlocked her car. "She'll feel like it's all her fault."

"She should have asked for ID or rung to check, so maybe it is."

"She knows nothing about this mess, Ben. What reason would she have to double-check what he said?"

"She is meant to be your gatekeeper. That's her job."

She jumped as a horn tooted right behind her. A bald, middle-aged man was leaning out the window of his truck. "Is this your car? I need to park here to unload."

"We're just leaving." Ben steered Careen towards the passenger seat.

She ducked her head to climb in. "No. No. No." Careen pushed herself out, stepping back quickly and almost throwing Ben off balance.

"Whoa, girl. Careful."

"The hat, Ben." She pointed at the hat while backing away slowly. "That's my Amalfi hat." And to ensure she didn't miss the point, sitting on the brim of the sunhat was another piece of jigsaw.

TWELVE

Ben had moved her car out of the loading zone but, given that Careen wasn't getting in her car, they took Ben's van. Careen always thought that Ben having a VW Kombi was a bit too much of a cliché but he insisted it was perfect for when he travelled. It had a bed and small kitchen and could hold all his painting gear.

"You okay if I park underneath?" He always checked before he parked at Careen's.

She laughed nervously. "It's either that or get three tickets in a week." Besides, Ben was with her.

Ben pulled the van into Careen's parking space. They walked hand in hand to the lifts, her eyes peering around the grey concrete pillars. She jumped as a door slammed. Ben squeezed her hand as he pushed the elevator button for the ground floor. Careen looked at him, a question in her eyes but he stayed silent. Still holding her hand, he pulled her into the foyer and walked over to the concierge.

"Good morning, Mr Seymour, Miss Tamley. How can I help?"

"Jim, isn't it? I'd like you to explain the hotel's security to me. I'll be away for work and I like to know that Careen is safe."

Careen cringed. After the dressing down she'd given Jim yesterday, this wasn't such a great idea. "Ben. Can we do this some other time?" Careen whispered.

Jim's expression didn't change, however, his normal affable

nature was absent. "Seems to be a popular question of late."

Careen gripped Ben's hand tightly. "What do you mean – a popular question?" She asked.

"Just a couple of potential guests. They wanted to check out how secure the building was."

"What did they look like?" Ben tried to extricate his hand as Careen squeezed it more tightly.

"The first one was a tall bloke. Pleasant chap. Glasses, moustache. Very polite. Ideal guest."

"Ben, it's him."

"Who?"

"Him."

"Careen, I'm sure it's not unusual for someone to check out a hotel before they stay." Ben pried his hand loose from Careen's, placed his arm around her and drew her close.

"Actually it is," Jim said. "Most people just assume a certain level of security in high-quality hotels and seldom worry about it at all."

"I see. So what did you tell the guy?" Ben asked.

"There were two gentlemen, and I told them both the same thing."

"Which was?" Careen prompted.

"If reception is unattended you need to swipe an access card to get in the front door. Everyone who isn't recognised by the staff is asked his or her business. You need a swipe card to access your floor or the lifts, and the swipes are apartment specific. In theory, no one who isn't entitled to should be able to get in. Even if they did, the security cameras would pick them up. The tall guy was paranoid. He asked what type of security system we had, where the cameras were and how often it was monitored. Must have a highly strung wife."

"And you told them all this?" Careen was incensed. "You gave complete strangers a full run-down of the security set up.

What the hell were you thinking?"

"I told them the building was secure and it is." Jim was on the defensive. "We're careful here. We're not like the residential building next door."

"What do you mean?" Ben queried.

"They're not so on the ball as we are here." Jim glared at Careen. "They had a guy slip under the car-park security grill and jump in the lift with a resident. He got off at the first floor. That's where their gym is. He was dressed in gym gear and waited until someone went into the gym and followed them in. He stole one of the resident's access cards. It was about an hour later when the girl noticed her card was missing and reported it. By that time the thief had been and gone."

"And you know about this how?" Ben asked.

"Joe from Reptic told me about it. They tracked the guy on the security camera but he was wearing a cap so they couldn't get a good look at his face. Don't know if they got him in the end."

The phone rang and Jim reached to answer it. "Excuse me."

Careen shook her head in disgust. "Anybody with half a brain would know you don't go around telling people your security set up just because they ask. We need to update our hiring practices."

Ben grabbed Careen's hand and pulled her away from the desk. "Enough. This is so unlike you." Ben turned her around to face him. "You know the security here is as good as it gets for a hotel. You helped test it."

"Then why did *you* feel you needed to ask?"

"Just checking things hadn't changed." Ben shrugged. "Actually I just hoped it would make you feel better. Just make sure you don't leave your keys lying around."

"What do you suggest? My bathers don't exactly have a pocket."

"You're right. From memory they fit snugly. All over." He grinned and Careen blushed. She turned away from Ben and surveyed the foyer. "I'm sure there are lots of other ways to get around the security."

"Like?"

"I'd rather not think about them right now."

They entered her apartment. Careen cautiously and Ben with a flourish, throwing open the door and striding in.

"Anyone here? Hello."

"Ben." She sounded as exasperated as she felt. He was not taking this seriously enough.

"Hey." Ben put his arm around her shoulders. "Easy, girl. You've known me long enough to know I joke around when I'm worried." He gave her a squeeze and released her. "How about you grab some clean clothes? We'll have a chat with Gordon and I'll take you out for lunch before I head to the airport."

"Thanks." She leant over, kissed his cheek and then headed into her bedroom.

Moments later, Ben called from the kitchen, "You're out of coffee pods."

"No chance. The stand is full and there's more in the cupboard. Top left where they're always kept."

"Only thing I can find is a jar of instant, which I must say, surprises me."

"Ben. I've never bought instant." Careen walked warily out of the bedroom still in her crumpled clothes. "I had plenty of pods on Saturday when I left."

"Are you sure?"

"Of course I'm sure. Have you ever known me to run out of coffee, or worse, buy instant?"

"Careen." Ben walked towards her, grabbed her hand again. "I don't want you to panic."

"What?"

"We both know you are rather pedantic about certain things."

Ben raised an eyebrow as if to indicate it wasn't a criticism, so Careen bit back the response she was about to make.

"Get to the point."

"I've never known you to leave anything on the kitchen bench when you go out. Given that you were in a bad state I want you to think very carefully." He pointed at the bench. "Did you leave that coffee cup half full on the bench when you left?"

Careen glanced at the mug on the bench and instantly moved back behind Ben as if he could protect her from what she'd just seen. She rested her head on his back, shutting her eyes to block out the picture. Sitting next to the half-empty mug were the pieces of the jigsaw that she'd thrown into the bottom drawer. They were all pieced together, along with the one she had thrown from her balcony onto the street.

THIRTEEN

They waited in the lobby downstairs, Careen alternatively pacing up and down or sitting next to Ben, rubbing her sweaty hands up and down her thighs to dry them out. Gordon arrived within half an hour, with a couple of security guys he brought with him to check out the place. Once they were in Careen's apartment, Careen and Ben ran Gordon through what had happened over the last few days.

"Mmm. He's stepping up his game." Gordon stood up. He called one of the techs over. "Might want to check for listening devices too."

"You're kidding me?" Ben, it appeared, was more surprised than Careen was.

"Do I look like the kidding sort to you?"

Gordon did have a point.

"Careen, you and I will go downstairs and get a takeaway coffee. Ben you can go now."

Ben looked at Careen, a questioning smile on his face. She nodded her head slightly indicating she'd be okay.

"I'm off. Talk later." Ben kissed her cheek. "I'm going to delay my Perth trip. Don't want to leave you alone."

"Come on, Ben. I'm a big girl. By the time Gordon and his crew are finished here, I'll be safe as houses."

"If you're sure?"

"Go." Careen pushed Ben gently towards the door and

leaned in to grab her handbag.

"No, leave your bag here. I want the guys to check that too."

Careen swallowed hard and placed her handbag on the floor, waving Ben off as he stepped into the lift.

"Wasn't smart, you know," said Gordon.

"What wasn't?"

"Letting your boyfriend go interstate. Best to have someone close."

"Number one, he's not my boyfriend. And two, he was on your list of suspects last week."

"Mm."

"He needs this commission. The family he's doing the portraits for have a lot of contacts in the art world and if he mucks them around he could lose not only this, but any future opportunities." She turned to Gordon. "And by the time your guys have done their work, I'll be living in Fort Knox."

"Even Fort Knox has a sentry or two."

Gordon pulled his notebook out of his blazer pocket before they'd even ordered coffee.

"So Logan comes and goes, and your PA Lei has a key. What have they got to gain? Why would they be trying to scare you?"

"It's Louise. It has to be. She knows my past and she's angling for a more sensational story."

"You seem very sure of this."

"I don't want to think of the alternative."

"Which is?"

A tune started playing close by. A tune she'd heard recently. The humming. Gordon reached into his pocket.

"Hey, honey. What's up? Dad's busy at the moment. Can I call you back later?" He glanced over at Careen, must have seen how pale she was. "Daddy has to go. I'll call you back real soon." He reached over and grabbed Careen's arm and she shook him off.

"You look like you've seen a ghost."

"Your ringtone."

"'Send in the Clowns'. My daughter loves clowns." Gordon placed his phone on the table between them. "Careen, I feel I'm missing something here."

"The clowns. Always the clowns." She put her elbows on the table and dropped her head into her hands.

"Careen? Ben mentioned the clowns are significant."

"I need a minute."

Their coffee arrived and Gordon took a sip. "When you're ready."

Careen raised her head, turned and stared at the ocean, watched the waves break over the shore, washing away the footprints of those who marked the sand as they passed. She wanted so much to forget. To have the waves wash away that part of her past. However, if it wasn't Louise frightening her it might be him. She needed Gordon's help. She suppressed a shiver.

"It was my nineteenth birthday. I was young and naive. Stupid." Careen shook her head. "I'd been out drinking with a few friends. I wasn't drunk, but I wasn't sober either. I'd parked in a high-rise station, the one over on Russell Street." The expression on Gordon's face clearly showed what he thought of her drink driving. She chose to ignore his silent censure and continued. "I caught the lift up to the third floor. It was late. About two a.m. The place was deserted."

Her voice was carefully monotone, like she was relating a story. Like it was someone else's past. She'd entered the dimly lit car park on a high. Her best friend Mel had just been offered a job in New York so they'd had a double celebration. Lots of champagne. Mel had offered to walk her back to her car, but she'd waved her off. Mel's feet were killing her, she didn't need the extra walk, and she always parked there, she'd be fine.

She sings softly to herself as she rides up the elevator, tracing the lines of the graffiti heart scratched on the door. Tracey loves Peter. That's so sweet. The lift shudders and stops at level three, but the lift doors remain closed. She stabs at the open-door button and with a screech the doors part halfway. Great. She shoves the doors apart, swears as she breaks a nail. She'd only had them done yesterday. She sucks on the finger and ambles towards her car; kicking an empty beer can and listening to it clatter away, echoing in the empty car park. Where were all the cars? She feels a tightening in her chest. She is alone up here. A white van is parked to her left, the light bulb above it flickering. She shivers uneasily, swallows. It's quiet, eerily so. She puts her car-park ticket between her teeth while she rummages in her bag for her keys. The light bulb above her head buzzes and dies. There are shadows everywhere. A car door slams shut and she hears the soft purr of an engine coming to life. Her eyes dart back to the van. Empty. Remembering some basic self-defence training she positions her keys so the individual spikes are sticking out from between her fingers; jumps as a car backfires in the street below. She picks up her pace, her high heels clanking in the silence, announcing her as loudly as a drum beat. She stops. Listens. Footsteps. Behind her. She wheels around. The floor seems deserted, or at least the parts she can see, but there are too many she can't. She pulls down her skirt, suddenly aware just how short it is. The grey concrete pillars look menacing in the half-light, holding secrets in their shadows. She pauses, holds herself still. Motionless. Alert. A steady drip is the only sound. She glances at the puddle to her left where water has pooled from the leaking pipes. Spots a movement in the reflection. She spins left. Nothing. Scans the floor again. There are four vehicles to pass before she gets to her car. The only sound she can hear is the hum of a generator or aircon on the next-door roof. She can't hear the traffic.

Could anyone hear her if she screamed? She grips her keys harder. Footsteps again. She doesn't stop to listen, just runs, her car keys firmly grasped in her sweaty palms. She veers around the corner and there he is, next to a shiny silver Audi. His face is in shadow, hidden. She stops suddenly, her bag swings down, jars her shoulder. She pulls it up quickly, but in the moment she glanced away, he disappeared. Her skin tingles everywhere. She's burning up; sweat is running down between her breasts, all her senses are on alert. Still she doesn't move. She needs to make a decision. Go back, or forward? She glances behind her, then twirls quickly, covering all bases. No one. Nothing. She remembers the red panic button on her car remote, hopes to startle him. She stabs at the button. Silence. She meant to replace the batteries, wishes now she had. She reaches into her handbag. Grabs her mobile. Starts to dial. "No signal in here, sweetheart." The voice echoes around her. She knows she's in trouble, but she's not sure where to go. She has no sense of where he is, where the threat lies. She gathers her courage, grips her keys more firmly and runs. He'll expect her to head for her car, so she sprints for the down ramp. Footsteps. Behind her. She glances back. Trips. Goes down. Screams in agony as her ankle twists beneath her. Kicks off her shoes. Groans out loud as she tries to stand. Limps away. His laughter echoes behind her, then nothing. The silence is worse. Where is he? She looks wildly around. He steps out from the shadows. Grabs her arm. "Enough games." His voice is harsh, gravelly. He is taller than her, wiry, but strong. She bites back a scream at the hideous mask he is wearing: a grotesque clown with bloody tears and filed teeth. He cackles, a hideous sound that chills her blood. He wrenches her arm, pulls her around, pinning her back against his chest. She stamps her heel on the arch of his foot. He curses, kicks her injured ankle. She moans with the pain. She moves her hips to the side, pulls her right arm free and stabs the keys as hard as she can into his balls. He screams. Releases her. She runs, ignoring the pain shooting from her ankle. He is back up. Running behind her. She ducks. Not fast enough. He grabs her loose hair and pulls her in. She uses the keys again, turns and scrapes them down his neck. Hard. He hollers. She kicks at his knee with her good foot. He buckles. Stumbles back. She runs.

"I made it down to the next level. There were people there. They helped me. Calmed me down. Called the police. By the time they got there, he was long gone."

"Did they catch him?"

"No." Careen took a gulp of her water. "The security cameras weren't working and I couldn't describe him. Tall, skinny, but strong. He was wearing a wig and a hideous clown mask." Tears started to fall and she wiped them away angrily. "If I'd been able to describe him, maybe incapacitate him properly, he wouldn't have gone on to kill eleven other girls. I should have done better."

"You aren't to blame for his actions."

"I know that logically, but it doesn't help."

"Did they get any DNA from the keys?"

"Yes, but they had nothing to match it with."

"How do they know it was him, that he killed the others?"

"He left a card with a clown face – the same card every time. Blood tears, filed teeth, grey skin. The face of death. Each card had a number."

"Number?"

"Numbers two to twelve."

"And number one?"

"They assumed that was for me."

"I see."

"It didn't stop there." Careen signalled the waiter, she needed more water. Gordon waited patiently while it was brought to the table. She took a large gulp. "Once a year on my birthday I'd get a card at home or at work. On the front would be a picture of a clown, and on the back, six words. 'You'll always be my number one'." She shuddered at the memory. "There were never any fingerprints. It stopped after five years. The police assumed he'd been caught for something else and locked up, or he'd got bored with torturing me. Either way, they closed the file."

"And you think he could be back?"

"That's the thing. It's the same, only different. I'm not sure where the jigsaw pieces fit in – other than it looks like he is building up a picture of a clown. Then there's the numbers, counting down from twelve, the number of girls he attacked. But it doesn't fit with what he did last time. And the 'princess' thing. Where does that fit? The humming of 'Send in the Clowns' is something new too."

"It could be a copycat with their own agenda. Someone using the same MO to frighten you."

"Well, it's working."

Careen needed to walk. The memories were too close to the surface and she needed to outpace them. Gordon ordered another coffee to go and strode beside her by the sand as he outlined his plans for the new security system and webcams. He would also work with security at the Montage office to put a trace on Careen's work line and mobile.

"Careen. Keep acting natural and then turn slowly to your left. I want you to look for a tall guy, six foot plus. He's been keeping pace with us the whole time we've been walking. I want to know if you recognise him."

Careen turned to study the gentleman on the boardwalk but in the short time it had taken Gordon to draw Careen's attention he had turned his back and walked away.

"Shouldn't you go after him?"

"And say what?" Gordon grabbed Careen's arm to stop her darting up the beach. "He was walking on the boardwalk, nothing more. That's not a crime."

"Describe him."

"Tall, about six foot four. Broad shoulders. Square jaw. Moustache. Hair was light brown with blond highlights. Short at the back, longer at the front. Obviously styled. In fact over dressed for the beach. Designer labels tailored to fit." Gordon paused. "He was quite blasé. Wasn't worried about me being able to describe him so he was either a random stranger or he doesn't think you can identify him."

"You got all that from a quick glance?"

"No, I've been keeping an eye on him for a while, and he was aware of the fact."

Careen shut her eyes and drew the picture in her mind from the details Gordon had provided. "I don't know anyone like that." Frustrated she kicked at the sand.

"It's unlikely you know him then. If he wasn't just a random stranger then he may know who I am and would know I would be able to describe him clearly."

"Which brings us back to Louise Mears. Her photographer was a short stocky guy. He doesn't fit. Maybe Louise has hired someone."

"Not necessarily." Gordon sipped his coffee and grimaced. "Luke warm." He swallowed nonetheless. "I'll keep investigating her but I also want to explore other options." He turned to Careen. "I'll also put a tail on you."

"No." Careen was emphatic.

"What you need to understand, Careen, is that you likely already have one." Gordon paused. "Isn't it better that we have one of our team keeping an eye out for you?"

Careen's back was ramrod straight and her laugh was bitter. "I thought talking to you would make me feel better and you've made things worse."

"My job isn't to make you feel better, it's to keep you safe. Have you considered making a report to the police?"

"Did that. They weren't that interested. They think it's a copycat and until he actually threatens or confronts me they can't do anything."

"That's correct, but it's always good to have a report on file in case things escalate."

"Escalate." Careen flinched. "To what?"

FOURTEEN

Gordon liaised with building management at the office and started working with them on a plan to improve security. The alarm system in her apartment would need another day to be up and running, so Gordon suggested Careen stay overnight at a friend's place or at another hotel. As Mel was arriving tonight Careen booked them adjoining apartment suites at the Conrad, the only one in the chain with a vacancy. She'd have to come up with a story for Mel as to why they were staying at the hotel rather than her place. One thing she was sure of, she wasn't going to tell Mel about the jigsaw pieces. Mel still blamed herself for not walking Careen back to her car that night.

Gordon had suggested that she stick to well-lit public places and she wasn't about to argue. She sat at the Conrad's bar, nursing soda water in her hand, while she waited for Mel. She loved this bar. John had designed it and it felt familiar, comforting. Lots of dark wood panelling and deep comfortable chairs ensured you could settle in for a drink and relax. There was a small private courtyard that was perfect for a sunny afternoon. The bar was busy enough for her to feel safe but, being for guests and their visitors only, meant that not just anyone could stroll in but, if they did, she had placed herself in a way that she could check them out. That aside, she just wanted to leave it all behind her tonight and enjoy time with her friend. It had been nearly a year since Mel's last trip to

Melbourne, and Careen was not going to put a damper on their reunion.

Soda water, Careen? Wanting to stay alert perhaps. And a hotel bar, one of your hotels too. Really? It wasn't that hard to find you. I don't think you understand the seriousness of your situation. Perhaps it's time to up the ante.

"Mel." Careen waved as Mel entered the bar. She hadn't changed a bit; still stylish and a little offbeat. She was wearing tight black pants, knee-high red boots and an amazing technicolour top that draped around her, emphasising her hourglass figure. She'd topped it off with a bright-red beret. It could have been the height of New York fashion or the fact that Mel spent so much time in Paris, but she was affecting an air.

"You look gorgeous. As usual." Careen hugged her.

"You don't look half bad yourself. A little conservative, but that's to be expected."

"Maybe I'll let you take me shopping one of these days – let you update my wardrobe."

"Still waiting. You've been promising me that for years." Mel perched on the stool next to Careen. "I'm parched. Up for a lychee martini?"

"Sounds perfect."

Careen didn't drink cocktails as a rule but lychee martinis were Mel's favourite and Careen had developed a taste for them. They chatted until the cocktails arrived then clinked glasses.

"So how's it all going work-wise?" Careen asked.

Mel owned a PR company in New York that often dealt with high-profile clients and some tricky situations. She had a knack for promoting clients, of course, but her speciality was troubleshooting when things took a bad turn.

"Have you seen the write-ups in the paper about Niptosa Computing? That's the latest mess I'm trying to clean up. Why they wait until things get out of control before calling us in is beyond me." She waved her hand in a dismissive gesture. "But I'm over work for the week. Tell me about what you're up to. How's the love life?"

"In one word: barren."

"And the beautiful Ben. Any change there?"

"No. And not likely to be."

"Have you told him how you feel yet?"

Careen laughed. "I tried that over lunch recently to no avail. He just laughed it off." Careen filled her in on the latest with Ben, stopping midway to order another drink, wine this time.

"Have you ever thought he's got Stuart syndrome?" Stuart was Mel's partner.

"I'm almost afraid to ask."

"Stuart syndrome is a man disease; mostly related to the size of their ..." She paused, laughing, "... ego. Ever since Stuart lost his job he's been acting like a real jerk. Seems he can't cope with having me earning more than him. A threat to his manhood or some such idiotic notion."

Careen laughed. "So what's he doing about it?"

"That's the thing. He's having trouble getting a job at the level he was at, so when a job came up working with me I suggested he take it. Idiot says he can't work for me. Having me pay him would make him feel like a kept man."

"What's that got to do with Ben?"

"Come on, girl, don't be so thick. Ben's a great painter, I get that. But he's not earning much yet. He gets his income from you, the profits *you* make at Montage." She finished off her martini. "You're not only more successful than him, you're paying him. Not too good for his ego."

"Don't be ridiculous. Ben's not like that." Careen was emphatic.

"Are you sure?" Mel tilted her head and looked directly at her friend.

They progressed from drinks to wanting a meal. Rather than walk too far they requested a table at the restaurant next door.

"Ah, Italiano. My favourite food. And my favourite men." Mel winked at the elderly waiter as they were seated.

"Down, girl." Careen was laughing. She missed Mel, missed the spontaneity, the fun. Mel had moved overseas for work shortly after the attack and Careen often wished she'd gone with her.

They were both hungry, so they ordered quickly and settled in with a fresh glass of wine each.

"So any more on the holiday? I've been practising my Italian you know, for when I visit – Ho bisogno di un altro martini."

"Glad to see you've learnt all the useful phrases."

"I can also order a beer, red wine and pizza. You'll be lost without me."

"God I miss you, Mel."

"Of course you do." Mel sipped her wine. "So spill on the holiday plans."

"I've put in a booking request for the place in Amalfi." Careen caressed the stone on her pendant. "Is it possible to be terrified and excited at the same time?"

"Absolutely. Fear is healthy, it keeps you safe." Mel leaned over and squeezed her hand. "You can do this. Start off with a short holiday and build up to a longer one next time."

"Mel." Careen paused. She'd never told Mel about the seven-year codicil in the will. "I'm not actually taking a holiday. I'm leaving Montage."

"What? Can you do that?"

"Can and am. I've asked Chris to take over as CEO."

"Did he do a happy dance or what?"

"Maybe on the inside." Careen somehow couldn't imagine Chris dancing around the office.

"So ..." Mel stopped Careen from picking up her glass. "No wine until I get the full story."

Careen grabbed at her glass and took a sip. "I've resigned, Mel. I'm leaving. All those years as a teenager pleading with Mum and Dad to take me when they travelled, all those nights cutting out pictures of exotic locations and pasting them in the scrapbooks. It's real now, Mel. I'm actually going to do it." If she said it often enough, pretended to be excited, perhaps she would learn to be. Perhaps the excitement would eventually override the fear.

FIFTEEN

A click, a scrape. Careen's eyes snapped open. Instantly awake. Her sheets were soaked with perspiration and she'd thrown the bed covers aside during the night. She shuddered as she remembered the nightmare. Careen pulled the sheet over her bare arms and strained to hear the noise again; the one that woke her. Silence. I'm safe here. No one but Mel knows I'm staying here. She'd even booked the rooms in Mel's name. She sat up, swung her legs over the side of the bed, every sense alert. She quietly crept to the bedroom doorway. She stuck her head around the corner telling herself there was no one there; this was just a peek, to make her feel safe. She checked the door; the security chain was fastened in place. She was alone. Careen dropped back onto the bed and lay down, still listening. A click of a lock and laughter, that's what must have woken her. Other guests getting home at some ridiculous hour. She was safe. She bunched up the pillow, relaxed into it and dozed off, dreaming once more.

He is here, the Clown Killer, dressed as he was that night, the black clothes that blend and hide him in the dark. The mask, grey pallor, eyes weeping blood instead of tears. He doesn't attack her in the dream. He just stands there, smiling, his uneven teeth poking out between the blood red lips. She can't move, just lies there watching him as he watches her. She knows it isn't real; the

Clown Killer wouldn't just look. But it doesn't stop the paralysing fear. He stands and he watches and she lies breathing softly, wanting to pull the covers over her head but unable to move.

She sees me yet she doesn't. Half awake, half asleep. Caught in a nightmare. I can taste the fear that paralyses her. She lies so still, so beautiful, with her eyes wide with terror, her breathing barely perceptible. Will she remember in the morning? Perhaps a message just in case.

The morning light filtered through the gap in the curtains and fell on her face, waking her. She reached for her mobile. Seven twenty. She never slept that late. She'd arranged to meet Mel downstairs at seven thirty for breakfast. She'd better get a move on. She'd unpacked last night. Careen always hung up her clothes and put her toiletries out ready for morning. She'd put away the hotel shampoos and other items. Regardless of the quality she always used her own products and liked them lined up ready for use. She threw her legs over the side of the bed, peeling her sweaty singlet top from her back. Her shoulders ached. The tension had tied her muscles in knots. She rolled her shoulders to ease the pain.

She stood, straightened up the bed, tucked in the sheet corners and pulled up the cover. She retrieved her navy suit from the closet, hung it on the doorknob, pulled a perfectly ironed shirt from the closet and slid the hanger over the opposite handle. Opening her jewellery pouch she selected a pair of moonstone earrings and her George Jensen ring and laid them neatly on the side table. She caressed the aquamarine stone as she removed her necklace and placed it next to the other items. She'd taken to wearing it everywhere but always removed it to shower as she'd been told by the jeweller that heat could cause the stone to fade; and she loved her showers extra hot.

She stood under the water in the shower and soaped herself, scrubbing off the sweat along with the memory of the nightmare. She reached for the shampoo and her knuckles hit the back of the shower cubicle. Her hand crawled along the length of the shelf and came up empty. She scanned the shelf. Neither the shampoo nor conditioner was there. Careen spun around and her foot hit something. She jumped back as if she'd been bitten. She glanced down and saw her shampoo and conditioner bottles, along with her face wash, lined up on the floor of the shower. How did they get there? She never put things down on the floor; they were always lined up in military fashion on the shower shelf. Order. Structure. She would not have put them down there. Careen had said no to any turn-down service, so no one should have been in, and even if they had, why would they move her shampoo? Careen abruptly turned off the taps, suddenly conscious that she couldn't hear anything over the noise of the water. She stepped out of the shower and wrapped her towel around her like body armour. The bathroom door was locked. It was okay. It would be okay.

She towel-dried her hair, not confident enough to run the hairdryer; too much noise, no way she could hear anything over that. She clicked open the bathroom door, peered out, listened. Nothing untoward. She walked back into the bedroom and stopped. She pulled her towel around her with one hand, grabbed the doorjamb for support, bit her lip to stop herself crying out. On the bed was her work outfit, neatly presented like a person lying on the bed. Everything was perfectly in place, her shirt tucked inside the jacket, the earrings sitting where her ears would be, the necklace nestled in place. But what scared her more than what he'd done to her clothes were the two jigsaw pieces that had been left, two eyes staring out, correctly placed and looking exactly like those in her nightmare.

She pushed herself away from the doorjamb and stood

straight up. "Who's there?" Her voice sounded small and squeaky so she cleared her throat and added, "And how the hell did you get in?" Her voice echoed in the suite. A small click. A shuffle. He was still here. She watched the bedroom door for any movement as she grabbed her mobile and edged back towards the ensuite and safety. She locked the bathroom door behind her, tried fingerprint control to unlock the phone and realised she was sweating so much it wasn't going to work. Passcode. What is my passcode? Her mind was blank.

She almost screamed as the phone rang, the noise loud in the tiled room. She bit her lip again, this time tasting the salty warm blood as it ran into her mouth. She hit the answer button.

"Mel."

"Careen. You're late. You're never late, my dear. Are you practising for retirement already? I'm at reception waiting to head out for food. Come on down."

Careen's words came tumbling out. "Mel. He's here. He's in my hotel room."

"Who's there?"

"Him." Then she remembered that she hadn't told Mel about what was happening.

"Are you okay?"

"No."

"Where are you?"

"In my bathroom." She kept an eye on the door handle, waiting for it to turn. "Get hotel security to come up. Now, Mel. Right now."

"I'm coming."

"Don't come alone. Bring security."

"Hang on." She heard Mel explain the urgency to the front desk. "They're on their way."

"Shhh. I just heard something." Careen put her ear to the bathroom door. No sound at all. She wanted to peek under the door but didn't want to be caught down low if he forced it open.

"Careen, the security guys will be there in a minute. Hold tight."

"Can you run?" She hated to be needy but right now she needed a friend and a couple of bulky security staff.

"Security." What sounded like a fist was pounding on the suite's door.

"Mel?" Careen called out loudly, hoping she could hear her. She wasn't ready to open the bathroom door yet.

"Miss Tamley, are you okay? It's hotel security. Your friend Melinda is with us."

Careen unlocked the bathroom door, keeping her foot wedged against it just in case he charged in. Peered through the gap.

"We're coming in Miss Tamley." She heard the door click as they used their swipe to enter.

"Hang on, I need to undo the security chain."

She threw on the bathrobe, moved towards the hotel door, and froze. The security chain hung down, unlatched and undamaged. There was no forced exit or entry, no screws loose. The hotel door had been opened from the inside.

SIXTEEN

Careen rang Gordon as soon as hotel security left. "Two pieces, Gordon. Why two? Does that mean he's escalating?"

"Slow down. Take a deep breath." He waited. "I don't believe this is an escalation. There are two eyes on a face. He needed two pieces to complete the image."

"He was in my room." She was still reeling from the fact that he must have been in the hotel suite with her all night. She'd put the security chain on when she'd come in and then, after a quick check that everything was secure, had gone to bed. He must have accessed the suite earlier and hidden.

"It does appear that way. What is interesting, however, is that he didn't harm you."

"Interesting. Interesting!" Careen could hear the shrillness in her own voice. She took a deep breath. "Could the dream have been real? Could he actually have been standing over me?"

"Slow down. What dream?"

Careen couldn't do this, not while she was in the bedroom. "Give me a minute." She moved into the dining area, took a seat facing the door, and only then felt she could tell Gordon about her nightmare.

"I don't know, Careen. This doesn't make any sense. The Clown Killer murdered eleven women. I don't think he would just stand there. It's more likely that someone is trying to scare you and using the clown makeup and jigsaw to do so."

"But what if it's not? What if he really is counting down to one and then he'll kill me. Gordon, he seems to be able to get to me just about anywhere."

"I've asked for the security footage from the hotel. I'm working on this. Stay another night at the hotel and I'll make sure your apartment is secure by tomorrow. I'd suggest you get a security guard outside your room immediately to avoid a repeat of last night."

"Already on it." One benefit of owning the hotel was everything she asked for was immediately actioned.

Mel wasn't letting Careen out of her sight. Careen made a quick call to Lei to let her know she would be in for her first appointment at eleven a.m., then they ordered a coffee. Mel was apologetic about being unable to delay her flight home. Her mother, who had moved to New York shortly after Mel, was undergoing chemo for early stage breast cancer. That was the reason that Mel's trip to Melbourne had been so brief in the first place.

"Mel, what do I do if this happens when I'm overseas?"

"Italy is miles away from all this. From Clown Man and from that hideous journalist."

"But you don't understand. I was useless. I locked myself in the bathroom."

"Which is what you'd do over there. And then you'd call the police."

"In English?" She shut her eyes for a moment. "I've booked an apartment not a hotel. It's not as if there's a security desk downstairs. Mel, my Italian is atrocious. I couldn't explain anything coherently in English I was so scared, so how the hell would I go trying that in Italian?"

"Careen." Mel reached over and grabbed Careen's hand, then gently unclenched her fingers before holding it tenderly.

"Whoever is doing this is sick and it's just a game to them. You need to remember that. It's not him, Careen. It's too different."

"It keeps coming back to me, Mel. That night. I dream about it again. I thought it was all over."

"It is." Mel dropped her hand and rubbed her temples. "God, I wish I could stay. Be here."

"Me too." Careen's smile was weak.

"Well tonight you have a kick-ass suite on the top floor and security will have someone in the hallway. I told your hotel manager that if anyone gets near your room, she'll have a vengeful Mel to deal with. No one messes with my friend."

"You sound like Bruce Willis in *Die Hard.*"

"Me and Bruce. We're like this." Mel crossed her fingers and laughed.

"Seems like I'm going to need a two-bedroom in Amalfi after all."

"Get me a good internet connection and Bruce and I are all yours." In typical Mel fashion she tamped down Careen's fears and then tried to lighten the conversation. "So how's the lovely Logan then?"

"Can't get what you see in him."

"You're his sister, if you could I'd be worried." Mel raised her iced coffee. "To the lovely Logan."

Careen laughed, clinked her cup with Mel's glass and proceeded to fill Mel in on the latest Logan antics.

She was on her way into the office when Ben phoned to check on her. She pulled herself together and gave him a light-hearted account of her night out with Mel. She casually mentioned she was staying over another night at the hotel; there was no point in worrying him while he was interstate. She was glad she'd taken that approach when he told her he'd been asked to fly directly to Italy to paint one of the family portraits. Apparently, the elderly gentleman was succumbing to pneumonia and they wanted his picture painted while he was still alive.

"I mean, really, the guy is on his deathbed and they want me to paint him. Give the guy a break. Let him be ill in peace."

"And what did they say when you mentioned that?" Careen knew Ben too well to think for a minute he wouldn't have said something.

"I was informed that the agreement was for seventeen portraits and I was required to fulfil the contract."

"So you're going then?"

"Not if you need me there, Careen. You're more important than this commission."

She wanted to hug him, then and there. "I'll be okay. I'm staying at the hotel. And ...", she added, " ... when all else fails, there is the indomitable Gordon."

Regardless of how much she wanted him here she wasn't going to ruin this opportunity for him.

Five meetings, four coffees and a mocha. She'd made it through the day and didn't think anyone had noticed how jittery she was. If so, she could always blame the caffeine. She called an Uber and texted Gordon to say she'd be at her apartment shortly.

Walking into her apartment was like being transported into Flinders Street Station at peak hour. So many people, touching things, moving things. Careen shuddered. She knew it was necessary but the disorder in her apartment was unsettling to say the least. The supervisor pulled Careen aside to give her a run-down.

"We found some pretty interesting stuff here – two audio bugs and two hidden cameras – in the living area and, sorry to say, in the bedroom." Careen shuddered again.

"And?"

"The VOIP phone was bugged. Good-quality stuff too."

"The front door?"

"Easy to get into. You do know you can buy key-swipe coders online? All he needs is an override master code for the building and he can cut his own."

"But what about the security chain?"

"Take your pick, excuse the pun. Rubber band, string – easier just to give it a good hard kick, but I suppose that leaves a trace."

"This doesn't help me feel very secure."

"Sorry about that. You should google breaking and entering one day – lots of helpful advice for the newly minted crim." His phone rang – the *Stars Wars* theme tune adding to the high-tech setting. "Hold fire."

While she was waiting for him to finish his call she couldn't help but overhear a conversation between two of the technicians.

"Swipe's easy enough to replicate and the security chain had some rubber residue on it. Nothing special there." His mate nodded in agreement. "However the rest of the stuff is really cool. Whoever he is he has access to some high-tech equipment and knows what to do with it. Great toys if you can afford them."

"Hey, remember that guy who used to test security for us? Could get in anywhere."

"Yeah. Ex con – jewellery and high-end art, wasn't it?" He bent down and started to pack up his equipment.

"That's the one. He used the same brand of gear."

Careen stepped closer. She wished everyone else would just be quiet so she could listen in.

"Can't be him, he got locked up a few years back. Seems his version of going straight had a few curves." He picked up the tool bag and grinned at his mate.

"Couldn't have happened to a nicer bloke." They both laughed and then strolled over to the door.

"Sorry about that." The supervisor pocketed his phone. "What you now have is a lot more secure with some monitoring to top it off. We've changed the lock to a seven-gauge pin and tumbler – almost impossible to pick."

Careen didn't like the "almost" bit but she supposed that was the point of the rest of the hardware.

"We've added a deadbolt, which isn't hotel spec, but figured you'd want the security. We'll leave the security chain in place although more for peace of mind than anything else. The security system will have two modes: perimeter, so you can have it on when you are home, and then the joint perimeter and motion sensor for when you're out and about. There's a six-digit code that we'll get you to set before we go. I suggest you keep this to yourself for now. We've installed a secondary camera in the corridor. Still sure about the living-room cam? It means we can catch him in the act."

"No cameras inside." She did not want her life ending up on a video to be watched by strangers at the security company's HQ. "Plus I thought the point of all this –" she gestured at the door "– was that he couldn't get in."

It was quiet after the techs left. She set the perimeter sensors and locked the deadbolt. She dropped her keys into the white marble bowl, straightened up the vase and looked around. It all seemed different somehow. Like someone else's place. It took her over an hour to move methodically around the apartment and put everything back where it belonged, moving things a few centimetres until they were perfectly positioned, cleaning surfaces that they had touched. Only then did she pick up her briefcase and head back to the office.

The taxi pulled up outside the Montage building. She surveyed the street before she opened the cab's door. Just across the street was a battered blue Nissan. Lei's car.

What's she doing here at this hour? It was almost nine p.m. Lei never worked that late and seldom drove into the city. Careen swiped her security card to enter the building and then, remembering how easily the Clown Killer had accessed her hotel room, asked the security guard to escort her to her office and check it before she entered. The guard appeared perplexed but did as he was asked. All the way up to the thirty-second floor Careen's mind was whirling. She'd hired Lei seven years ago and never regretted it. But that was before Gary. Could Lei be the leak? Could she be sneaking back after hours and ferreting through Careen's papers? Had she found out about Careen's retirement? Lei was one of the few people with access to Careen's private line and had an apartment swipe. She often ordered Careen a takeaway to the office when she was working late and knew the places she would order from and her favourite meals.

"No." Careen's voice was loud in the confines of the lift, startling the guard. There'll be a logical reason for Lei being here.

The lift bell chimed as she reached the thirty-second floor. As the door slid open Careen looked straight into Lei's frightened eyes.

"It is late," Lei croaked, tears streaming down her face. "You are never at the office this late."

"And neither are you. But it appears we've both changed our habits." Careen's voice was hard. "The question is why?"

"I am sorry. So very sorry."

The guard was standing in the lift, his hand on the open-door button, watching. Careen stepped out of the lift and turned to the guard. "Thank you. I'll be okay from here." He held the door open a few moments longer, shrugged his shoulders and released the button. Once the door had closed Careen turned back to Lei. "Why are you doing this?"

"He ..." Lei stopped as she gulped in air.

"He what?"

Careen grabbed Lei's arm to stop her backing away. Lei yelped and tried to pull away.

"You are hurting me. Please let go."

"Not until you tell me what's going on." Careen's grip was unrelenting.

"Please." Lei was cringing against the wall.

"Who is *he*?"

"Gary." Her voice was desolate and the tears were falling freely now. "He is back on the drink."

"But what does Gary have to gain? Why is he pretending to be the Clown Killer?"

Lei appeared confused. "I do not understand."

For the first time in a long while, Careen studied Lei. She looked tired, bags under her eyes, and pale as if she were seriously ill. Careen let go of Lei's arm and Lei rubbed where Careen's fingers had dug in.

"Lei, answer me one question. What are you doing here?"

"Gary needed money. He said he would stop drinking if I got it." Lei stood up straight. "I could not do it. Not even for him." She looked Careen straight in the eye. "Not even for him."

"What couldn't you do?"

"He said I had to do it. He said he drinks because he is worried. He owes some nasty people a lot of money. He said if I could get him $20,000 it would all be okay." Lei blurted this out, her eyes now downcast. "I came into the office and got the cheque book. I tore a cheque out of the back. You would not notice it for a long time. I can write your signature." She glanced towards Careen the dropped her eyes back to the floor. "It was wrong. I knew that. I did not want to. Not for him. Then

I started to think. I am here. I could get away. I can take a few cheques, write them out for different amounts, cash them at different banks. But where do I go? He found me last time I left. He threatened the friend who helped me." Lei slumped down to the floor. Lei who was always so proper. Lei who would never even perch on the side of a desk.

Careen cringed at the thought of the carpet – dirty street shoes walked on this carpet – then chided herself. She wasn't going to get answers towering above Lei like this. Careen joined Lei on the floor. The silence stretched out.

"Please forgive me," Lei beseeched. She rubbed her arm; the long sleeves of her top rode up, exposing the marks from Careen's grip.

"I'm not sure what I'm forgiving you for yet."

The finger-marks on Lei's arm were red and angry. Like the ones Clown Man had left on her arms that night so many years ago. The bruises that went away, that everyone forgot about but her.

"I'm sorry, Lei. I didn't mean to hurt you."

"What will happen to me now?"

"Did you write out the cheque?"

"Yes."

"And ...?"

"And then I tore it up. I could not do it." A panicked look crossed her face. "Please do not fire me. My job is all I have. If I lose my job Gary will be even more angry."

"Any angrier than when you come home empty handed?"

She'd only met Gary a couple of times. He'd come up to the office when Lei was running late in the evening. Careen had introduced herself the first time and they'd shook hands. He was a skinny guy, wiry and muscled. He wore a sleeveless tank top that showed off his tattoos and tight jeans that emphasised his anatomy. He'd gripped her hand tightly and squeezed as if he had something to prove. She'd smiled sweetly at him and released her hand from his sweaty palm. He'd sneered at her then told Lei they were leaving – now. A man with very little respect for women. She had wondered what Lei saw in him.

"Lei, why didn't you tell me about Gary?"

"You have your problems. You do not need mine." Lei was clearly more observant than her.

"You need to get out you know."

"I love him. When he is sober, we are good."

"And how often is that?"

Lei's forlorn expression answered the question. "What do I do?"

"Lei, you didn't do anything wrong. You thought about it, and thinking about something isn't a crime." Careen's voice suddenly got hard again. "Was it you that leaked the information about my retirement?"

"You are leaving?" Lei appeared bewildered. "You did not tell me you were leaving. Why? Am I not to be trusted?" Lei lowered her eyes, dropped her head. "I am not to be trusted."

Careen leant back against the wall. Could things get any worse?

"I do trust you." And she realised she did. This whole mess had her doubting everyone. She turned to face Lei. "Look at me, Lei. You were the fourth person I was going to tell. Ben is aware I'm leaving, and I've told Chris and Logan. I was going to tell you today but things, well, there are other things happening that ..." Careen paused. "Is it Gary that is impersonating the Clown Killer?"

"I do not understand. What is a clown killer?"

"The Clown Killer is a who, not a what." Careen sighed. "Lei, I need you to be honest with me. Is Gary the person who is sending me jigsaw pieces?"

"Why would he be sending you jigsaws?"

"I don't know, Lei. Someone is. Has Gary been acting strangely lately?"

"No. He is the same as always."

"Which is?"

"He is nice to me most of the time. When he drinks, he loses his temper. It is my fault most of the time. I will do something that sets him off. If I was more careful, he would not hit me. He is always sorry later. He does not mean to hurt me." She looked up at Careen. "He loves me."

"Lei. Love is about caring, not about dominance and fear."

"He does care."

"And how caring will he be when you go home without the cheques?" Careen couldn't miss the fear in Lei's eyes. "Lei, you can't go back."

"He will find me wherever I go." The tears were falling again. "He told me …" She stifled a sob. "He told me not to come home without the cheques. He wanted me to cash them first thing in the morning."

"So you're not going home." Careen's mind was mapping out a solution even as she spoke. "I have an apartment above the Perth hotel that you can use. We'll get you on a flight today. Don't worry about clothes, I'll give you some money for that." How easy it was to fix a crisis when it was someone else's. "How about you ring Gary and tell him that I caught you leaving with the cheque and that you've had to go into hiding from me, that the police may even be after you. He won't go looking for you then."

"But my job. Do I still have a job if you are leaving?"

"Yes, Lei. You will always have a job at Montage. I have a number of options for you to consider. I was going to go over these with you when I told you I was retiring."

"If I go and hide, what happens then?"

Careen took that question as a good sign. Lei was considering the possibility of not going back to Gary.

"Your move to a new role just gets delayed for a while."

"But what about money? I don't have any savings."

"I would have thought you were quite good with money."

Lei looked down at the floor. "Gary gets my pay and gives me an allowance. He said that is what couples in love do."

"Did he now? And I suppose you have a joint account."

"No. Just Gary's account. My pay goes in there. It is easier to manage that way." She must have seen the expression on Careen's face because she quickly added, "He owes people money. I cannot just spend my pay on myself. I have to pay these people back or they will hurt him."

Careen stopped to think. "You must have a stack of leave accumulated – use it. It's paid leave and you are due your mid-year bonus so that'll be your spending money. I do, however, insist that you open a bank account in your own name for this money. You'll need this money to live on. Gary will need to find a way to pay his own debts."

"I do not think he can." Lei looked scared. "They will hurt him."

"Yes, they probably will."

"I cannot leave him to get hurt."

"What are your options, Lei?" Careen was trying hard to control her frustration. "If you go home without the money, he gets hurt. If you steal the money you go to jail, he still doesn't get the money, so he still gets hurt and so do you." She reached over and squeezed Lei's hand. "How did he get into this mess?"

"It was not his fault. He had a bad run at cards. He tried to win it back, but lost again. He says they cheated."

"I see." Careen decided not to labour the point. "Where were you meeting Gary?"

"At home."

Their apartment. "Lei, whose name is your apartment leased under?"

"Gary's. He wanted me to move into his apartment. He did not like my neighbours. He said they were rude to him." She smiled sadly. "I miss them. They were friendly and they cared about me."

And that is why he didn't want you there.

"I have a plan." Careen stood up and held her hand out for Lei. "But I'd prefer to discuss this somewhere more comfortable." And cleaner, she added to herself.

Careen washed her hands in her office bathroom while Lei made them cups of tea. They sat on the sofa as they discussed options.

Lei looked lost. "Why are you doing this?"

"Lei, we have worked together for over seven years and I don't know what I would have done without you over that time. You organise my life, notice when I'm having a bad day and make it better. I consider you a friend. And as your friend I should have noticed you were in trouble. Let me help you now."

"I am scared."

Careen faced Lei and touched the bruise on her cheek. "I'd be more surprised if you weren't."

"What if he finds me?"

"He won't." Careen's voice was icy. She would speak with Gordon. He would be able to help.

Lei was safely on a plane to Sydney with a connecting flight to Perth. There were no direct flights that night and Careen wanted Lei away from Melbourne immediately. It had taken a while to organise. Careen had caught a taxi with Lei to the airport and waited until Lei's flight had departed. Lena, the hotel manager in Perth, would have the apartment key waiting when Lei got there.

She hadn't told Lei the reason she had chosen Perth. That prior to moving into hotel management Lena had been a social worker and Careen hoped that Lena's skills would help Lei to realise that she needed to stay away from Gary.

SEVENTEEN

It was strange without Lei in the office. Careen's finger kept hovering on the call button and then she'd realise that Lei wasn't around. They'd spoken after she had arrived in Perth. Lei loved the apartment and Lena had taken her under her wing. Lei sounded decidedly cheerful for someone who had walked away from her life. Perhaps I'll be like that when I'm no longer CEO, Careen thought.

She'd spent a few hours today finalising the renovation project specs for the new Wellington hotel before handing it over to Chris. A quick check of her emails and she'd head off while it was still light. She hadn't received any more calls from Clown Man. Perhaps now because her apartment was a fortress, and he didn't know her movements, he'd decided to give up. Or had he? What if it really had been Clown Man? He didn't give up last time, he just chose easier targets. She sat up in her chair, her throat dry. Had she jeopardised someone else's safety by ensuring her own? Was it happening all over again? No. She wouldn't get wound up. She couldn't do anything, she didn't know who it was. Just like last time, her subconscious whispered, and look what happened then.

"It wasn't my fault," she enunciated slowly and clearly. "It wasn't my fault."

Her therapist said she needed to repeat that constantly until she started to believe it. She had survivor's guilt. She'd been lucky. The others had not. Her death wouldn't have stopped him – he'd have kept going regardless – and she would've been dead. She wasn't to blame for living.

She moved to the liquor cabinet and poured herself a Maker's Mark. Almost choked as she knocked it back. She poured herself a second one and sat back at her desk. She needed to let the past go.

She glanced at the screen as an email popped up. The subject line was a direct challenge: *Accident or Murder? You Decide.* Careen took another gulp of her drink before opening the latest email from Louise. She figured she was going to need it.

The death of Careen's parents was a terrible accident according to the coroner. A distracted driver and his drunk wife. The question that remains unanswered in the report is: What was it that made him distracted and what drove his wife to drink?

Let us consider the details set out in the police report. Our dear friend Careen had argued with her father, apparently quite violently prior to them leaving that evening. The argument centred on Careen's desire to attend university to study accounting – a skill that would come in useful later. We will never know why her father resisted Careen's desire for education, perhaps he realised that too much knowledge in the wrong hands is dangerous. Careen knew her father drove erratically when he was angry, she knew her mother drank when her father was irritable and yet she still pursued the argument right up until the moment they left. Did she drive him to his death? I will present the facts; you will need to draw your own conclusions.

"Jesus."

Careen had blamed herself. She knew in her heart that her parents would still be alive if she'd waited to have that conversation, if she hadn't argued with them before they left. Her therapist had worked with her to try and make her understand that having an argument did not make the accident her fault. She knew different. She'd learnt to live with it, pushed it deep down inside her, knowing she couldn't change the outcome, knowing that she also couldn't have changed who she was. Who she is. She'd spent half her life arguing with her father. He believed a woman's place was in the home, not out there in the real world. Her mother was such a fine example of this – bored and drunk – she'd countered. That's where it had all started – again.

"How dare you speak about your mother like that." Careen's father took a step towards her. He liked to tower over her, diminish her. Not this time. "Apologise now."

"What, for speaking the truth? I love my mother but she doesn't do anything but lunch, shop, entertain and drink. Let's not forget the drink."

"Your mother knows her place."

"Under your thumb."

"Look, young lady. This is not a discussion I'm going to have with you again. A woman does not need an education. You will get married, have children and stay at home to care for them and your husband. An education is a waste."

"And what if I don't get married? What then?"

"With an attitude like that I'll be surprised if anyone will have you."

"Let's work with that then. I'm a spinster. How am I going to support myself?"

"That will be up to you. There are plenty of good jobs for

women, especially if you go to secretarial school or become a nurse."

"That's it. I'm to be a secretary or a nurse?"

"They are important jobs."

"I want be an accountant." It was a skill she knew she could use anywhere in the world. She could work in London, New York and hopefully one day in Rome. Sit high in an office overlooking the Piazza di Spagna during the day and wander the streets eating gelato on the weekend.

"Not going to happen."

"I got accepted by Melbourne Uni." There – it was out.

"You applied without my knowledge?!" His voice was thunderous and in the silence that followed she could hear her mother pouring herself another tipple in the dining room.

"I'm going to uni, Dad. This is important."

How could he not see?

"Not while you're living under my roof."

"That's settled then. I'm moving out." She'd got her stubbornness from her father, a fact he never understood.

"I want you gone before we get home tonight. In my house you live by my rules."

"Jimmy. Now, let's not get hasty," Mum finally cut in.

"Celia, this is none of your business."

"She's my daughter too." Mum took another healthy swig. "And I don't want her to leave."

Dad looked stunned. Mum never stood up to him.

"We'll discuss this tomorrow." He turned and stormed down the hallway. "Celia, are you coming? We'll be late."

And that was the last time she saw them alive.

Careen stopped to pick up an Indian takeaway on the drive home. She'd had the car locks changed and the remote reset. It was good to be driving again. She'd organised to call the concierge on arrival and either Jim or Bill would meet her in the car park and walk her to the lifts. She knew they thought it a strange request but she'd decided she could put up with the sideways glances and whispers to feel safe.

Her mobile rang as she was turning into Bay Street. An international number.

"Ben?"

"Ciao."

"Picking up the lingo already." Careen laughed.

"When in Rome."

"Is that where you are now?"

"Florence, actually." She could hear a murmur of voices in the background. "Can't talk for long. How are things at your end? Are you okay?"

"Yes and no. Louise is busy writing sensationalist tabloid fodder and sending me snippets. The last one was about Mum and Dad's accident. It took me by surprise." Careen felt tears welling up. She'd held it in but now she was talking to Ben it was all coming back.

"Shit. What angle did she take?"

"If I hadn't argued with Dad they'd still be alive." Careen heard the catch in her voice. "I'm okay, Ben." She quickly added before he could respond.

"You know that's not true."

"What? Me being okay or about the argument?" She didn't want to go there right now. "I don't want to go through this again, Ben – the doubting myself – but she brought it all back." She hit the steering wheel with the palm of her hand. "If I let it get to me she wins and I will not have her win."

"That's my girl. Anything I can do?"

"Fly me to Florence for some time out?" she suggested, only half jokingly.

"Plenty of spare rooms here. I'm sure they wouldn't mind. Do you want me to find you a flight?"

They wouldn't mind. But what about you, Ben, would you want me there?

"I was only kidding. I have work to do." She wouldn't let him see it mattered.

She could hear more murmurs in the background.

"Careen, I have to go, but what about Clown Man?"

"He appears to have gone to ground. Now I've got top-notch security he seems to have made himself scarce."

"Pleased to hear it. I have to go now. Stay in touch. Arrivederci."

After he'd hung up Careen drove quietly on, the thickness in her throat signalling the onset of tears. She would not cry. What she wanted was a hug, but the best she was going to get tonight was butter chicken and hot roti – comfort food.

She jumped as her mobile rang again. The car bluetooth obligingly relayed the number and requested her to answer or decline. It wasn't Ben. It was the private line in her office. Careen ordered the phone to cancel the call. It was eight p.m. when she'd left the building and it had been all but deserted. She had locked her office door behind her, pulled it twice to make sure. She hit the answer button as the phone rang again.

"I thought you'd gone away." Her voice sounded more confident than she felt.

"Did you miss me?" A deep chuckle.

"Not so much."

"Very calm and collected, aren't we? Perhaps I need to up the ante." It was the same guttural voice from the late-night calls. "Do you know where I am?"

"Security are on their way up."

"I doubt that. They are busy attending to an altercation outside the office." He chuckled. "That was fun to set up, I must admit."

"So the point of this call is?"

"Just to let you know that nowhere is safe. I can get into your car, your home and your office. There is nowhere to hide."

Careen froze. "No."

"'No' is such a negative word. Me, I'm more of a positive type of person." He chuckled. "I can and I will."

The phone went dead.

Careen searched her contacts and dialled building security. It rang out. She dialled again and listened to the phone ring as she pulled out into the traffic.

"Answer dammit." She ran the orange light and put her foot down.

"Building Security, Warren speaking."

"Where the hell have you been? It's Careen Tamley. We have a break-in in my office. Take back-up and go immediately and detain whoever is there. Lock the place down, ensure no one leaves."

"I can't do that. We have a situation here. All the exit doors and stair doors have unlocked simultaneously. We can't lock them. There's a crowd of people trying to get in. They're all dressed as clowns and they keep saying there's a prize for the first person to get to the thirty-second floor."

"You have a lift swipe. Use it."

"I had to lock the lifts down." Warren sounded tense. "If I try to use the lift there'll be a stampede."

"I need you to stop the person who is in my office from leaving."

"I'm sorry, Miss Tamley. The police are on their way. There's nothing I can do until they arrive."

Careen hung up. He'd planned it well. He would either be long gone or just one of the crowd by the time she got there. And there was no way in hell she was going anywhere near a crowd of clowns.

EIGHTEEN

"Louise Mears speaking." Her voice purred down the line, self-satisfied and arrogant.

"It's Careen Tamley."

"Ah, Careen, darling. So lovely of you to call. Sorry I didn't get back to you. So busy ferreting out wonderful titbits of information about your life. What can I do for you this lovely morning?"

"You can stop it right now."

"The podcast is going ahead, darling, with or without you. Your lawyers will have advised you of that by now."

"I'm not talking about the damn podcast. I'm talking about the clowns."

"No idea what you are talking about." Careen heard the clink of a cup and saucer.

"You're a bitch, Louise, but even I didn't think you'd stoop that low. Not after what happened to you."

"Clarity, dear. How you can run a company with such scattered thinking is beyond me."

"You were mugged, raped and left for dead in a field outside Byron Bay. Remember that night, Louise? Fun, wasn't it? Want to relive it over and over again?"

Careen had googled Louise shortly after her initial contact and had been horrified to read about the attack. One of the reasons she'd agreed to work with Louise on the original article was that she felt they had something in common, a shared history in a way. She'd not raised it with Louise at the time and had been surprised when Louise had brought up the Clown Killer in Careen's office in such an offhand manner.

The silence on the end of the phone stretched out. Careen could hear the hiss of a coffee machine and a murmur of early-morning chatter.

"You bitch. What gives you the right to bring that up? Do you have any idea what it's like, what happens every night I go to sleep? How I feel every time I leave the safety of the city? How dare you." Her voice was harsh with anger and distress.

"What's good for the goose."

"What the fuck have geese got to do with it," Louise hissed. "I knew you were a bitch but that is low. I will destroy you for that, Careen Tamley."

"You seem to think that taunting me, making me relive the attack at the car park, the deaths I couldn't prevent is okay, but not when it's you. Well, two can play that game."

"What the hell are you talking about?"

"The clowns. The fucking clowns."

"Oh my God. He's back." She heard Louise take a sharp intake of breath. "It's not me, Careen. I wouldn't. I couldn't. It's not me." Louise was pleading with her now.

Careen froze, her mind refusing to believe Louise. Because if it wasn't Louise …

"Careen, are you there? You must believe me. I've been through the same thing, the nightmares, the panic, the terror. I wouldn't do that to anyone. No one. Ever."

"And yet you brought it up in my office. For someone who wouldn't do that you have a short memory."

"Shit, Careen." The condescending tone was gone. "I saw your reaction, knew you hadn't got past it. Left it alone. You have to believe me. It's not me."

"If it's not you …" Careen left the sentence dangling.

"He was never caught, Careen." Louise's voice was soft, understanding. "It might be him. He might be back."

"No." Her voice was adamant. "That was twenty years ago. Why would he come back now?"

"Why do they ever?" Careen, I know you don't like me, don't trust me. I don't expect you to. But you must believe me when I say it's not me and if he is back you need to be careful. Very careful. Go to the police, Careen. Now. Right now."

Careen laughed, a cold and empty laugh. "What and have them tell me that they can't do anything because he hasn't hurt me, attacked me. It was twenty years ago. A threat is not an action, Louise; you know that as well as I do. I have no proof it's him and the police will do nothing." Her voice was bitter.

"I'm sorry, Careen. I really am sorry."

Louise was saying the words but Careen was sure that she was already thinking about how this would add to her story.

"Warren. A moment please." Careen had stopped by the security office on her way in.

"I'm sorry about yesterday, Miss Tamley. It's that social-media thing. Makes people crazy." Warren was in his sixties, Careen guessed, slightly overweight and definitely out of touch.

"Did you eventually get up to my office?"

"Yes. As soon as I could. It was locked. I used the master to get in but nothing appeared to be out of place. Would you like me to go up with you now?"

Careen was about to suggest that perhaps they could walk up together but she took pity on him. It appeared that the fracas yesterday had shaken him considerably. Given her current predicament, however, she needed a security team that was on the ball; she would speak to HR.

"No. What I would like is for you to check the security-camera footage of the building, starting with this floor, the elevator and the staircase."

"Ah about that." Warren looked decidedly nervous; he was wringing his hands now. Careen waited. "The police asked to check it too and there was nothing."

"He got in somehow. There has to be some record of it."

"No, what I mean is *nothing*. The security system had been shut down."

"Of course it had," Careen mumbled, shaking her head as she walked away.

As she exited the lift she hesitated. With Lei in Perth the office felt abandoned. She would have welcomed a friendly face today. Careen unlocked her door, placed a hand on the doorknob, took a deep breath and pushed open the double doors. Despite Warren's observations, she hadn't been sure what to expect, but the office seemed exactly as it had when she left it last night.

Placing her briefcase next to her desk she slowly walked around the room. Something was different. Then she realised what it was – the smell – a faint smell of aftershave. Warren? No, it was the same smell she had noticed in her car. Ben's aftershave; but not quite his. Something on the bookshelf caught her eye. One of the pictures was facing backwards. It was the photo taken on the opening day of the Conrad. She picked up the silver frame, smiling at the memory.

It was ready. She had started with a dream and today it became reality. She was twenty-eight years old and her future stood before her, laid out like a stairway to the stars. Standing on the front steps of the Conrad she'd surveyed the crowd. They were all here for her opening, to see the hotel she had built, to learn about the new boutique-hotel chain she was starting. John had just arrived by limo – he always did like to arrive in style. The architect she had nearly driven mad seemed very pleased with himself and the interior designer had a satisfied air about her. There seemed to be a good turnout from the press, which meant Logan, as media liaison, had made all the right calls.

"Excuse me." The noise died down as she called everyone to attention. "My name is Careen Tamley and I am Managing Director of Kudos Hotels, a division of the Montage Group. On behalf of the owner of Montage, John Seymour, and myself I would like to welcome you here today. Many of you will have stayed with us over the years, enjoying the service and finesse of our Montage hotels. We would now like to offer you an opportunity to experience something new. The Conrad opens today as the first in the Kudos range of boutique hotels. The Kudos brand is all about you – *your* stay the way *you* want it to be. A small, boutique hotel offering total luxury, sophistication and personalised service."

She had talked about the Conrad, outlined the plans for their new chain of luxurious hotels and then welcomed them all inside for a preview. What a day. She'd been flying high that afternoon. The photo had been taken standing with John at one of the grand fireplaces in the dining room, John's arm draped around her shoulders as he grinned like a proud father.

Why this photo? Perhaps he'd just knocked it as he walked past. Given how carefully he'd orchestrated the whole break-in scenario, she doubted that. She figured it was placed like that to remind her of the night at the Conrad last weekend. She scanned the office again, expecting to find his calling card – a piece of the jigsaw. She was about to replace the photo when she realised that the back of the frame was loose. She levered off the clips and tucked up neatly inside was another piece of the puzzle – only this one had teeth; the same teeth her attacker had – sharp, pointed and dangerous.

A notification pinged on her phone. She had a meeting in fifteen minutes. With shaking hands, Careen replaced the back of the photo frame and returned it to the shelf; she then placed the jigsaw piece in her top drawer. She pulled out the disinfectant wipes and wiped over the bookshelf, her desk, her leather chair and the photo frame. She would get the cleaning team in to thoroughly clean the office this evening. In the meantime she would restrict her movements and hold her meetings at her desk.

Since Lei had gone, Missy was working for both Chris and Careen and Careen had agreed that she would no longer have a daily briefing. She missed Lei and the usual routine of her day. She checked her phone for any upcoming appointments. Damn. She'd forgotten that tonight was Chris's birthday. Edward, his partner, had arranged dinner at Donovan's in St Kilda and Edward had decided that everyone should dress up twenties' style. She knew she couldn't get out of the dinner and her wardrobe contained nothing suitable. This unfortunately called for another shopping expedition, and after the last one, Careen wasn't sure she was quite ready for this.

Careen buzzed Chris's office. "Chris, I need Missy for a couple of hours about three p.m. – any problem?"

"No problems. Just make sure she's back by six or Ed will have my hide."

Missy was thrilled to be asked to help Careen clothes shop. She had an unerring sense of style that Careen was hoping to tap into. Careen steadfastly refused to even think about the fact that she felt better having someone around, just in case. In case of what? Her mind wandered back to her last shopping trip and she shuddered.

"Ready when you are." Missy bustled into Careen's office right on three. Twenty minutes later, she was steering her into a huge vintage-clothing warehouse in Flinders Street. Missy raced up the stairs with Careen following at a more sedate pace and they were now busy trying on a range of outfits from safe to quite risqué.

"That's it, that's the one." Missy appeared very pleased with herself, her eyes shining.

Careen turned slowly in the mirror – an unusual choice, but she had to admit it looked fabulous on her. The deep burgundy background with the black lace and fringe was classy and the cut highlighted her slim figure. The headband was fun, the white feather a great contrast to the outfit.

"We'll take it." Careen was smiling and realised she was actually enjoying herself. Missy's enthusiasm was contagious.

"Shoes. We need shoes." Missy clapped her hands. "Myer has some fabulous ones. I got mine there."

With the dress carefully wrapped and paid for, they walked the short distance to Myer. The selection was vast, but Missy knew exactly what she was after. Burgundy dancing shoes and they even had Careen's size. "Two down," Missy grinned. "You head down to the jewellery department, I'll grab the gloves and meet you there." Missy flounced off.

"So, who's the boss?" Careen laughed softly.

"Can I help you?" The sales assistant caught her eye.

"Yes. I'm after a 1920s' style piece. The dress is burgundy and black lace, so it needs to work with that."

"I have just the thing. Follow me." She was right. The necklace and earrings, although pricey, were gorgeous. Careen held the pendant against her neck and looked in the mirror – perfect.

"Paging Miss Careen Tamley. Miss Tamley, if you are in the

store, please come to the information desk on level two. Miss Careen Tamley – information desk, level two."

Careen started and glanced around. Missy obviously couldn't find her and was having her paged.

"Excuse me. That page is for me. What's the quickest way to the level two information desk?"

"Up the escalators, to your left. Do you want me to hold this for you?"

"Yes please. I should only be a few moments."

"Missy." Careen saw Missy as soon as she arrived on level two.

"Is everything all right?" Missy enquired, a concerned expression on her face. "I heard you paged and came up."

"You didn't page me?" Careen felt a cold chill creep down her spine.

"No." Missy appeared confused.

Careen marched over to the information desk. "I'm Careen Tamley. Who paged me?"

"A gentleman." The information clerk glanced around. "He doesn't appear to be here at the moment, but if you'd like to take a seat I'm sure he won't be long."

"Don't count on it," Careen mumbled under her breath. "What did this gentleman look like exactly?" Her voice was loud and firm and sounded as if she was in control, which was very far from how she was feeling.

"Hang on. Stella?" the clerk hollered back over her shoulder to the elderly woman sitting at the desk behind her. "The guy who got you to page a Careen Tamley, what did he look like?"

"No need to yell, it's my eyesight's going, not my hearing," Stella yelled back.

"Is everything okay?" Missy was standing beside Careen. "You've gone pale."

Careen glanced at Missy and turned away. "Too much shopping, probably. Out of practice."

Missy did not appear to be convinced.

Stella, by now, had ambled her way to the front desk. "You the one asking about the guy?"

Careen nodded.

"Tall he was, strong shoulders. Cold eyes though."

"What do you mean by cold eyes?"

"Just what I said – cold – no feeling – guy gave me the creeps. You know him then?" Stella had picked up something was wrong.

"No, I don't. Did he leave anything – a parcel or a message?" Careen held her breath.

"No, should he have?"

"No, just wondered."

"He did leave his name," Stella volunteered. "But I was only meant to give it to you if you asked specifically." But she went on quickly, covering her tracks. "You did ask if he left anything."

"His name." Careen stood very still. "He gave you his name?"

"Tony. He said his name was Tony. Said he hadn't seen you in a long time. Said he was dying to see you," Stella said. "Said I should use those exact words. Dying to see you."

Careen gasped. She only knew one Tony and he was supposed to be dead.

Careen didn't remember much of the trip back to the office. Missy had asked her over and over if she was okay, but Careen kept staring ahead, walking one foot in front of the other. Thinking, remembering ...

Thanks to Ben introducing her to John, Careen had secured a job working at Montage. Six months in, when an opportunity arose to transfer into HR at Head Office, she had jumped at it. She'd worked her way through HR, did a stint in marketing and wound up as part of the business development team, working for Tony Fisher, John's golden boy and heir apparent was the word around the office.

There were rumours that Tony was John's illegitimate son but when Careen had asked Ben if the rumours were true, he'd just laughed. Tony and Ben had been best friends since primary school. Tony's parents believed that children should take responsibility for their own lives as early as possible, meaning they left him to his own devices, and Tony had spent most of his teenage years at Ben's house – Ben's dad, John, and his mum, Cindy, were Tony's surrogate parents only. Ben's complete lack of interest in the hotel industry was a constant source of antagonism to his father, but Tony helped smooth the edges between John and Ben and proved himself invaluable to John in the business.

She'd loved working for Tony and, as her skills and confidence grew, he gave her plenty of scope to make changes and try out new ideas. He was only three years older than her, but his style, combined with his business acumen, made him exceptional. It was always expected Tony would take over the business from John when he retired. Tony had been good to Careen and had taught her well and, combined with her natural ability, she had become a key player. She, Tony and John often met to discuss new ideas and hers were often implemented. She was flying high. Tony never saw her as a threat – he was, and would always be, John's successor.

Then one night, when he was returning from a business dinner, a drunk driver had hit Tony. His injuries were extensive and the doctor induced a coma that lasted three months. John, Ben and Cindy were distraught and each coped in different ways. John became hard headed, allowing no one to dispute his orders; Cindy started drinking; and Ben hid himself away and painted. Tony's parents didn't let this 'hiccup' inconvenience them, they scheduled a 15 minute visit to the hospital once a week in order to keep up appearances.

Careen decided to take control at work and, after her

initial personal distress, she grabbed the reins of the business development department and made it hers. She got John to approve access to Tony's files, she pulled the team together, set the direction and continued to market Montage to the best of her ability. No one questioned her right to take the role.

She'd been managing well, but the budgets were due and she had no idea how to go about it. Tony had always managed the financial side of the department and although she'd asked, he'd never quite had the time to show her how it all pulled together. Careen freed up a weekend and pulled all the financial files for the last two years – she needed to understand what they were spending the money on, why, and how the allocations worked for pulling together a budget for the following year. At first she thought she was missing something, but the more she delved the more inconsistencies kept popping up. She decided she needed help and asked Quentin, the Chief Financial Officer, to spend a day with her explaining why the books didn't balance by over half a million dollars for each of the last two years. She was doing something wrong, and until she figured it out, she would never understand the budget figures.

That's where the trouble started...

Careen pulled herself up short. Reminiscing wasn't going to help. It was all in the past. Tony was dead. Why would someone choose to bring it up now?

Back in her office, Careen turned her chair so she could stare out of the window. The light was already fading. She wasn't sure how long she sat there, but she stiffened as the phone rang.

"Careen Tamley," she said harshly.

"Careen. Hi, it's Chris." Relief surged through her. "Just checking you hadn't forgotten about tonight."

"As if I would."

"Actually, you did forget last year, so I just wanted to make sure it was in your diary. Seven thirty for cocktails."

Careen glanced at her watch. It was seven o'clock already. She never missed a work appointment but she had so few social engagements that she often forgot about them completely.

"Just thought a reminder was in order. See you shortly." Chris chuckled and hung up.

Careen grabbed her briefcase and the shopping bags then ran her eyes across her desk to ensure everything was in its place. She set her new office alarm, locked the door behind her and headed for the lifts.

Fifteen minutes later, Careen entered her apartment foyer.

"Miss Tamley. A parcel was left for you earlier." She turned to see Bill walking towards her with a parcel in his hand and the expression on her face hardened.

Bill took a step back. "Everything okay, Miss Tamley?"

"No, Bill, it's not. Who left the package?" she demanded, her usual polite demeanour completely absent.

"A gentleman. Said you'd left this behind at the Myer jewellery department."

"Don't suppose he left a name?" Careen asked, knowing the answer already.

"Tony. Said he was looking forward to seeing you wear it tonight."

Careen shivered. "Is he now?" She put out her hand to take the parcel. "Hate to disappoint Tony then, wouldn't we?" She snatched the parcel and marched towards the lift, a mixture of fear and anger stirring her blood.

Careen disabled the alarm and pulled the door behind her securing the chain. She surveyed her apartment. Nothing out of place, but she could smell a brief hint of aftershave. Diesel –. Ben's choice. She smiled. A friendly fragrance to linger over. Except Ben was overseas. Don't get ahead of yourself, girl; it was likely one of Gordon's guys. She placed her keys in the marble bowl, her briefcase under the side table, and then stood in the middle of the room with her shopping bags in one hand and the parcel in the other. She looked around again, noticing every little detail, but this time feeling the emptiness of the place. She sighed softly, reached for her shopping bags and headed for the bathroom. She was going to go to Edward's birthday, she'd promised Chris she'd be there, and she was damn well going to wear the necklace.

NINETEEN

Careen tucked a stray wisp of hair behind her ear, straightened her shoulders and took a deep breath. As she entered the restaurant she scanned every face, but kept her stride confident. *Where are you, you bastard?* The bar was full, as was each of the tables. "Tony" could be any one of the diners. And she didn't know if she was looking for Tony himself or someone pretending to be him.

Careen had spent the afternoon trying to remember who knew Tony and would know that John called her Princess. The list was remarkably short – herself, John, Ben, Logan – and then it got murky. Logan was apt to talk after a few beers, so, basically, she could include any of his drinking buddies or, in reality, anyone within hearing distance at a bar. With Ben overseas her thoughts kept coming back to Logan. What perplexed her was that it had all started before Logan knew about Murray taking Chris's job, so if he *was* playing games she was at a loss to know why.

Her thoughts were interrupted by a squeal from Edward as he spotted Careen. "You are gorgeous. Very risqué for you, my dear. Very short, very appealing. Lots of nice single blokes here. Now you have some spare time you could fit in a date or two." He clapped his hand over his mouth and looked sheepishly at Careen.

"It's okay, Edward. I don't think anyone was paying attention." Or she hoped not.

As usual, Edward was talking non-stop, barely pausing to take a breath. "Sorry," he whispered. Then raising his voice again continued, "Let me introduce you to ..." and off he went running names and occupations faster than Careen could keep up, " ... and this is Anthony."

Anthony. Tony. Careen started, steadied herself and studied Anthony – short, bald and, judging by the leer, decidedly sleazy. She wrote him off as an unlikely suspect and continued to survey the other guests. No face registered, no tall men that met the description from Gordon's beach guy or from the Myer information desk. She hadn't actually expected him to be part of the group, but in one way she'd hoped he might be. She took her seat and absently lined up the cutlery, moving the glass to the tip of the knife. She picked up her napkin and folded it neatly into squares before centring it on her side plate. She'd briefly filled in Gordon after the incident at Myer, omitting the name Tony. He'd said he would have an agent at the restaurant but a quick glance at the bar didn't help identify him – which undoubtedly was the point. Gordon's man would be watching for someone watching Careen. She absently fiddled with her necklace as she sipped her wine.

Ah Careen, you can still surprise me. You wore the necklace. I am proud of you. Your back is straight, your expression unconcerned, but your eyes, they betray you. I wonder how long you can take this. How long before you break?

"So, you're single then?"

Careen glanced over the table to see Anthony leaning towards her. Great.

She spent most of the dinner avoiding conversation with Anthony and then, just as dessert was being served, she ended up speaking with an interesting trio who had a website and search engine for marketing hotels. There were already a large number of these in the marketplace, but they had a unique twist and she had spent a fascinating couple of hours throwing ideas around with them. Their enthusiasm was contagious and she was enjoying herself immensely.

A tap on her shoulder had her turning towards the waiter. "Excuse me, Miss. The gentleman at the bar asked me to bring you a drink. I told him you were on champagne."

Careen turned towards the bar, grabbed the waiter's arm, spilling the drink.

"Which gentleman? Point him out," she said shrilly.

All the conversation at the table stopped and every head turned towards her.

The waiter glanced back to the bar, pointing at an empty barstool. "Sorry. He left straight after he ordered. Bumped into another guy as he was leaving, spilt his beer down him. I thought they were going to come to blows. Something about him made me think it wouldn't take much. The other guy must have seen it too. Backed away. Apologised."

"Which other guy?"

He looked around the crowded bar. "Sorry, can't see him. It's pumping in here tonight."

"Did he give you anything else?"

"I'm sorry?"

"Did he give you a piece of jigsaw?"

"Ah that makes sense now."

Careen gripped his arm tighter. "What makes sense?"

"He said if you ask about a jigsaw to tell you not to be so impatient. He'll get there soon enough."

Careen shivered. It was him. Where was Gordon's agent? Why hadn't they noticed anything? Why had they let this happen?

"Could you let go of my arm, please?" The waiter was obviously uncomfortable now.

She dropped her hand.

"What did he look like?" she asked sharply, knowing the answer.

"Tall, dark, moustache, designer jacket, possibly Armani, black t-shirt – new, not worn in, Rolex watch – worth a bob or two."

Careen's surprised expression must have registered. He laughed.

"I'm studying to be a police profiler. I practise on the clientele."

"Anything else?"

"Actually, yes, his hair was dyed, not naturally dark, and his moustache was odd – not his either, I would say."

"And his eyes?"

"Deep blue – contacts would be my guess. Expensive dental work or naturally good genes, manicured nails and a ring. Unusual, he showed it to me when I asked about it – said it was a family heirloom. Black onyx on silver. Snakes circling the stone. The workmanship was superb."

Careen's blood went cold. Tony had always worn a ring just like that – said it had been in the family for generations. He never took it off – ever. It was the one item that hadn't been found with Tony's clothes on the beach.

She shivered again. Tony had been pronounced dead. But was he? The body had never been found. What if …?

"Excuse me." Careen pushed herself away from the table. "I have to go." She smiled weakly. "Thanks, Edward. Happy Birthday. Have to fly."

She wheeled around and ran out of the restaurant.

A taxi dropped her off outside her apartment building and she walked swiftly up the steps. The shadows drawn by the streetlights looked sinister tonight. Suddenly something inside her snapped and she felt fear, real fear. She ran, her chest heaving, air rasping through her lips, not seeing, not hearing just running. She had to get inside. Swiping her security pass she almost fell into the foyer.

"Miss Tamley. Are you okay?" Bill's concern pulled her up short.

"Fine. Just fine."

Her breathing was laboured and her pulse was racing. She smiled at Bill who gave her a perplexed look then moved his glance to something behind her. Careen pivoted sharply and collided with one of the tenants. A small gasp left her lips and she moaned.

"Miss Tamley?"

"Fine. Just fine." Careen repeated then spun around spooked by a noise behind her. "Lifts. Just the lifts."

She waved to Bill, who seemed to be quite unsure what to do, but had obviously decided she needed a hand. He headed towards her, but she backed away towards the lifts.

"Fine. Everything's fine."

She made herself turn around and walk towards the lift – her every step slow and measured, proving that she was in control. She entered the lift, jabbed the level-seventeen and the close-doors buttons simultaneously avoiding making eye contact with the woman who was reaching out her arm to stop the doors closing. As the door whooshed shut in the woman's face, Careen let out a sigh and leant back on the mirrored wall. She'd apologise next time she saw her.

She shut the apartment door behind her and slid the security chain across. Dropping her keys in the bowl she went straight to the liquor cabinet, poured herself a bourbon and skulled it, enjoying the burn as it cascaded down her throat. She knew she should have called Gordon from the restaurant, or even the taxi, but she'd needed time to think, to regroup. She moved to the sofa, settled herself and called him.

"It's late. Better be important." Gordon yawned. Careen must have got him out of bed.

"Would I have rung otherwise?"

"Who knows?" She heard a creak and figured he was climbing out of bed. "You were at a friend's birthday tonight were you not? What happened?"

Careen filled in Gordon on the last few hours, leaving out Tony's name. She wasn't ready to go there yet.

"Okay. That justifies the call." Gordon paused. "I'll call you back in about ten minutes. I need to speak with the agent who was covering you tonight."

"Call my mobile."

Careen started to pace before stopping herself. A cup of tea to settle. One of Lei's phrases – she missed having her around. She'd ring her tomorrow and see how she was going.

She placed the teabag in the mug, topped it up with boiling water and walked over to the balcony doors to stare into the night. I wonder? She put her mug on the side table and unlocked the balcony doors. Stepping out, she leaned over the railing, staring down onto the dimly lit street below. A man was standing brazenly under a street lamp; the mask he wore covered his face. He saw her, blew her a kiss and turned away. Careen grabbed onto the balcony rail to stop herself falling. Shut her eyes. Breathed. In for three. Out for three. In for three. Out for three. She opened her eyes, searched the foreshore. He was gone.

Careen took a slow step backwards and then jumped as her mobile rang. Recognising Gordon's number, she picked up the phone.

"Gordon, he's here. Outside. Now."

"Where?"

"Beach Street. On the foreshore. He's walking towards St

Kilda. Tall. Skinny. He's wearing the mask. It's him, Gordon. It's him."

"Hold." She heard the phone click and held her breath while she waited. "My agent is onsite – the only people she can see is a group of guys drinking beer."

"They must have seen him. He should ask them."

"He is a *she*. They appear to be a bit wasted so she's hesitant to approach them. Unlikely they'll be able to tell her anything."

"Do any of them have a ring on?" she interrupted Gordon as the thought hit her. "A silver ring with a black stone."

"What's this about a ring?"

"Just ask her to check. Please."

"Hold." The wait seemed interminable. "She can't get close enough to see. They mostly have their hands in their pockets." Gordon paused. "Careen, my agent found a business card at the spot where you say you saw the man in the mask."

"What's that got to do with anything?"

"It's your business card."

"I don't understand."

"Your name has been crossed out and written above the title of CEO is the name Tony."

A moan escaped Careen's lips.

"Careen. Who is Tony?"

Careen arranged to meet Gordon the next afternoon to give him the background on Tony. Gordon's final advice was to lock up securely and get a good night's rest. If whoever he was at the bar and outside her apartment had wanted to hurt her he could have easily managed it when she ran out of the restaurant alone. Gordon, in his usual brusque manner, had made it abundantly clear what he thought of her actions.

Even though she agreed with Gordon that it hadn't been her finest hour, she did point out that she had assumed that his agent was keeping an eye on her and would be following close by. Though, actually, it hadn't crossed her mind. She'd just wanted to get out, needed the fresh air, had to get home, lock herself in. Be safe.

Now that she was home, with the door secure and the alarm set, she discovered she didn't want to be alone at all. With Ben overseas and Logan acting strangely she decided she needed a pep talk with Mel.

"Hey, Mel, it's Careen."

"What's up? Oh my God, is everything all right. You never call me during the day. Isn't it the middle of the night over there? What's happened?" Mel didn't stop for a breath.

"Whoa. Everything's fine. I just had a bit of a scare and need to chat. Have you got a minute?"

"Always." She could hear Mel's shoes striding across a hardwood floor, then the click of a door closing. "That's better, a little quieter in here. So spill."

Careen filled her in on the shopping trip, the necklace and the fact that the Tony person was getting bolder, following her to Edward's dinner.

"Confused here, girl. What has Tony got to do with Clown Man?"

"Tony is ..." Careen stopped, dropped to the couch. "Mel, what if there are two of them?"

"Come again?"

"Two people. What if they aren't related? What if Clown Man is back and this Tony guy is someone else entirely? People have given me different descriptions – both tall but one is underfed, and the other bulked up."

"You have two stalkers? Come on, Careen, how likely is that?"

Careen was crunched up on the couch, her head resting on her knees. "I don't know anymore, Mel. I just don't know. And how does Louise fit into this?"

"Let's think this through. Clown Man is leaving pieces of jigsaw each time he does something. Did you get another piece of jigsaw with the necklace?"

"No." Careen bit her lip. "Just the necklace."

"And when he bought you a drink?"

"No. But he did give the barman a jigsaw-related message."

"And on the pavement it was your business card, not a piece of jigsaw."

"Correct."

"That doesn't gel. Why pick a signature item and then ignore it." She could hear Mel pacing in the background. "Unless he wants you to *think* there are two of them. That's quite clever really – puts you right on edge."

"Great. I've either got two stalkers or one clever one. Those are my choices. Thanks, Mel. Just what I needed to hear."

"Sorry. But you know me, Careen, I think best out loud." A squeak in the background indicated that Mel had lowered herself into one of the chairs. "What did Gordon's guy have to say?"

"Gordon's girl, actually. Nothing to add. There was a group of guys around, that's all. They appeared wasted so she didn't approach them. Couldn't see if any of them was wearing a ring."

"What ring?"

"Tony used to wear this distinct ring, never took it off. It wasn't found with his clothes so he must have worn it into the water."

"And this links how?"

"The guy who's pretending to be Tony is wearing a similar ring according to the barman. I thought if the skinny guy was wearing the ring then it all tied together. But there seems to be two of them. It's doing my head in."

"This ring is an important link then." Mel paused. "Clown Man never wore a ring did he?" Mel hated the way the media had dubbed him the "Clown Killer" and refused to use that name.

"No. That's what I don't get. How does this Tony guy fit in with the Clown? One is tall, broad shoulders, good looking and is pretending to be Tony." Careen shivered. "The man I just saw was stringy like the Clown but he left a card with Tony's name on."

"So there's definitely two of them working together?"

"You are meant to make me feel better, Mel. Not worse."

"Sorry."

"Look, I'm getting confused now. How about you start where I left off when I flew home? I'm going to jot down a timeline. It always helps me think."

Careen walked to the kitchen, switched on the jug and grabbed a mug. It was going to be a long chat. She'd got as far as the barman/police profiler-in-training description when she realised that Mel had gone quiet.

"Mel are you still there?"

Silence.

"Mel?"

"Can you describe the ring again?"

"The ring. Why?"

"Careen, just describe the damn ring for me."

"Black onyx set in silver with a weird pattern of snakes surrounding the stone."

"Careen, I think I know who one of the guys is." Mel sounded shaky.

"What are you talking about?" How was Mel tied up in this? "Mel?"

"Stuart and I broke up briefly. While we were separated I dated this guy, Michael, for a few weeks. He wore a ring just like that."

"When? Why didn't you tell me?"

"It was a brief fling. You and I hadn't spoken for a few months and it was over just as quickly as it started."

"Mel."

"Shit, Careen. He was the strong silent type." Mel went silent. "He did ask quite a lot of questions about my life in Australia." Mel was shuffling. "Careen I told him quite a bit about you. I was missing you at the time and he seemed interested in our friendship. My God. What have I done?"

"Have you got a photo of him?"

"No." Mel was obviously upset. "Actually, that's the thing, I did have some on my phone but he must have deleted them just before we broke up, because when I went back to look at them later they were all gone." She heard a catch in Mel's voice.

"Mel, hold it together. What do you know about him? Anything at all you can remember."

"Other than what he looks like, very little. It wasn't until after we split up that I realised I knew nothing about him. He never talked about his family, I never met any of his friends and we, well, we spent most of the time in bed or just chatting." Mel paused. "We talked about Australia and about you. He said he was thinking about heading to Melbourne and would I mind if he looked you up. Careen, I gave him your phone number and your address."

"That answers that question at least."

"How could I be so thick?"

Careen wouldn't let her friend take any of the blame. "I agree. I mean when you think about it Mel everyone asks their lovers if they're thinking of stalking their best friend on the other side of the world. Comes up in conversation at lot."

"You're taking this rather well."

"Not really." Careen was curled up on the sofa. She was scared, but it wasn't Mel's fault. "Whatever game he's playing it's taken a while to set up."

"You're not kidding. We dated months ago."

"Okay, fill me in. On everything."

Careen picked up her iPad and started typing. By the time Mel had finished it was two a.m. and Careen was drained. She decided not to wake Gordon again that night; she'd call him first thing in the morning. She got up and stretched, eyeing the door. Gordon had installed deadlocks and a security system but it didn't seem enough tonight. She wasn't going to get any sleep without a back-up plan. She spied an ornate crystal vase, a present from John's wife Cindy many years ago.

She'll forgive me.

Careen double-checked that the door was secure, set the perimeter sensors and placed the crystal vase precariously on a chair leaning up against the door. No one was getting in without her knowing about it. If anyone opened the door there would be an almighty crash and then the alarm would go off.

TWENTY

The crash made her sit up in bed with a start, every muscle taut. An icy chill spread over her. The alarm; why didn't the alarm go off? Maybe the chair wasn't balanced properly and the vase slid sideways. That was it. Nothing to worry about. If anyone had opened the door the alarm would have woken her, not the crash. That's how the sensors worked. Open the door. Beeping. Thirty seconds to disengage. She listened for the beeps. There they were. She held her breath. The alarm would start screaming soon. He would leave. Silence. Why wasn't it beeping anymore? Had he turned it off? Could he do that? Gordon's man didn't tell her he could do that. She grabbed the sword; glad she'd taken it from the hallway. Protection. Strength, Courage. She forced herself to climb out of bed. The vase had just been to make her feel better. It wasn't actually meant to work. She had an alarm, for God's sake. Grasping the sword with both hands, she took one step forward then froze. Footsteps. Not possible. She grabbed her phone and dialled 000. The footsteps were closer now. She ran to the bathroom and locked the door behind her. Leant on it. Not again.

"Triple zero. Do you require Police, Fire or Ambulance?"

"Police," she whispered.

"What is your location? Suburb and state, please."

"Port Melbourne, Victoria."

"Putting you through."

She heard a click. "Police. May I have your exact location please."

"Apartment 1705, 85 Beach Street, Port Melbourne."

"What is the nature of your emergency?"

"Someone's in my apartment. I'm here alone. Please come quickly," she whispered frantically into the phone while watching the door intently.

"Is there another way out?"

"No. I'm seventeen floors up."

"Can you see anyone?"

"I've locked myself in the bathroom. I need someone here *now*."

"A car has been dispatched. I'll stay on the line until they arrive. Can you answer some questions for me?"

"Yes."

"Did they come through the front door?"

"I think so. The vase fell down. It wasn't meant to work. I have an alarm. It didn't go off."

"I'm sorry, what is this about a vase?"

"Footsteps. I hear footsteps. He's coming. He's …" She listened intently. "He's stopped."

"Are you safe in the bathroom?"

"Is anywhere safe?"

"An officer will be with you shortly. The station is only a few minutes away."

"Don't go. Please don't go."

"I'll wait on the line."

She no longer heard movement outside the door. No shuffling. No footsteps. Silence. Careen stood up and faced the door, sword held in front of her. Come on you bastard. Just you try it.

A distant knock made her jump.

"Hello. It's constables Mather and Stanton here. May we come in?"

"Is he still here?"

"We're just checking the place now."

"How do I know if you're who you say you are?" Her paranoia was showing.

"Miss Tamley, it's Bill here. It's the police. I came up with them."

"Dispatch has identified two officers on site," the emergency operator confirmed.

"Thanks."

She hung up the phone and unlocked the bathroom door, holding the sword in front of her like a weapon.

"Please put down the sword," said a female officer.

"How do I know you're real police? Anyone can hire a uniform. Can I see some ID?"

"I need you to drop the sword."

Careen lowered the point of the sword but didn't let it go. The female officer flipped over her badge while the male kept his hand hovering over his gun. Careen studied the badge intently, using the time to get her equilibrium back. She nodded her approval and placed the sword gently against the wall. She walked towards the two police officers, her eyes all the while searching the apartment. She saw nothing out of place but the shards of broken vase that littered the floor near the doorway.

"How did you get in?"

"The concierge here provided access up and your front door was wide open."

"So he's gone then?"

"Miss Tamley, I'm Constable Mather. Perhaps you might like to put something warmer on before we talk," said the female officer.

She glanced down, realising that she was dressed only in a singlet top and pyjama shorts. Walking into her bedroom, she grabbed her silk kimono and pulled it on, tying the sash tightly, all the time searching the room for movement.

"Did you catch him?" she demanded. "Did you at least see him?"

"No, we didn't." Constable Stanton shook his head.

"Then he could still be here." Careen looked around wildly. "Please can you check?" Her voice was shaking now.

"Constable Mather, if you will stay here with Miss Tamley, I will re-check the apartment." He moved towards the bedroom.

"Thank you." Careen sank into the sofa.

"While he's checking the apartment how about we start with a few questions." She turned to Bill. "Thank you for your assistance. We'll take it from here."

Bill looked offended. "If you need anything, Miss Tamley, just let me know."

"Thanks, Bill. I will." She watched him cross the room, counting his steps. Bill's tread was heavy, unlike the person who had been in the apartment. His footsteps had been light, quiet. He hadn't wanted to be heard.

"How did he get past my alarm?" Careen stood up to check the alarm pad. "It was on. I turned it on when I went to bed."

"Miss Tamley. Take a seat. We'll get to that in a minute."

Careen perched on the edge of the sofa then jumped up. "Tea. Would you like tea?"

Constable Mather smiled. "If you are having one that'd be nice. We both take it white, one sugar."

Careen filled the jug, trying to calm down. Breathing deeply she made two teas, the sugar spilling on the bench as her hand shook. She hated appearing out of control, always had. Breathe. In for three. Out for three. In for three. Out for three. By the time the tea was ready Careen was feeling more composed.

Pulling the sash tightly around her again, she picked up the mugs just as the other constable reappeared.

"No one is in the apartment other than the three of us," he responded to her unasked question.

"Are you sure? Did you check under the bed and in the closets?"

"I looked everywhere a person could possibly hide. Whoever was here has gone."

"Oh." Careen passed out the tea and sunk back down into the sofa directly across from Constable Mather, her eyes on the now closed door.

"Miss Tamley, we will need you to answer a few questions. Are you up to it?" Constable Mather pulled out a notebook.

"Yes." No.

"What alerted you to the fact that someone was entering your apartment?"

"I'd placed a vase on a chair by the door. When the door opened it tipped over the chair and the vase fell off and smashed. The noise woke me."

"What time was this?"

She told them.

"Did you see the assailant?"

And on the questions went: Can you describe what you saw? Has this happened before? Who has access to this building? Have you lost a set of keys lately?

"Miss Tamley. The door had been unlocked, not forced, and then the security chain was neatly cut. Whoever broke in knew what they expected to find – someone at home and the security chain in use. The alarm was turned off."

"How can he do that?"

"Who else knows your code?"

"No one. The alarm is new. I told no one."

"Why did you have a vase balancing on a chair behind the

door?" asked Constable Stanton, watching her closely now.

Careen looked him straight in the eye. "I've had a few prank calls that have made me nervous. It's just for peace of mind, to help me sleep."

"Miss Tamley." She could see in his eyes that he wasn't convinced she was giving him the whole story and he raised his eyebrows questioningly. "I would have thought that a security chain and an alarm would be sufficient to help you sleep if it was only prank calls." He looked straight at her and she felt herself blushing.

"Someone has been stalking me. I don't know who. He leaves odd gifts. Makes sure I know he's following me."

"Have you lodged a report with the police on this?"

"I tried. You can talk to Sergeant Lawson at Russell Street Station. He said that unless they actually harm me there's nothing the police can do."

"I'm afraid that's the case. Sending someone presents isn't illegal, but breaking in is. Are you sure it's the same person?"

Careen snorted. "Are you suggesting there's a whole team of them?"

The constable ignored her comment. "Are you sure the door was secure when you retired?"

"Absolutely."

"You have a very sophisticated alarm system here." Constable Stanton was leaning over the alarm. "There appears to be a few wires loose. Was it like this before?"

"No."

"Then it appears whoever broke in knew what he was doing." He straightened up. "We'll get someone in to dust for prints in the morning, but I don't think it's likely that we'll find any." He tucked his notebook into his pocket. "We'll also check the security-camera footage from the building."

If he could get into a secure building, unlock deadlocks

and override a sophisticated security system, Careen doubted anything was going to show up on the security tapes.

Constable Mather stood up. "I think it would be a good idea if you stayed with a friend for a few days."

"I'll call someone and have them come over. I'll be fine."

It wasn't until they'd left that Careen noticed the photo. The missing picture of Ben, Logan, her and John was back and sitting on the side table near the key bowl. Her face had been neatly cut out of the picture and the photo had been put back into the frame.

She called Ben but hung up after the international beeps. She didn't want him worrying when there was nothing he could do. Logan, however, was a different matter. She left a message for him but he still hadn't called back by the time she was due to meet with Gordon the next morning. Didn't he ever check his voicemail?

She hadn't slept at all after the police had left, so she went to the office early to tidy up a few matters, and then she would drive to Gordon's office. She hitched the lift down to the car park with Chris who was also heading out to a meeting. She was safely in her car with the doors locked before he was out of sight.

She was nearly at the exit when a figure leapt out in front of the car. Careen jumped on the brakes automatically and the car skidded to a stop. It was daylight. The car park was full. It was all wrong. She hit the lock button on her already locked doors before looking frantically around, her hand poised over the horn, hoping it was just some idiot not paying attention. Knowing it wasn't. A knock on the passenger window. Careen hit the horn, hard. Its siren echoed in the car park.

"What the fuck are you doing?"

She looked out her passenger window. Gary? She released

the horn and wound the window down slightly, leaving the doors locked.

"Jesus, you nearly ran me over and then tried to deafen me. You're completely mad."

"What do you want, Gary?"

"What the fuck do you think?"

"Always the charmer, I see."

"Where is she?"

"I haven't seen Lei since Tuesday." Careen tried to make her voice sound harsh, unforgiving.

"I know you know where she is."

"What makes you say that? Last time I saw her she was writing out a cheque and signing it. Don't you think perhaps if I knew where she was, I'd let the police know?"

"You didn't call the cops."

"What makes you think that?"

"Spoke with that tart, Missy. Said Lei was away on holiday."

"I don't tell my staff everything."

"If you'd told the cops they would've been around."

Why didn't it surprise Careen that Gary would be known to the police? "Even if I knew where she was, I'm hardly going to tell you." She pushed the button to raise the window.

"You'll lead me to her one day. I'll be everywhere you are, right on your tail."

"Join the club," Careen said softly as she closed the window.

McNaughton & McEwan Investigations' reception wasn't what she expected at all. Modern and sleek, glass and stainless steel, but with enough decorator touches to make it warm, not cold. It didn't suit Gordon at all. The receptionist had been polite and made her a delicious coffee – nothing like PI offices in the movies.

"Careen?" A woman was walking towards her, her hand

extended. She was wearing a smart tailored suit and high shoes, and seemed decidedly uncomfortable in both. "I'm Jill, Gordon's partner. He's filled me in the details of your case. I won't be sitting in today as I'm heading out to another meeting, but I wanted to say hi."

"Hi." Careen shook Jill's hand. "Nice office."

"Nothing like on TV is it?" Jill laughed.

"That obvious?"

"It's okay, I'm used to it. I'll get you settled in my office before I head off. Gordon's office is having a refit at the moment." Jill's office was more edgy than modern. Rugs scattered on the floor, antique filing cabinets with piles of papers on top, family photographs littering the shelves. Jill indicated a solid leather chair and Careen sat down, surprised to find it more forgiving than it appeared.

"Gordon will be with you shortly. Got to fly." Jill turned and looked at Careen and smiled. "It was nice to finally meet you."

She shut the door with a quiet click.

Moments later, Gordon appeared.

"Ah. Jill said she'd put you in here." Gordon moved some papers off an old armchair and sat down. "So, let's start. Who is Tony?"

Straight to the point.

"Tony Fisher. Tony was my boss, my mentor and my friend."

"Was?"

"Tony's dead."

About forty-five minutes later Careen was getting hoarse.

"Coffee break," said Gordon.

Careen stood up and stretched while Gordon went out to ask the receptionist for fresh coffee. She was admiring Jill's collection of canopic jars when Gordon returned.

"Not sure why she likes them. The Egyptians used to put

old body parts in them, preserving them for the afterlife. Personally, I'd rather keep my bits inside."

Careen laughed. "You don't believe in the afterlife?"

"I'll start believing when someone comes back to tell me about it, and not before." Gordon placed her coffee on the table.

"Might be sooner that you think." Careen sat down again, taking a sip of her coffee.

"Doesn't happen. Only way someone's coming back is if they were never dead in the first place. Okay. We have Tony in a coma from the accident and you are investigating anomalies," Gordon prompted.

"Once Quentin, the CFO, had been brought in there was no stopping him. He agreed that the money was in fact missing and the books had been fiddled. He then did a total audit of the finances and traced the missing funds, which had been routed straight into Tony's personal account. Quentin was quite excited. He'd always been jealous of Tony's relationship with John so, now that there was a trail to follow, he was like a bloodhound. I tried to tell him it was all a misunderstanding, but I had to admit it didn't look good."

But, she thought, how hard did I try to convince him? Could I have done more? Was I thinking more about me, my ambitions, than the fallout for Tony? Did I hope deep down that Tony was guilty and that I would get his job?

"Careen. Pay attention."

"Sorry."

Gordon shook his head, muttered under this breath.

"Anyhow, a few weeks later I was a nervous wreck, Quentin was like a pig in mud and we had a problem. Neither of us had told anyone about what was going on and now we had to speak to John."

"I take it that didn't go well."

"That would be an understatement. Quentin approached

it in a roundabout way, he explained the missing funds, the reason for investigation, and the results. As soon as Tony's name came up, John started cursing and swearing and threw both of us out. To be honest, I was worried he was going to have a heart attack."

"And then?"

"John called me back in."

Careen would never forget that meeting.

John's usually benevolent face had been bleak and pale and his eyes held tremendous pain.

"What made you look?" His eyes accused Careen.

John was like a father to her and she needed him to believe in her. However, the reality was that Tony was his successor, his second son, while she was the poor cousin. She knew she'd wear the blame – there was always a scapegoat and she'd be it. She straightened her shoulders and took a deep breath. She would go down honestly and with dignity. And then find a job sweeping floors, a little voice twittered in her head.

"I wasn't actually looking. The budgets were due and with Tony in hospital I wanted to get them done." She was looking John straight in the eye, he'd taught her that. "When I first found some inconsistencies, I assumed my lack of knowledge meant I was missing something and so I asked Quentin for help."

"Not helping yourself to a promotion, then? With Tony out of the way you would be the key mover and shaker." John's voice was hollow.

Careen understood his bitterness, but this she wouldn't take. "You know me better than that," she countered. "I've worked with Tony for four years. I've always respected and admired him. He was a great teacher and mentor to me. I would do nothing intentional to harm him." Her voice was hard. Convincing.

"But it seems you have."

"Yes it does, doesn't it?" Her shoulders slumped and her eyes were downcast. "John, Tony is my friend as well as my boss – I don't want this to be true." She stood up, turned to leave, then turned back. "If I could turn back the clock, I would. I want no part in destroying a friend. Even a dishonest one." Careen paused, her hand on the door handle as John rose.

"And if he wasn't in a coma, was working here and you found out – what would you have done then?"

The question was loaded and Careen knew it. The answer would determine whether she kept her job or not, whether she remained a part of John's life – but what was the right answer?

"Answer from the heart. Don't think," John said harshly.

She turned to face him. "What would I have done? I would've confronted him, asked him why, told him to stop."

"And if he didn't?"

"And if he didn't ..." She lowered her eyes and raised them again to John. "And if he didn't, I would've come to you. I suppose I'm not such a good friend after all."

"Depends on which friendship you're referring to." John turned his back to her.

"What happens now?" Her voice was cowed by John's coldness.

"For now, nothing. You are to speak to no one about this." His tone demanded acquiescence and Careen nodded to his back as she left the room.

For the next few weeks it had felt as if she was walking on eggshells. Tony had come out of the coma and was convalescing at John's. At the office, everything continued as normal and Careen kept wondering when the explosion would occur. John must have told Ben and he was avoiding her. She doubted the friendship would survive. Logan had a new love interest and was so wrapped up in her that he hadn't noticed Careen's world falling apart. She'd never felt so alone. Her job was all she had and so, in spite of the tenuous hold she had on it, she spent twelve hours a day, seven days a week, with her head down, working hard – it kept her mind from dwelling on Tony.

Sixteen days after her meeting with John, she received an email advising that due to poor health, Tony had resigned his position as Business Development Director and Careen was taking over his role in an acting capacity until a replacement could be found. For him or me? she thought sadly.

"Zoned out again, Miss Tamley?" Gordon appeared perplexed. "Do you do that a lot in business? It's quite disconcerting."

"No, never happened before." She smiled. "It must be you that does it to me."

Gordon didn't even crack a smile. "Back on track, please. Tony disappeared one night."

"Three days after the memo, Tony let himself out of John's house and walked to the beach. His clothes were found on the wet sand with footsteps leading into the water. He'd left a note. 'What I did was wrong, but for the right reasons. I hope you can all say the same.' His body was never found."

"And Quentin?"

"John sacked him after he caught him talking to the press."

"I checked around. There's nothing about Tony stealing money."

"John had friends in high places. Got it hushed up."

"Could he be involved in this somehow?"

"No. Quentin went a little loopy after John let him go. He got all paranoid, thought he was being followed, that people were breaking into his home and moving things around. He started drinking. His wife left him, took the kids. Last I heard he was in rehab, but that was years ago."

"Being followed, break-ins, moving items around. Sound familiar?"

Careen froze. "Oh my God!"

"It's unlikely that we'll get any help from that angle."

"You don't think ..."

"It's a possibility." Gordon's voice was quiet and calm.

"Tony is *alive*." Her gaze shot up. "He paid Quentin back and now it's my turn."

"As I said, it's a possibility."

"We need to find him." Careen paused. "Exactly how do you go about finding a dead person?"

"Some things are harder than others, but very little is impossible. We have a long afternoon ahead of us. Let's get a fresh cup and then you can tell me everything you know about this Tony Fisher."

TWENTY-ONE

Another sleepless night – Careen looked at herself in the mirror. The face that stared back was not hers, but that of an old, worn-out woman. Today was the day she officially handed over the CEO role to Chris. But she was so tired she felt no emotion at all. She'd expected to be sad or excited, not drained and uncaring. She purposefully turned away from the mirror and went to prepare for the day.

The boardroom was buzzing when she arrived. All the senior management had been called to attend, and although some may have had an inkling what this was about, they were seeking confirmation before they shifted alliances. She searched the room for Logan and her heart stilled briefly when she realised he wasn't there. They would all notice, and once she left they would comment. Couldn't he see he was undermining his own position, damaging his reputation?

"No change of heart?" Chris whispered to her as he surveyed the group.

"No, Chris, no change of heart." Careen smiled. She moved up to the head of the table, her corporate persona in full force now she was here.

"Please be seated." She raised her voice to make herself heard.

Everyone took their place, coffee cups clinking on the glass table as they made themselves comfortable.

She paused and looked around. Murray was nervously scanning the room. It appeared he was aware Logan was missing.

"Thank you. Many of you …" She paused as the door burst open and Logan entered.

"Oops, late again. Sorry." He threw himself down into one of the vacant chairs. "Missy, be a love and grab me a coffee – black. Was a late night." Logan grinned. "Sorry, did I interrupt something important?"

"Logan, please." Why did he decide to play the fool today of all days? He wasn't doing himself any favours. Even on a bad day he was usually a bit more circumspect in the boardroom.

"Sorry, sis. Will have a coffee soon and will dutifully shut up and await my impending doom."

Careen sighed. "Missy, can you pull the door shut, please?"

As Missy closed the door, Careen glanced over at Chris. He was clearly not amused. It suddenly occurred to Careen that Logan and Chris were going to have to work this one out without her. God help Chris, she thought, or perhaps it's Logan who would need assistance.

"Careen, you were saying?" Chris's words gently nudged her out of her reverie.

She smiled. "I remember when I started Kudos. My dream was to build the best boutique hotel chain on the globe, to take the Montage brand and make a mark on the world, something unique. This has been achieved, but not by me alone. Each one of you has made a valuable contribution to what we are today, and I'd like to take this opportunity to say a heartfelt thank you to all of you."

"Oh gee whiz, sis. That's sweet. Makes me all gooey inside."

Chris shot Logan a look so filled with antagonism that even Logan couldn't miss it. He smiled at Chris and reached across Murray to grab a croissant. As his hand came back, he deliberately knocked over Murray's hot coffee. Murray jumped up, scalded and cursing.

"Oops, so sorry."

"Bloody hell, Logan, that was deliberate." Murray's face was red and angry as he glared at Logan. "Just remember that—"

"Murray." Chris cut off Murray before he could continue.

"Okay, since Logan seems determined to make this meeting a fiasco, let's get straight to the point," Careen said, her voice raised and sharper than she intended.

Murray looked over and sat down, still wet and steaming.

"As of today, I'm appointing Chris as CEO of the Montage Group. His appointment is effective immediately. Many of you have worked for him as part of the Kudos brand. Chris will now take up the reins for the entire organisation. Chris, I'd like to officially handover the Montage Group to your care." Careen stood and indicated the chair at the head of the table. "This is now yours."

Congratulations were passed around the room and each person stood up to shake hands with Chris. Logan remained seated and Careen silently pleaded with him to stand and join in. Didn't he see the damage he was doing? Logan glared at her and she mouthed the word "please". He shrugged, but stood and offered his hand to Chris across the table.

"Best man for the job," said Logan to Chris. He turned and glared at Murray. "Some jobs go to the right people, anyway." Logan pushed back his chair, blew a kiss to Careen and walked out of the room.

Could have been worse – how she wasn't sure, but it could have been.

"Chris. Over to you, this is your team now." She indicated her vacated chair and he picked up his papers and moved across.

Careen and Chris had decided that as she handed him the reins and the head chair, she'd depart. She paused, her hand on the door. She turned to her old team who were all watching her. "Thank you all. I know you'll support Chris in his decisions and help take Montage into the future." She turned and walked out of the door.

And that, she thought, was that.

Careen headed back to her office to collect her handbag and a few personal items. It still was her office and would remain so, to be used for any other projects she chose to initiate. Chris had known her well enough not to ask for the office – it had been John's and therefore was sacred to her.

She walked past Lei's empty desk and sighed. She was so tired. Perhaps, like Lei, she needed to get away. Go straight to the airport and catch a flight. It wouldn't matter where to. But that would be like running away and Careen prided herself on never backing down in the face of a challenge.

"And I am not going to start now," she said out loud as she entered her office.

"Start what?"

Careen's heart jumped and then settled. "Logan, what are you doing here?" She sighed. "What you did over there wasn't very smart."

"I know." He looked sheepish. "I couldn't help it. Murray's been pushing my buttons all week and this morning I decided to pay him back."

"What do you mean pushing your buttons?"

"Ever since you told him last week, he's been giving me these sly looks – whispering behind my back, making decisions to thwart me."

"Since when?" Careen queried.

"Last Tuesday."

"Logan, Murray was only offered the position yesterday, he knew nothing about it before then."

"Are you sure his mate Chris didn't spill the beans?"

"I was there when Chris asked Murray – he was genuinely surprised. I can spot a faker most times." Or can I?

"Why was he surprised?" Logan queried.

"Bad choice of words." Careen walked to the window and gazed out at the view for a few moments before turning to Logan. "Logan, you have to work with Chris now. I think you should apologise to him for this morning." And to me. Careen held her breath.

"You mean he can sack me?" Logan's voice had an edge.

"Only if you give him good cause." She continued before Logan could interrupt. "If you undermine him, Logan, you'll give him no choice and I can't protect you from yourself or from the consequences of your actions.

"No." She held up her hand to stop him speaking. "Logan, if Chris accepts poor behaviour from you, he sets himself up to fail with the other managers, you must understand that."

"So he can sack me?"

"Yes, Logan, he can."

"Bitch!" he said under his breath, but loud enough to make sure Careen heard.

"Call me anything you like, Logan, but if you want to continue as Head of PR, you'll need to do your job. You are exceptionally good at it when you choose to be."

"Shit, Careen," Logan slumped into a chair. "I'm not good at this nine-to-five stuff, it's not for me."

"So talk to Chris about your hours, talk about targets and KPIs and reaching those in flexible hours – it worked for us – there's no reason for Chris to want to change that."

"I can hear the 'but' in your voice."

"Logan, your attitude has to change. Chris is in charge and he's very good at what he does. Recognise that and give him the respect he deserves."

"And Murray, the wimp?"

"Murray is Chris's choice and he'll make a great 2IC – he's still a bit raw, but he's committed, intelligent and has the aptitude to eventually take over one day. You may not like it, but those are the facts."

"Factual as always. Everything in its place." The bitterness was pronounced now. "So, basically, if Chris leaves, Murray gets his job and I'm left behind again."

Careen was getting angry now. "Yes, Logan. Unless you have a miraculous turnaround you will always be left behind." She was looking directly in his eyes and saw the anger there.

Logan stood, towering over her. "I quit," he spat out. "I can work for Chris but I will not work for Murray, so I quit." He turned to leave.

"If you quit, Logan, you lose your salary and your car. Think about it."

"I can make it on my own without you, you know."

"I know you can, Logan," Careen said softly. "But, selfishly, I don't want you to. I like having you close." She sat down and looked up at him. She felt incredibly sad. Perhaps it was the stress, the lack of sleep or maybe it was the end of an era. She smiled. "Remember how we used to spark off each other, ideas flying, laughing and building our dreams? Where did all that go? When did we lose that?"

"Trying the soft-soap approach now?" The bitterness was still there.

"No, Logan, just wondering where it all went wrong – us, me. Why is it all so hard these days?" The tears were spilling down her cheeks unchecked.

It was the tears that did it. Logan had only seen Careen cry once – at their parent's funeral. Never again for any reason, no matter how bad things got.

"Shit, Careen, don't cry. I didn't mean it." He was floundering now in unfamiliar territory.

"Don't worry, Logan, it's me, not you. Go home to Samantha. I'll be okay in a moment."

"Careen."

"Go, Logan."

He handed her a box of tissues and quietly shut the door behind him. Doing what Logan did best, running away when the going got tough.

Careen spent the rest of the morning tidying away her office. Chris dropped in briefly to give her a summary of how the meeting had gone and appeared very much the man in charge. He deserved it and would look after Montage well.

She stood up and looked around her office – it was different now – nothing physical had changed but it no longer felt the same. Her mobile rang and she smiled.

"Gordon. Good morning." Perhaps he had the answers already.

"I take it you haven't logged into the Montage Facebook account then."

Careen put Gordon on hold and opened up the app on her phone. She skimmed the first few posts then stopped at the third: *Coming soon, a new* True Lives and Lies *podcast – Montage's Careen Tamley.* Over 760 likes. She shut her eyes.

Miss Careen Tamley is known as one of Melbourne's leading lights in the hospitality industry. She has run Montage since taking over the reins following the death of John Seymour, the company's founder, seven years ago. But who is Careen Tamley really? How did she make such a name for herself? Was her inheritance luck or meticulous planning? Did she genuinely deserve to inherit one of the most successful hotel chains in the country? Did she beguile John Seymour's son, luring him away from the prize and then kill Tony Fisher when he became a rival for the inheritance? Why is she giving it all up? This tell-all podcast reveals the strategy behind Careen Tamley's climb to the pinnacle, interviews with those who helped her along the way and reveals a real-life glimpse behind the scenes from those who have worked with her.

Careen Tamley – True Lives and Lies is a tale of murder, deceit and manipulation. The ultimate story of one woman's climb to power and those who fell by the wayside.

It seemed Louise had a flair for sensationalism. Careen shut her eyes, shaking her head. This couldn't be happening. She thought after her conversation with Louise something had changed.

"How did she get that onto our feed?" she asked when she'd reconnected to Gordon.

"It's easier than you think. I suggest you get your IT people to take it down immediately. I'll call you later."

As Gordon hung up, Careen's email pinged. She turned to look; knew she'd have to face the fallout. The email subject was short: *Seven years exactly – you just couldn't wait could you?*

Dearest Careen,
I do hope you saw my podcast post. Quite catchy I thought. Don't want to spoil the surprise for all my listeners but I thought you might like a little more.
Please understand this isn't personal – I won't include anything about the attack – I'm not that callous, but I do have a contract to fulfil. Given that you haven't reported anything about your clown attacker to the police, I do wonder if the whole upset phone call to

me was a ploy to get me to stop. And a clown crowd - if that was for my benefit, to get me to feel sorry for you and back off, you need to know that I'm not that easily manipulated. I've jotted down a quick summary of where the story is heading so far. Something to tide you over until it goes live.

It appears that she didn't want to wait a minute longer than legally required. After the untimely death of Tony Fisher, seven years ago, Careen lined herself up to inherit the Montage Group. A little history here for our readers. Careen met John Seymour via his son Ben. Careen has tried to woo Ben on a number of occasions, a way in to the inheritance. Ben was a little too savvy for our young Careen and avoided any entanglements. However, once Careen discovered Ben was not the heir apparent, she set her sights on Tony Fisher, Ben's best friend and John Seymour's illegitimate son. Tony started to suspect Careen was using him but just as he was about to confront her, an unfortunate accident put Tony into an induced coma for a number of months. Careen saw her chance. She doctored the books, and then invited the CFO, Quentin Malance, in to audit them knowing what he would find. When Quentin and Careen took the altered records to John Seymour, Tony was thrown out of the company and Careen quickly stepped in to fill his shoes. Once Careen had Tony out of the way she took no time in ingratiating herself in the high echelons of the business. She had one focus – to inherit Montage. Even her brother Logan was left behind in the climb.

(I have a wonderful quote I recorded in a conversation with Logan that will fit here perfectly – "Careen is all business and outcomes. She has no time for friends and family.")

"Oh Logan." Careen's voice was filled with sadness.

> Careen climbed to the top of the pile and there she waited, working closely with John Seymour, ensuring when the will was redrawn after the death of his beautiful wife, Cindy, that Careen was the one who would inherit the lion's share. Poor Ben. With Careen whispering in John's ear all he got was twenty per cent of the profits but none of the control. Careen was in charge and Ben must remain on good terms with her or he will lose what little he has. There's no way out for him. He must continue with his facade of friendship until finally he makes it in the art world. We hope for your sake, Ben, it's soon. No one should have to put up with this treatment.

Careen bit her lip until it bled. Louise was tearing apart her family and friends. Not Ben. Please not Ben. Her tears were falling freely now, but she kept reading; had to see how bad it really was.

> It's seven years since John Seymour passed away. According to his will he insisted that Careen must remain in charge for seven years before she relinquishes control of the business. Why seven? Did you know it takes seven years for someone to be legally declared dead? Was that the reason for the codicil? But true to form, Careen has moved on, seven years exactly. She doesn't like to waste time. So what will become of Montage? Does she care?

> Hope you like it.
> Love, Louise.

Careen left a message for Logan and another for Ben. She needed to talk to them both although she wasn't too sure what she was going to say. Especially to Ben. What if Louise was right? What if Ben stayed close to keep an eye on her? No. Ben wasn't like that. They were friends. Real friends. Then why the flirting and nothing else? Keep her hoping? That didn't make sense – she had nothing to gain by being with Ben other than, well ... being with Ben. He hadn't seemed upset when she told him she was handing over to Chris; in fact he had supported her. Was that because he wanted the power with Chris, not her? Oh God. It was all so screwed up. Louise had her doubting Ben and she hated her for it.

TWENTY-TWO

She drove home in a daze, poured herself a glass of wine and plonked herself down in a Cape Cod chair on the balcony. "It's all gone wrong, John." She wished he was here to talk to. Talking out loud to a ghost seemed slightly crazy today but after the day she'd had, ... if anyone heard her they could think what they liked. She took a long sip of the cool wine. "I'm not sure what I did to deserve this. It was meant to be an exciting time, not a mess. What would you do if it was you?" She sat, listening to the wind and the waves, letting the sounds wash over her as the tears fell.

"Hi Ben." She answered the call nervously.

"Hey. You okay?"

"Not so much."

"Logan called me. Louise copied him in on the email. Careen, it's all rubbish and you know that. Don't let her get to you."

"Oh, Ben. It was meant to be so good. Handing over to Chris, finally getting away, travelling. Going to all the places I've dreamed about. It's all gone, all the joy, all the planning, everything."

"No one will believe it. It'll all be okay."

"Tall-poppy syndrome, Ben. It's rife in Australia."

"It'll blow over."

"I'm so tired, Ben. I just want to pack up and run away from this mess."

"No you don't. You need to take charge and sort this out. You can't let her win."

"You don't want a visitor then?" There went the idea of a week in Florence with Ben. She couldn't remember the last time she'd had a holiday. Every time she went away on business, she'd planned to take a few days for herself, give herself a taste of the freedom that she'd spent her teenage years yearning for, but she'd never stayed. Business travel was full of meetings and dinners, there were appointments and timetables, she was seldom alone. Holidays were different.

"No point. I'm coming back Careen. I'm not leaving you to deal with this on your own. We'll get Logan on board and figure this out."

"Not sure Logan isn't feeding Louise. Things are a bit rough between us at the moment."

"Logan's feeling like shit right now. He can't believe she used that. Yes, he said it, but it was when he was pissed off about not getting the 2IC role. He doesn't mean it, Careen. He loves you."

"Fine way of showing it."

"Don't hold it against him. He really is sorry."

She wanted to tell him not to come back but she remembered something John used to say. Sometimes you need help. Never be afraid to ask. Now was one of those times. "When are you back?"

"I'm flying out tomorrow morning. First flight I could get and it's a bit roundabout so it'll be a couple of days. I'll phone when I land."

Ben was coming home and she didn't want him thinking she'd just been sitting around wallowing. "Well, John, another thing you taught me was that if I have a problem, put pen to paper.

Lay it all out. There's very little that can't be solved. So, if Tony's still alive, what does he want?"

The piece of paper in front of her was blank. She stared at it for a while then picked up her fountain pen and started to write.

About an hour later she had five pages of notes and was feeling back in control. She'd written down every anomaly, even The Hollies CD in her car, although she didn't think it was particularly relevant. She studied the descriptions she'd been given of this current Tony – tall was a constant, dark hair although probably dyed, moustaches or not, again likely fake. Designer label clothes – so not short of cash. The descriptions varied a bit from lean and skinny to broad shouldered, which was a little confusing. When it came down to it, Tony had been tall and fairly nondescript; it was his personality that shone. The sort of guy you would pass in the street without noticing unless he smiled at you. In fact, she was having a tough time remembering what he looked like at all.

I wonder if Logan would recall? she thought. He could accurately describe just about every female in the place, so perhaps the skill applied to everyone he met. Careen was somewhat sceptical, but it was worth a try. It was a great way to find out if Logan actually was sorry.

"Logan's Passion Pit. Your pleasure is my pleasure. Leave a message and we'll touch base. Cheers." Always a new message. How did he find the time? Why did he bother? Careen found herself shaking her head. She hung up and was just about to put her phone down when it rang.

"Hi Logan."

"Hi, back. You called?"

"I have a puzzle I need your help solving and—"

"Since when have you started doing puzzles?"

"Just a new hobby I picked up," Careen responded, in what she hoped was a conversational tone. "Logan, we need to talk."

"Ah, about that. Look, sis—"

"It's okay. I know you didn't mean it," Careen interrupted. "Ben called. He's on his way back but I need your help in the meantime."

"Anything."

A contrite Logan might be useful. "Tony Fisher?"

"What about him?"

"Can you describe him? Physically that is." Careen held her breath waiting for the questions to come.

"Bones and rotting flesh by now I'd say, but with immaculate nails. He'll have had the fish giving him a manicure I'm sure of that." Back to the old Logan. That didn't last long.

"Nails. What do you mean about the nails?"

"Guy was a ponce. Had a manicure twice a week, every week."

"And you know this because?"

"Had a fling with the chick at the salon. She said Tony had been going there for years."

"Where was this?"

"You're joking aren't you? Do you have any idea how many beauty chicks I've scr— ah, dated?"

"Logan." Careen let her annoyance show. This was going nowhere fast.

"Okay. Okay. Likely to be the one in the mall opposite the office. But it's gone now." he added thoughtfully. "Jewellers now. Run by some old crone."

"You mean the Oasis Gallery?" Careen had shopped there a number of times.

"Yeah. That'll be it."

"Logan, that old crone is forty-five – only a few years older than you are." She had to smile.

"Shit, I don't look that old do I?" Logan sounded seriously worried.

Careen laughed. "To a nineteen-year-old beauty chick, as you term it, yes Logan you probably do."

"Ouch."

"Logan. Back to Tony. Other than his nails, can you remember much about him?'

"Not really, wasn't my type."

"Anything at all?" She wasn't going to give up that easily.

"Actually, best person to ask is Anna. Used to work in HR. Moved across to Mantra, I think. She had a thing for him. Quite serious as I recall."

"Didn't you date Anna for a while?" Careen vaguely recalled an Anna.

"Dated might be too strong a word, but she had a crush on me and used to drop by a lot and sometimes I was lonely."

"Logan, you aren't alone long enough to ever get lonely." Careen laughed at the idea.

"How little you know me, sis." Logan's voice was serious now. "Being surrounded by people doesn't mean you don't get lonely sometimes."

This wasn't the Logan she knew. The laughing, joking Logan she had grown up with. How do I respond to this? she thought. We haven't had a serious personal discussion in years. Not since Mum and Dad died. Not going there. Definitely not going there.

"Logan. I ..." Careen was floundering.

"Hang on a tick, Sam's just arrived home. Got to fly. Talk to Anna. Cheers, sis." And he was gone.

Anna agreed to meet her for lunch the next day. Careen kept herself busy in between by cleaning her apartment from top to bottom. They met at a coffee lounge in Fitzroy that Anna had suggested. Careen wasn't quite sure what to expect, but Goth Anna definitely wasn't it. Anna wore pale makeup, black lipstick and eyeliner, and black nail polish. She was dressed completely in black and seemed determined to prove how worldly she was. Careen had devised a cover story about writing the history of the Montage Group and wanting to paint an accurate picture of Tony. Anna seemed quite excited and after asking if she would be mentioned in the book was happy to fill Careen in, although not much had come out of the conversation. Apparently Logan was correct about Tony and his nails. He'd apparently also had a thing about messy tables at restaurants and a penchant for always being early for a date. He was skinny, just over six foot tall, sandy hair that he had streaked with blond highlights and he had a crescent shaped birthmark on his left shoulder. He had liked movies; gourmet takeaway dinners and hated pubs with bands.

Anna leaned forward and drew on her cigarette. She was very busy playing the part of the cool Goth. She blew a smoke ring and smiled smugly. "As I told the podcast lady ..."

"Wait. Louise?"

"Yes. She was quite lovely."

"And you told her everything you're telling me?"

"I'm going to be on the podcast." Anna's black-rimmed eyes lit up. "She recorded me and everything."

Careen ground her teeth.

"Anyhow as I was saying. I kept hoping, you know, that it was a mistake. That he hadn't drowned and one day he'd turn up on my doorstep. I waited you know. I didn't date for two years cos Tony didn't feel dead. I know this sounds silly, but I thought I would know if he'd died – sort of like a light going out." The conviction in her voice was unmistakable. "I still think it was a mistake and one day he'll come back. They never found his body you know."

Careen shivered. "Oh believe me, I know."

She had just returned to her apartment when her mobile rang.

"Hi, Careen. It's Missy."

"Chris has you working weekend's now?" She couldn't think of any other reason Missy would be calling on a Saturday.

"Just for a few hours this morning. Anyhow, a large box arrived in the office this morning addressed to you. I wondered what you wanted me to do with it."

"Does it say who it's from?"

"There's no name on the return slip and the address is Fry's Storage in Port Melbourne. There's an envelope on the outside. It might have a note in it."

I'm sure it does. Careen's heart sank. Fry's Storage, the place she'd put all of her parents' things after their death. She hadn't been back since. It was her history. How dare he?

"Are you still there?" Missy sounded concerned.

"Can you read the card please?"

"It just says, 'You need to be more careful with your belongings.'" Missy paused. "The box seems to have been opened, the masking tape has been ripped off and left hanging."

Careen bit her lip to stop herself moaning out loud. "Can you put it in my office for now? I was planning on coming in Monday. I'll get it then." She was about to hang up when she had another thought. "Missy, was there a piece of jigsaw in the envelope?"

"Hang on. I'll check." Careen heard the rustle of paper. "No. Should there be?"

"No. Just thought I'd ask."

No jigsaw piece. That means it probably wasn't the Clown. Was someone else involved? How did Mel's Michael fit into this, and why did he have Tony's ring?

Firing up her laptop Careen entered her Google search criteria – Tony Fisher, drowning. Sorting through the thousands of items on Tony Fisher was going to take time but time was something she currently had. There was no way she was just going to sit around and wait for Gordon to come up with something. Now she was no longer CEO of Montage she needed a project – and Tony Fisher was it.

TWENTY-THREE

The insistent ringing woke Careen. Grabbing for the phone she glanced at the bedside clock. Eleven o'clock. She'd only been asleep for half an hour. She hesitated, wary of who was calling at this hour, but pushed the answer button before she woke up properly and realised how bad an idea that probably was.

"Careen?"

"Gordon?" She sat bolt upright, instantly awake. It was late. Why was he ringing at this hour?

"I take it you're awake then."

"I am now."

"We found Tony. Martin's been researching his death. Turns out he isn't dead at all."

"Whose Martin?"

"My nephew. He works for me. Keep up."

"I was asleep you know."

"Concentrate, Careen. Tony is alive but he's mentally incapacitated and is in a managed care home. He was found shortly after his disappearance wandering the streets, stark naked, no ID. He'd suffered extensive brain damage from oxygen deprivation. Tony barely functions on a day-to-day basis. He's not your stalker."

"He's alive. I don't understand."

"Tony is not your stalker. Someone else is orchestrating this and using Tony as either a cover or an excuse. I think we need to go back and investigate your clown attacker."

Careen shivered. She pulled the covers around her and stared at the bedroom door, her mind in a whirl.

"Hello? Zoned out again, Careen? I do wish you would stop that. Pay attention—"

"Gordon, someone broke into my personal storage cage today," she interrupted him. "They found the box where I'd put all my things after my parents died. They opened it, presumably rummaged through it looking for something and then delivered it to my office to make sure I knew."

"Is there anything missing?"

"I haven't checked it yet."

"Make sure you get onto that first thing in the morning." She could hear him scribbling notes at the other end. "Back to Tony. I have a few questions about your boyfriend."

"Boyfriend?"

"Ben Seymour."

"Ben. What's Ben got to do with this?"

"Not sure yet. His father, John Seymour, set up a trust to pay for Tony's care. On Mr Seymour's death the trust transferred to his son, Ben. Ben has been paying Tony Fisher's bills."

John knew Tony was alive and so did Ben. Careen felt completely betrayed. How could they? She thought they had loved and trusted her. Tears rolled down her cheeks and she sobbed.

"I get that this has come as a surprise but I haven't finished yet. Can you save your tears for later?"

"It gets worse?" Careen checked her emotions. She needed to hear the rest of the story.

"I have some leads and they worry me. There's a man called Michael who visits Tony every week."

"Michael. Mel's Michael?"

"I take it there is something else you have neglected to tell me."

Careen filled him in.

"Timing fits. Can you come to the office tomorrow, about three p.m? We'll sit down and go through this."

"Why not now?" Careen knew she wasn't going to get any sleep.

"Because it's late and I'm tired. Miss Tamley, this Michael character has a history and not all of it above board. Can you call a friend and have them stay with you?"

"Is he dangerous?"

"He had more than a few run-ins in the lock-up. He had a row with his cellmate who ended up dead later that day, but he was never convicted of his killing. Always hard to get a witness to a murder inside. So, is he dangerous? Very possibly. It's better if you're not alone."

"I'll call Logan."

"You do that. Goodnight, Careen."

She sat holding the phone, listening to the dial tone. Why didn't Ben tell me about Tony? Why didn't either of them tell me? Is that why Ben's coming back? Am I getting close to something he wants hidden? My God, does he want his inheritance back? Is this some sort of revenge? Careen's mind was whirling.

"No." Her voice was loud in the quiet of the night. Ben wouldn't do that. He knew he only had to ask. But did he? And would she relinquish the money and lifestyle so easily – what else did she have after all? Pulling on her robe she wandered absently around the apartment. Her movements were distracted but wary. Who was Michael, and was he a serious threat? She checked the security system and then reached for the kettle to make a cup of tea. It was going to be a long night.

She was on her third cup of tea when she realised that she needed to talk to someone – and that someone was Mel. She checked the time difference and decided it was a good time to call.

"Hey, girlfriend. What's up?" Mel sounded like her usual chirpy self.

"Just ringing to say hi and to see how your mum is."

"All good. She's on the mend and driving me bonkers. To be expected, I suppose. How are things going at your end? Any progress?"

Careen updated her on what had been happening since she left.

"So wish I was there for you." Mel sighed. "I assume you've checked the box to see what's missing."

"Not yet. I suppose I'll find out when I go in on Monday." The thought of going into the quiet and empty building on the weekend unnerved her.

"And the storage cage?"

"I know, Mel. I'll get the lock there changed as well. Ask them to check the security cameras." She paused. "I'm nervous about going to the storage cage."

"Because he might be there?"

"He's everywhere so, no, that's not why. It's ..." She pulled her legs up under her on the sofa. "Mel, I haven't been near any of that stuff since Mum and Dad died. It's like a chunk of my past that I don't want to revisit."

"Why not?"

"That's the me before the attack. The stupid, naive, unworldly girl. The girl who had dreams to travel. The girl who thought she could take on the world." She shifted into a more comfortable position. "Mel, it's like there are two of me, a before and an after. I'm not sure if going back and digging through all the boxes is a good thing."

"God, I so much want to hug you, Careen. To tell you it'll all be okay. I hate being so far away."

"I'll assume a virtual hug then, shall I?"

"An almighty big one."

Mel asked after Lei and Careen realised she hadn't spoken to her recently. She'd call her tomorrow. She needed to remember she wasn't the only one with problems.

She hung up from Mel and made herself a fourth cup of tea. Standing staring out at the darkness of the bay she wondered what her life would have been like if she'd gone to uni and studied accounting rather than starting work with Montage. She might be in New York at some upscale office, catching up with Mel on weekends. She may not have been in the car park that night and ... No. She wasn't going there.

Sometimes she was jealous of Mel's life. She loved Mel and her bubbly personality and envied her choices and where they had taken her. Mel had done what she'd wanted. She'd escaped to New York, worked for a leading PR firm for eight years and then launched her own company. Her business on her terms, in the town she wanted to live in. Inheriting Montage had been a wonderful thing for Careen but she often wondered what it would have been like to have started her own company. *Her* success not someone else's. She'd once said this to Ben who'd laughed at her and reminded her that Montage had expanded considerably since she took over – it was Careen's success as much as his father's. That didn't stop her feeling like a fraud, that Montage wasn't hers, that she was just the caretaker. And now, after seven years, she wasn't even that.

Careen woke with a crick in her neck. She'd dozed off on the couch, the teacup still upright in her hand. She sat up, stretched and automatically checked that the replacement vase by the door was still in place. The apartment buzzer rang at the same moment and Careen jumped, spilling the cold tea down her front, the stain darkening as it spread over the green silk. Was that what woke her? It was still early. Who comes visiting at ... she glanced at the wall clock – seven thirty a.m. on a Sunday morning?

She padded over to the monitor deducing that Michael, whoever he was, was unlikely to bother have reception call up. Careen pushed the audio button. "Yes."

"Miss Tamley. There are two detectives here wanting to speak with you. Can I let them up?"

Careen shivered. The only reason police called upon you at this hour of the morning was with bad news. And detectives meant that it was seriously bad news.

"Have you checked their IDs?"

"Yes. It's all in order."

"You can send them up."

She acted quickly to remove the vase and upright the chair it had been resting on. She then raced into the bedroom and slipped out of her soggy robe. She pulled on a pair of jeans and lifted a t-shirt from the top of a perfectly aligned stack. Glancing in the mirror, she ran her hands through her hair and her finger over her teeth. Yuk, morning mouth. That'll teach them to arrive so early.

Careen suddenly plonked down on the bed. I don't want them to come in. I don't want to hear what they have to say. Not again.

A sharp rap at the door made her start. She rose, took a deep breath and walked down the hallway. She opened the door to two hard-faced gentlemen, both dressed in ill-fitting suits. "Detectives Minters and Hatchkey from the Melbourne West Crime Investigations Unit. Can we please come in?"

"What's happened? Is it Logan? Is he okay?"

"I don't know a Logan, Miss Tamley, but if you will let us in, we would like to speak with you."

They were sitting face to face, like opposing forces, on the two conversation couches. They had let her make them tea. The way they were watching her had her on edge. She wiped up the bench and folded the dishcloth into a perfect square before placing it at the top left corner of the sink. There was no way to delay this any longer.

"I'm ready." Her fists were clenched and she knew she looked pale. "You said it wasn't Logan so that leaves Ben. What happened?"

"Miss Tamley, do you know a Gordon de Paul?" Detective Minters took the lead.

"Gordon. What's this got to do with Gordon?"

"Miss Tamley, please answer the question."

"I thought I did." Careen was confused now. "How does this relate to Ben?"

"Miss Tamley, who is this Ben?"

"Ben is my ... my friend. Please tell me he's okay." Careen held her breath.

"Miss Tamley. Gordon de Paul was seriously injured in a hit-and-run last night, just as he was leaving the office around eleven thirty."

"Is he going to be okay?" Careen sank further into the couch. Gordon. Hurt. My God. What if this Michael had run him over because he found out about him?

"At this stage Mr de Paul is in a critical condition." He opened up a notebook. Took out a pen. "Given Mr de Paul's business dealings, we need to find out if in fact it was an accident or whether it was deliberate." They were watching her carefully now.

"What do you want from me?" Careen was confused.

"When was the last time you saw or spoke with Mr de Paul?" Detective Minters pulled out his notebook.

Careen paused. They probably already knew the answer and

she had nothing to hide. "We spoke at eleven o'clock last night."

"Was that usual?"

"No. Gordon was tracking someone down for me and he rang to give me an update."

"At eleven p.m.?"

"I know it sounds odd. He was concerned. There'd been some issues and he wanted to make sure I wasn't alone."

"And were you?"

"Yes, I was. I don't have a partner and I'm way too old for sleepovers." Careen could hear the high-handed tone in her voice.

"Can anyone verify where you were between eleven p.m. and one a.m. this morning?"

"You aren't serious? You think I ran Gordon over? Good God. Gordon was on my side. He was helping me find him. Keeping me safe. Why the hell would I hurt Gordon?" Careen was standing now, her anger having propelled her to her feet. "I would like you to leave now." She moved towards the front door.

"Miss Tamley. If you would just answer the question."

"Where was I? If you must know I was here, on the couch, alone. If you need to verify this there are security cameras everywhere. You will find I didn't leave my apartment all night."

"I see. Is this building security or personal security?"

"Some building, some personal."

Detective Minter raised his eyebrows. "And you feel the personal cameras are necessary because ...?"

"Gentlemen, I'm in a high-profile job. I'm a single woman who is very successful and therefore considered to be well off. I chose where I live carefully and secure it accordingly." She heard the defensiveness in her voice, bordering on haughtiness.

"If we could just ask you a few questions regarding the case that Gordon was working on for you."

"I suggest you speak with Sergeant Lawson at the Russell Street station. He has the details."

"We will. These are just preliminary enquiries at this time but we may need to come back to you with further questions."

"I take it we are finished for now then." Careen opened the door and looked pointedly at the two detectives who were by now standing.

"One more question. How well did you know his colleague Martin?"

"I've never met him. He was with Gordon at the office last night. Is he okay?"

"Thank you, Miss Tamley. We'll be in touch." They turned away and walked out in silence.

Careen pushed the door shut behind them and then leant back against the cold wood. She slid to the floor, pulled up her legs and wrapped her arms around them, hugging herself tightly. It couldn't be about her. But it happened right after Gordon called her. What had he found out? Was it worth killing for? How did Michael know? Careen double-checked the door was locked and moved to the window, idly watching a drone hovering over the bay. It turned; the red light flickered. Careen stepped back from the window and pulled down the blinds.

TWENTY-FOUR

"How's it going over there?" Careen had rung Lei to check she was okay. Careen also needed to take her mind off her own troubles.

Sending Lei to Perth hadn't been just an easy solution; it had been one she hoped would help Lei. Lena and Craig, the couple who managed the Perth hotel had lost their daughter a number of years ago. She had committed suicide after battling depression and an abusive partner. They hadn't known anything about the violence their daughter lived with until after her death when friends had come forward. Lena had never forgiven herself for not being there, and even though she lived thousands of miles away she felt she should have known, that she should have sensed something was wrong. Lena initially channelled her pain into social work but she found the emotional toll on top of losing her daughter was too much for her. She changed careers, started working in hospitality and had worked her way up to management. When Lei had arrived in Perth, Lena and Craig willingly took her under their wing.

"I am good, I think." Lei sounded unsure. "It has been hard, Careen. I have lived with it for so long it is like there is a hole in my life now. I know what he did was wrong but it was not all bad."

"It's okay, Lei. You don't need to talk about it if you don't want to."

"Lena says I should. That I need to talk, to tell others, to ask for help." She could hear the catch in Lei's voice. "Have you got time to talk now?"

"Yes. And any other time you need to talk too."

"Hang on." Lei blew her nose. A dainty sound, so typically Lei. Careen smiled.

"Somehow it is easier over the phone," Lei started out. "It is like I am talking to myself. Trying to get it clear. Are you sure you want to hear this?"

"Lei, if you're ready to share I'm ready to listen."

"It was good early on. He was such a charmer. Nothing like the quiet studious boys I used to date. We used to have so much fun. He would take me out to exciting places, he had such interesting friends, and it was like a whole new world for me. He did not drink much then. Yes, he would get angry when I did something silly but it was only a slap, never more and he was always sorry afterwards. He would buy me a new scarf or a pair of earrings he knew I would like." Lei stopped, blew her nose again.

"He was working at Ford. He lost his job with all the redundancies. He started drinking then. A lot. We were living together so I started paying for everything. What other choice was there? He got angry if I went out with my friends in the evening, said he was alone all day, that I did not love him enough to stay home with him at night. I stopped going out. I thought he just wanted to spend more time with me. That he loved me so much he did not want to share. Lena says this is all about control. That he did it to separate me from my friends. I did not see it that way. He applied for another job and was rejected. He started drinking again. He started to hit me more often, if dinner was not to his liking, if I was late home from work. Once I dropped a glass and he beat me quite badly. I am so clumsy."

"No, Lei, you were scared. Being scared would have made you clumsy."

"He was sorry afterwards. He always was. Things would be different he said, he would not drink. The drink drove him to it. He was always good for a while after but it never lasted long." Lei sniffed. "I believed him when he said he was sorry. How could I have kept believing he would change?"

"Lei."

"I hid the bruises. He had never hit my face until that day. He never left a mark that was obvious. He would check how I was dressed each morning before I left. Made sure nothing showed. And I let him. Once after he threw me down the stairs I said I was leaving. He promised he would change. I believed him. He even went to counselling with me once. It helped. I thought he had changed. He stopped drinking for while. Every day I came home, hoping he was sober, knowing it was not likely, but I still went back. He started coming to the office, would be there to pick me up every day after work. He started getting mean. He would make fun of my English, ridicule my ancestry, my history. He said he was joking and I thought he just did not understand my culture, how important it was to me." Lei paused. Took a breath.

"Several months ago he started drinking again, said I drove him to it. He was gambling too, losing a lot of money. That is why he sent me to the office that night. How could I even think about doing that? What sort of control did he have over me? He said if I left him he would hunt me down. I was his and if he could not have me no one would."

Careen recoiled at the thought of living in fear constantly. She'd had one night of violence and it had sparked years' worth of nightmares, had fuelled her fear of dark places, empty spaces and had jeopardised every relationship she'd had in her twenties. Spooning with her boyfriends was impossible. If he breathed on her neck she would panic, leap out of bed flailing. If a boyfriend put his arms around her from behind she had to stop herself from screaming, from kicking out. Most of her partners had found it too hard, had tired of her nightmares and her withdrawals. She couldn't imagine what sort of scars living with violence everyday would incur.

"Careen, I do not want to go back to that. I like not being scared every day, not having to watch every word, being careful to move quietly."

Careen decided now wasn't the time to tell Lei that Gary had been trying to track her down. She'd warn Lena and Craig to keep an eye out.

"Lena has told me to get an intervention order. Will you help me with that?"

"Of course I will."

Lei then changed the subject completely, telling Careen about the wonderful things she had been doing. She'd been to the planetarium, the art gallery and spent hours just wandering around the botanic gardens. Lena and Craig were taking her away for the weekend to Margaret River soon and she couldn't wait. Lena had asked her to select a bed and breakfast and Lei had narrowed it down to two but wanted Careen's opinion – she wanted to make sure she chose one that Lena and Craig would like. She said she would email the links to Careen as soon as she hung up and Careen promised to look at them straight away.

After the phone call, she made a cup of coffee, tidied up and moved across to her desk, placing the coffee cup exactly centred on the coaster. When she opened up her emails she saw Lei hadn't sent the links yet so she scrolled through her other emails while she waited. There was one from Louise. She almost hit delete but decided it was better to know where the next attack was coming from. She counted to sixty as she sipped her coffee slowly, breathing in and out to slow down her heart rate and to delay the inevitable.

Careen darling,
Long time no speak. Did you know you didn't respond to my last email? Did your mother not teach you any social etiquette?

I was sorry to hear about Martin. He was a good kid, still learning the ropes. He didn't deserve to die.

Martin had been with Gordon that night. They'd been working on her case together. They'd left the office and were just saying their farewells when the driver had struck both of them. Martin had taken the brunt of the accident and had gone under the car. He didn't make it. Gordon was tossed over the bonnet and had landed head first. He was still in ICU and heavily sedated. Jill had filled her in on the details when Careen had rung earlier that morning. Careen knew they'd been working on her case. Was she somehow to blame for Martin's death and Gordon's trauma?

But moving on. I had a delightful afternoon yesterday. Some kind person dropped off a box of goodies at my front door. So many scrapbooks, Careen. There was a note too, signed by Tony. Very intriguing. My research says that Tony is dead so how can he be sending parcels? I will have to follow that one up.

Careen shut her eyes not wanting to read more. Who the hell had given her scrapbooks to Louise? Why would they sign the note "Tony"? None of this made sense.

But, back to the scrapbooks. You were a busy little bee. One with expensive tastes, I must admit. I'd not even heard of the Grand Resort Lagonissi in Athens. Forty-seven thousand dollars is a little steep for one night in a

> hotel – a bit out of my price range. Was that your dream,
> to own that hotel?

Louise had got it wrong again. Was always getting it wrong. Careen dreamt of *travelling*, she wanted to work at the world's top hotels, to live on the edge of their world, to get a taste of the freedoms they enjoyed. Her ambitions as a teenager were to stay at backpackers' and hope a tiny bit of glamour rubbed off from the places she would work at. Owning the hotel had never even crossed her mind.

> Ah, and the romantic places – the Maldives, the Bahamas.
> Who did you plan on sharing them with? Ben? Or perhaps
> a sugar daddy? John? Interesting angle there.

What was wrong with that woman? How dare she tarnish John's memory; he was like a father to her. The supportive, loving parent she wished she'd had.

> Some outdoorsy stuff which surprised me. Hiking the
> Inca Trail in Peru, a river boat on the Amazon, a safari
> in Tanzania. Doesn't seem your sort of thing at all, but
> maybe it's just because I've never seen you out of your
> designer heels. Climbing Mount Kilimanjaro was also in
> there – but that shouldn't surprise me – the more I find
> out about you, Careen, the more I realise you do like to
> climb, just usually over other people to get what you
> want.
>
> Anyhow, darling Careen, the box disappeared from my
> home as mysteriously as it arrived. Luckily I had removed
> the diaries and put them somewhere safe.
>
> Love and kisses.
> Louise.

Careen dropped her head into her hands, dragged her fingers through her hair. If Louise had her old diaries things were about to get worse.

TWENTY-FIVE

Careen was glad Ben was back today and she'd messaged him to say she'd pick him up at the airport. She needed to talk to him about the trust; to find out why he hadn't told her about Tony. Given that she wouldn't go near the airport car park, Ben would message her as the plane landed and she'd swing past the pick-up zone. She'd been planning to go into the office on the way and pick up the box that had been sent there, but Ben's flight had been delayed by four hours and she didn't want to go to the office late. Mind you, she didn't want to be driving on her own this late either.

She'd made herself poached egg on toast for dinner and sat down to eat the bland meal. Now that she was retired, perhaps she could learn to cook. Takeaways were fine after a long day at work but seemed wrong somehow if she would be home all day. Ben had once bought her a voucher for cooking lessons but she'd not had the time and the voucher had lapsed. Now, a few courses would help fill in the empty hours. Ben seemed to enjoy cooking so it couldn't be too bad.

She washed up the dishes, dried them and put each item away neatly in its correct place. She stopped at reception on her way to the car park and asked Bill to escort her to her car. He turned the volume down on the TV and, with a last wistful glance at what appeared to be the final few minutes of the football, called the lift to the basement.

Bloody hell he's close. Careen touched her brakes in the hope that the car behind her would drop back. The bright white light from the rear-vision mirror blinded her for an instant. Idiot. He'd turned up his high beams. She sped up, indicated left and he followed. She turned left, then right, but the car remained tucked in tightly behind her. She took the next light just as it tipped red and he followed her through. She slowed as she googled the closest police station. The problem was he didn't. Wham. He'd hit the back of her car. She grabbed the wheel trying to keep control as the car started to slide sideways. Grappling with the steering wheel she corrected the car and pumped her foot on the accelerator, the tyres screeching as she took off.

She pushed the horn long and loud to attract as much attention as possible and turned left, right, left, winding through the streets as fast as she could. She glanced in the rear mirror; saw he was dropping further behind. She ran through an orange light and took a sharp left onto Melrose Drive. She wished she'd used the freeway, roadworks or not, at least there were plenty of cars. She floored it. One hundred and ten kilometres an hour in a sixty zone. Where were the cops when you needed one?

She sped into the airport departures area, narrowly missing a man dragging a heavy suitcase across the road. She watched the car come closer, staying in the right lane. She knew they had security cameras here and that someone would be along quickly to move her on. She double-checked the locks on the door. His car stopped next to hers. Her hand hovered over the horn but her eyes were fixed on the car, on the window. She wanted to see him, to see who was doing this to her. His window wound down and it took all of Careen's willpower to keep her eyes focused. She gripped the steering wheel harder to stop her hands shaking.

"You damaged my car you bitch," Gary screamed at her from the other car. "Don't you know how to drive?" His voice was slurred; he must have been drinking. "I'll make you pay for that."

He revved the engine and with a screech the car sped off down the ramp.

Gary.

She leaned back in her seat, relaxed her grip on the steering wheel. It was only Gary.

Ben's flight had been further delayed. She couldn't stay there any longer, she didn't know if Gary was still around. She sent Ben a quick text explaining she was exhausted and would appreciate him getting a cab. She added that she'd be at Martin's funeral on Wednesday but would catch up with him after that. She'd talk to him then.

TWENTY-SIX

Her black boots sunk into the mud and then squelched as she lifted her feet, the noise accompanying her as she trudged through the graveyard. The southerly wind cut through her ankle-length, black woollen coat and she shivered, pulling the collar more closely around her neck and moving her umbrella to block the driving rain. She'd never liked graveyards. The modern ones were so impersonal and the older ones were usually run down and neglected, the dead forgotten. This place was different somehow; it had a sense of peace. As if the people buried here had accepted their time had come and were at rest. She glanced around, admiring the wrought-iron fencing built sturdily upon huge bluestone blocks. The gatekeeper's house was also bluestone, well built by the look of it, in about the 1860s.

"Too small for a hotel," Careen murmured. "But it would make a great bed and breakfast." She smiled to herself – perhaps the location wasn't quite right.

As she approached the mourners gathered at the graveside, Careen looked around uneasily. She hardly knew Martin and felt like an interloper, standing amongst those who were genuinely mourning. She wasn't here to grieve, more to try to understand. She had asked Logan to come with her but Chris had meetings lined up for him. He hadn't resigned and was, for the moment, toeing the line.

As she stood shivering beneath her umbrella, Careen scanned the small group of mourners. The men seemed stoic, their faces registering resignation. The women looked ravaged, the desolation worn clearly in the lines on their faces. Martin's family, she assumed that's who they were given that they had the same nose as Gordon, stood apart from the rest, quietly sobbing by the graveside, some of them gripping bibles in the vain hope that somehow prayer would bring him back. Jill was with the family and she nodded a hello.

A movement distracted Careen and her gaze lifted to the dark man behind Martin's family, hunched into his coat. He didn't seem to fit in. His expression was not one of sorrow; more patient and alert, like he was waiting for something. He must have felt her gaze because he lifted his eyes and looked straight at her. She stopped her scrutiny as he smiled at her; she was embarrassed to have been caught staring at his lovely, long dark eyelashes highlighted by the raindrops.

A few moments later, a soft voice spoke into her ear. "Excuse me."

Careen jumped, her already taut nerves jangling and her heart beating wildly. She had been lost in her own world.

"Sorry, I didn't mean to scare you."

"Well you did," she retorted. The sweat seeping out of her palms cooled as it hit the lining of her gloves. Eyelash Man.

"I'm sorry." He smiled and Careen watched with fascination as the water droplets cascaded down his nose before launching off, like a hundred miniature skiers hurling themselves into oblivion.

"Do you mind if I share your umbrella? I left home early this morning and didn't think to bring one with me. It's rather wet out here."

She surveyed the crowd and realised that most people were sharing umbrellas. It appeared that he hadn't been the only one caught short.

"Yes. Of course." She transferred her umbrella to her left hand and lifted it up to accommodate his height. She judged he must be at least six foot three.

It couldn't be.

About the right height but no moustache, real or otherwise. Eyes are a different colour too. She was getting paranoid now. She couldn't go around suspecting every tall, broad-shouldered male.

"Let me." He took the umbrella from her hand and held it above them both making sure that she was sheltered. The minister raised his bible to silence the crowd and the service began.

While the minister was delivering the oration, Careen risked a glance at Eyelash Man to find him looking directly at her. He raised his left eyebrow and smiled. She shivered involuntarily and turned back to the service.

As the minister concluded the funeral, the family were given handfuls of sand to sprinkle on the coffin. A few traditionalists scooped up a handful of mud and the mud pies landed on the coffin with a splat. Then one by one the mourners turned, and with bowed heads walked back to their cars.

"I'm Mitch Smithson." Eyelash Man turned towards her, his gloved hand outstretched.

"Careen." She forced a smile, deliberately not taking the outstretched hand.

"Did you know Martin well?" he enquired.

"I know the family," Careen replied. "You?"

"Client of Gordon's, actually. Martin was working with him though."

Careen nodded and held out her hand for her umbrella. Again, the raised eyebrow. He handed her back the umbrella and stepped backwards into the rain, the umbrella scraping the top of his head as Careen brought it back to her height.

"Will you be going back to the house for the wake?" Mitch asked, the skiers assembling on his nose again.

"No."

"How about a coffee then? I could sure use a warm up. There's a great café across the road – Potters Field Coffee Shop – an interesting choice of name given the location, don't you think?"

"No thanks."

Mitch stood for a moment and then nodded towards the umbrella. "Thanks for sharing."

Careen stood still, clutching the umbrella handle tightly, and watched as he strode purposefully through the rain towards the car park.

She was unsure of how long she stood there but soon she found herself alone. Even the minister had left. The graveyard didn't feel historical anymore, just empty and menacing. Shivering she turned and trotted back towards her car, carefully avoiding the puddles. The café lights shone like beacons in the gloom. She'd skipped lunch to get to the funeral and was now cold and hungry. and the smell of fresh percolated coffee drifting from across the road was irresistible.

"So it was me and not the coffee you were rejecting?"

Eyelash Man. Mitch. Now that it was dry his nose appeared somewhat ordinary. Without his coat she saw he had a solid build, strong shoulders setting off the line of his Tom Ford suit. His square jaw was softened by the small crescent-shaped scar above his lip. The divine eyelashes framed his brown eyes, the exact colour of a walnut just ripened.

"I'm sorry?" Careen realised she had been staring.

"I hope you've changed your mind and have decided to join me for a coffee after all."

"Thanks. But no. I'm not great company at the moment." Careen joined the queue for takeaway.

"That's okay." Mitch moved to stand beside her. "Asking a girl out for coffee at a funeral is in extremely poor taste. You just looked so pale and lost out there. I thought some warmth and a coffee might put some colour back in your face."

The waitress approached to let Mitch know a table had become free. He asked for a soy latte and raised his left eyebrow in a question.

Careen saw the length of the takeaway queue and then glanced out the window at the gloom.

"Skinny latte please." One never knew what one could learn over coffee.

Mitch ushered her towards the table and pulled out a chair for her. He remained standing, a perfect gentleman, while she hung her dripping coat off the back of the chair. Although she was glad to be warm and dry and off her feet, Careen felt on edge. She pulled her shoulders back, tucked her hair behind her ears and stared straight at Mitch, saying nothing.

"So let's start again, I'm Mitch Smithson."

"Hi Mitch. Careen." She peeled off her scarf and folded it neatly on the table beside her.

"Still no last name?"

"No."

"Can I ask why?"

"You can ask."

"But I won't get an answer, right?" His eyes held a hint of merriment. Not cold eyes at all.

Careen tilted her head to acknowledge his comment. "So you are a client of Gordon's then?" She had decided to do a bit of digging.

"Yes. I met him about three months back," he said. "I deal in art. Expensive, original art. Someone in my circle is ripping me off and I hired Gordon to investigate." Mitch shuddered. "I'm a little worried that Gordon might have been getting close to the answer and had to be removed."

"It was Martin who died."

"Martin was a researcher only. He was likely just in the wrong place at the wrong time." He sighed.

"So you think they were aiming for Gordon because he found out something he shouldn't. Are art thieves really that deadly?"

"This lot are."

Relief coursed through Careen. If Mitch was legit, and maybe he was, this was a more likely scenario than Clown Man. That wasn't his style.

"Have you spoken to the police about your suspicions?" Careen asked.

"I did. The problem is that mine is just one of six cases Gordon was working on. The cops say it could be related to any of them. It'll take them some time to go through them all. Have they spoken with you yet?"

"I said I was a friend of the family."

"Yet you didn't go back to the house."

They sipped their coffee in silence.

"Actually, I am a client of Gordon's."

"I see."

"I hired Gordon to find out who is harassing me."

"And did he?"

"I don't know. We were due to meet on the day he got hit." She tried to read the expression on his face. It was blank, no twitch, no telling signs.

"What sort of harassing, if it's not too personal a question?"

"The usual. Midnight phone calls, ringing the doorbell and then running away, moving things around." Careen stopped. "Trying to unnerve me I think." Her eyes met his with a challenge.

Mitch opened his mouth as if to ask another question and Careen quickly interjected. "Tell me more about the art world you inhabit."

Mitch wasn't all he seemed and something wasn't quite right here; something subtle had shifted. She had built up Montage negotiation by negotiation, knowing the subtle signs of a lie in the making and learning to follow her intuition. She would play this the way she would in business – by her rules.

Forty minutes later Careen had learnt a lot about the art world, none of it particularly useful, but interesting nonetheless. Mitch showed an obvious passion for his work, so maybe that part was real. She had mentioned Mel's name in passing and watched for a reaction. She was quite disappointed when there wasn't one. She had asked if he was familiar with Ben's work but apparently Mitch's subject area was the Impressionists. He didn't dabble in other areas.

Mitch glanced at his watch and stood up abruptly. "Must go. I have an appointment at five. I've enjoyed talking with you this afternoon. If there is anything I can do to help with your situation, let me know. Here's my card."

"Thanks." She glanced down. It was an everyday business card. She had to stop being so paranoid.

"Call me?"

"Business or pleasure?" Careen smiled, trying for a flirtatious look.

"If pleasure is an option, how about dinner on Thursday?"

"I'd like that." The uneasy feeling remained and she wanted to dig some more. She'd let Gordon know. Not Gordon. She'd tell whoever was picking up her case. She hoped they were competent.

"So, Careen with no last name, where do I pick you up from?"

She bit her tongue, as the temptation to say 'home and you

know where that is, don't you' almost overwhelmed her.

"I'll be coming straight from work so it's probably easier to meet in the city." If he knew who she was he would know that was a lie. Again nothing. "How about Cecconi's in Flinders Lane?"

"Seven thirty okay?"

Careen nodded.

Mitch stood, and shrugging his coat on, turned and asked, "And do I get a last name over dinner?"

"Depends on how good the dinner is."

"There's a challenge." The raised eyebrow again, and smiling, he left.

Careen turned over Mitch's card in her hand. She hoped she was doing the right thing.

TWENTY-SEVEN

Careen was pleased when Jill, Gordon's business partner, called that evening to arrange to meet the next day. When she arrived a few minutes early, a red-eyed receptionist showed her into Jill's office. Today Jill was wearing a brown-and-black striped jersey dress with black leggings, knee-high boots and a tiger-print scarf. Her lips were painted bright red and she was wearing large round tortoiseshell glasses that didn't quite hide the redness of her eyes. She did, however, appear to be more comfortable than she had been in her business suit.

"Careen." Jill held out her hand.

"I'm so sorry about Martin. How's Gordon?"

"They still have him in an induced coma but they can't see any major head trauma in the scans."

"I hope he gets better fast. He's one of the good guys."

"That's nice of you to say. We all know he's gruff and tactless." She smiled. "He is, however, damn good at what he does."

"Perhaps he's a bit rough around the edges but I get the impression some of it is an act. Like he doesn't want people to see his soft side."

"It seems you're more perceptive than most." Jill indicated the chair. "Take a seat Careen." Jill moved some papers and perched on the side of her desk.

"Before we start. Have the police found the car that hit them?" Careen held her breath waiting. They wouldn't tell her anything when she rang the station.

"Not at this point. They've tagged the hit-and-run as an accident. Martin and Gordon were in the wrong place at the wrong time. They aren't connecting it to any of our open cases at this stage. They're still combing CCTV footage in the city. They'll find them."

Jill opened the file on her desk. "I've read through your file, including the notes that Gordon made the night he called you." She heard the catch in Jill's voice. "I've also done a bit more research on Tony Fisher. Tony had supposedly walked into the water at Elwood Beach sometime between eight p.m. and midnight on the eighth of August 2008. His body was never recovered. As his only surviving relative, his brother, Michael, inherited all his belongings."

"He has a brother?"

She'd known Tony for years. He'd never mentioned a brother. The CD – "He Ain't Heavy He's My Brother". Her unlocked car. Was that some sort of clue? And who left it? Careen made a mental note to tell Jill about the CD. She didn't want to interrupt her now.

"Michael is the older of the two and has spent most of his life on the wrong side of the law. He was sent to boarding school early, got expelled a number of times and ended up in juvenile detention. He must have learnt a few tricks there because he went on to high-level crime, became quite an expert in breaking and entering. He only got caught because someone ratted him out."

"Any other crimes? Gordon did mention something about a cellmate."

"There are a couple of incidents he spent some time in jail for, fraud mainly, but he got off on appeal." Jill ran her hand through her auburn curls. "Michael was all good looks and charm according to—"

"Do you have a photo of Michael?" Careen interrupted.

"Only the one on file when he was convicted. It's not a recent one." She glanced down at the papers in front of her. "Current description states he's just a touch over six foot, sandy brown hair …"

"Brown eyes and a small scar above his top lip." Careen finished for her. It was him. Mitch and Michael were the same person. This was all tied to Tony somehow.

Jill's eyes opened with surprise. "You know him?"

"It appears that Michael, as you know him, and I have a date on Thursday night."

"I see." Jill removed her glasses, polished them on her scarf and replaced them. "Gordon didn't make a note of that."

"Mitch, Michael, whoever, asked me out at Martin's funeral."

"I see. And were you planning on telling me or just going on a date with a criminal without any back-up and hoping it would be all right. I would have thought with your past you would be a little more careful."

"Ouch. It appears some of Gordon's charm has rubbed off on you."

Jill stayed silent, waiting.

"I'm not stupid and I did learn my lesson. I was going to tell you. I wasn't planning on going without someone to watch my back." Careen held up her hand to stop Jill interrupting. "Can we come back to that? Tell me about Tony."

Jill picked up her notes again. "Tony is mentally impaired. He was found naked, no ID. It took them a while but they tracked him down to his listed next of kin – John Seymour."

"What I don't understand is why John kept it a secret." The betrayal still stung.

"That's not a question I can answer. What I do know is that Mr Seymour paid for his care and set up a trust so that should something happen to him the care could continue. Ben

Seymour, John's son, is currently the trustee. I've left a message for Ben to call me. I'd like to see if he knows anything more."

Careen wanted to move away from that subject. She hadn't had a chance to speak to Ben yet. It hurt that he hadn't trusted her enough to tell her about Tony being alive. That he would keep something like that from her. "Where does Michael fit in, and why now?"

"Michael has been incarcerated for burglary on and off over the last few years. He was released six months ago. Over the last few months Michael has been visiting Tony on a regular basis." Careen was about to interrupt again but this time Jill held up her hand to stop her. "According to the nursing staff Tony is very agitated and angry after Michael's visits and keeps calling out John's name."

He remembers. Careen shivered. "The timing fits. Michael started with Quentin and now is after me. He used Mel to gather information."

"Who's Quentin?" Jill was flipping through the notes but couldn't seem to locate any relevant details. "And Mel?"

Careen filled in Jill and then told her about meeting with Michael/Mitch at Martin's funeral.

"And you agreed to meet him for a date, knowing he was likely the guy who has been stalking you and breaking into your apartment and office?" Jill sounded astonished.

"What is that saying? 'Keep your friends close and your enemies closer.'"

"I don't think the great Sun-Tzu quite had this in mind."

Careen smiled. "I'm impressed."

"What, that I know about an ancient Chinese general? What you seem to have forgotten is that he also said, 'He will win who knows when to fight and how to fight.'"

"I was going more with 'Pretend inferiority and encourage his arrogance.'"

Jill laughed. "That might even work."

"So tell me more about this Michael guy. If I'm going on this date, I need to be prepared."

"I spoke to a contact of mine. Michael is known to them. His speciality is art theft and fraud. He breaks in, steals an original, reproduces it and, when the press prints details of the theft, he leverages that to sell a number of 'originals' to collectors. He's somewhat of an expert in forgeries. He's also quite cocky. From time to time he's put a note on a painting he's left behind stating it's a fake. Apparently, he's been right more often than not."

"Assuming that anyone with valuable art would have decent security, it means he's good at breaking in and standard locks or alarms wouldn't stop him," said Careen. She repeated the conversation she'd overheard when Gordon's team were refitting her locks, relaying to Jill what they'd said about the ex con they'd used to test security. "Could it be him?"

"I'll check that out."

"So if he's on the wanted list why don't you let them know where he'll be on Thursday? They can swing by and pick him up. After he pays for dinner, of course."

Jill laughed. "I somehow thought you'd be the type to pay for your own meal."

"Usually, yes. We'll be at Cecconi's from seven thirty."

"Not quite that simple. They need to catch him in the act. He's no amateur and he doesn't leave behind any evidence."

"Other than the notes of course."

"Unfortunately, he doesn't sign them."

They'd chatted about the security for Careen's date and the types of questions she should ask. Jill would have someone drive Careen to and from the restaurant, and would arrange for one of her people to be seated at the next table. Careen needed to believe she was up to it. He had made her afraid and she hated him for that. Somewhere deep down inside she would find the self-control she would need to sit opposite him and have a conversation.

"There is something else we need to consider." Careen was wondering if she was overreacting but she didn't want to regret not mentioning it. "I get the feeling that someone else is tied up in this." Careen explained about her conversation with Mel, the CD in her car and the man who had left the business card with her name crossed out and Tony's name written above the title.

"If this is about Tony, and it's Tony's brother, is someone trying to give me clues as to who I should have been looking for?"

"Or perhaps he wants you to know and is providing the clues himself."

"No, that doesn't make sense. The guy outside my apartment that night was a slim build; Michael is bulky. And if he thinks I already know who he is and what he wants, why go to the funeral and ask me out?"

"Maybe he thinks you haven't connected the dots yet and he's enjoying the game."

"Is that what you really think?"

"Careen, I'm not sure what to think. This is getting more convoluted by the minute."

They talked a few minutes longer before Careen grabbed her coat and put it on. It was getting chilly in the afternoons now. She put one hand in her pocket and moved the other forward to shake Jill's hand. She didn't get that far. Wedged in the bottom of her pocket was a jigsaw piece.

"Careen. What's wrong?"

Careen dropped back into the chair behind her and drew out the piece of jigsaw. She turned it over. Number four.

"Breathe, Careen."

Careen took a deep breath. She turned the jigsaw piece over

in her hand. He'd put it in her coat. She'd sat down and had coffee with him and hadn't seen him slip it in the pocket. How did he get it in there without her noticing? He stood next to her for a while but she'd had her hands in her pockets most of the time. At the café? No. She'd hung her long wet coat over the back of the …

"I wore a different coat to the funeral. It wasn't this one."

"Careen, I need you to explain to me what's going on in your head."

Careen handed the piece of jigsaw to Jill. "I was thinking that he'd slipped the jigsaw into my pocket at the funeral. He didn't. I wore a different coat that day."

"When was the last time you wore this one?"

"I took it with me when I met with Anna." Careen paused to think. "I left it over the back of the chair when I went to the ladies. He must have put it in then."

"That means Anna may have seen him. I'll talk to her, see if she remembers anything."

Careen shuddered. "Four, Jill. I'm down to four. What happens when he gets to one?"

Jill opened her mouth to respond but Careen cut her off. "No. Don't answer. I'm freaked out enough already."

"Careen. We'll keep you safe."

"Can you do that? Actually keep me safe? For how long, the rest of my life while I hide away? He said I'll always be his number one. Does that mean he plans on letting me live or plans on finishing what Clown Man started?"

Careen checked her phone as she was leaving Jill's office. The first message was from Missy. Chris wanted Careen to meet with him early next week and Missy had provided a couple of options that might be suitable. She texted Missy that eleven a.m. next Tuesday would work for her.

As she pushed send the phone rang and she pushed answer automatically without checking the number.

"Careen. Thank God. It's Ben. Where are you?" He sounded quite breathless.

Forgetting she was angry with him, Careen was concerned. Ben was seldom flustered.

"What's wrong, Ben? Are you okay? You sound strange. Are you in Melbourne?"

"Yes. Finally got in around midnight. Was buggered. Slept like a log. Careen, I just had the strangest phone call."

"From who?"

"I need to see you, Careen. Now. Where are you?" he demanded.

"I'm in Elizabeth Street. Ben what's wrong?" Careen was really concerned now. Ben was always so relaxed. Then she twigged.

"This is about Tony isn't it?" she said, her voice hard. "Did the rest home call you and tell you that someone's been trying to find out who's paying for Tony's care?"

"Who's Tony?"

"Tony Fisher. Remember him?" There was no softening in her tone.

"Tony. What's he got to do with anything? He's been dead for years." Ben sounded exasperated.

Does he not know or is he lying?

"Careen, I'm not far away. Can you meet me at The European in Spring Street? I can be there in about fifteen minutes."

"Ben, if this isn't about Tony, what is it about?"

"Just wait for me. I'll explain when I get there." Ben hung up before Careen could ask any more questions.

Careen was turning to cross the road when she caught a movement in the reflection in a window. Turning, she spotted

Mitch. Michael, she corrected herself. Mitch was just the name he gave her at the funeral. He was entering a shop across the road.

"Curiouser and curiouser," she muttered. Without thinking too much, Careen jaywalked across the street and into the art gallery that Michael had just entered.

"Can I help you?" The salesman was in front of her immediately. Careen glanced around but there was no one else in the gallery.

"A gentleman, six foot, sandy hair, just came in." Her eyes searched the shop, checking for telltale legs sticking out under easels.

"He did." The salesman hadn't moved and was standing directly in front of her.

"Where did he go?"

The salesman glanced behind him.

"Out the back. Interesting." Careen moved to follow him but the salesman stepped into her path.

"This is not a walkway, a thoroughfare or, in fact, offers any kind of access." His voice was haughty. "If you want to get to the market you can go around the block like everyone else." His eyes flashed a challenge.

"Everyone but him," Careen countered tersely.

"Everyone." He was not going to budge.

With another quick glance at the back door Careen turned to leave and then stopped, frozen in place, her mind unable to comprehend what she was seeing.

"It's good, isn't it?" The salesman came up behind her. She could hear the admiration in his voice.

"No, it's not." Careen snapped – then stared at the picture. "It's personal." Her voice caught in her throat.

"That's what makes him so good. He gets right inside a person."

Careen shut her eyes and slowly re-opened them, hoping the picture had gone away, but she was still staring at herself when she opened her eyes again. The picture Ben had painted the morning after her breakdown at his apartment. The picture that was so personal, so much a reflection of her pain, that she couldn't even begin to comprehend why Ben would sell it. It wasn't a fake, she knew that – she had dripped coffee on the edge of the canvas by mistake and the coffee stain was there. Proof of Ben's treachery.

"That picture." She pointed at it as if it was evil. "How much?"

"That is a Ben Seymour painting. This one is titled 'Distress'. Ben is renowned for his—"

"I don't want a lecture, I just want to buy the damn thing," Careen snapped, turning to face the salesman who took a step back at the venom in her eyes.

"It is very expensive." His expression clearly conveyed that she, a madwoman, couldn't possibly afford it.

Careen's emotions were running riot. "How much?" she barked.

"Four thousand eight hundred dollars. It has a full certificate of authenticity. Signed by the artist himself." He was in full sale mode now.

"Sold. Remove it immediately and wrap it. I'll pay now and collect it later." Her voice reflected the chill in her bones.

Recovering quickly from his surprise he turned towards the counter.

"I said, remove it from the easel. Now." Careen enunciated every syllable.

Startled he moved towards the painting, then paused, turned to stare at Careen and back at the painting again. His eyes widened.

"Yes." She stared back at him issuing the word like a challenge.

"I'll just wrap it." His eyes were alive with excitement now. She knew she would be the talk of the local art scene for the next few days. He picked up the painting and carried it carefully to the counter to wrap.

She was numb as she left the gallery. Her phone rang. She glanced at the incoming number, and, as she registered who was calling, all the emotion she had been holding so close came out.

"How could you?" The accusation was furious and full of hurt.

"Careen." Ben's voice was distressed but Careen barely registered this.

"Don't you ever call me again. I never want to see your face ever again. Never, ever again." As she hung up the tears were cascading down her face.

Why did Ben sell it? And why that gallery? Ben had needed to see her urgently but only after she had said she was in Elizabeth Street. The coffee shop he'd suggested was in the opposite direction. Was that a deliberate attempt to make sure that she didn't walk past the gallery? She massaged her temples, hoping to forestall the headache she knew was building.

TWENTY-EIGHT

Careen couldn't recall getting back to her apartment or how long she had been sitting staring into space but she did know she was cold – icy cold. She shivered, but didn't move – she was so tired. So very, very tired. The doorbell had been ringing constantly since she got home but she'd ignored it – ignored everything but the pain.

She heard a knock on her door. "Miss Tamley. Are you there? It's Bill here. Miss Tamley."

She ignored the knocking. The entreaty.

"Miss Tamley. I have your brother and Ben here. They are very worried." He knocked again. "Are you there?"

"For God's sake, Careen. Open the damn door." Logan had never been the patient type.

"Careen?" Ben's voice. Worried.

Someone slammed against the door. Probably Logan.

"I don't think you should be doing that." Bill sounded nervous.

"Damn it, Bill. I'm worried about her." Logan swore as he hit the door again. "Careen, open the damn door. I don't want to have to break it down but I will."

Careen sighed. She shuffled towards the door, unlocked it, released the chain. She turned around and walked silently back to the couch. Lowered herself down.

"Thank you, Bill. That will be all," said Logan.

"I think I should stay."

"No, Logan's right. Thanks, Bill." Ben confirmed.

Logan sat down next to Careen. Put his arm around her. "Are you okay, sis?"

"Careen, thank God. I've been so worried," said Ben.

Suddenly the tiredness evaporated and she shook Logan off. She stood up and turned to face Ben. "You were meant to be my friend." She dropped her head, then raised it again, tears streaming from her eyes. "I thought you cared. I thought I meant something to you. Why Ben? Why?" Careen sank wearily to the couch and dropped her head in her hands. "Please just go. I don't want company tonight." Her voice echoed her exhaustion. "Just go. Both of you."

"No," said Logan firmly, but tempered with understanding. "You need to listen to him, Careen."

She felt the couch give as Ben sat down beside her. He placed his hand on her shoulders and turned her to face him. She went with the motion, too tired to fight.

"Careen. I didn't sell the painting. It was stolen from my apartment." He tucked his finger under her chin and lifted it up, but she wouldn't meet his eyes. "Look at me, Careen." She raised her eyes and looked directly into his, noticing the pain he was also feeling, but still no words would come. "I noticed it was missing as soon as I got in the other night. I was exhausted, it's been a long few days, I just figured you had taken it for some reason."

"Why would I do that?"

"I don't know. Nothing else made sense. There were forty to fifty other pieces in the studio. It couldn't have been a theft. Why take that one and not the others?"

"Good point." By now Logan had seated himself and was listening intently.

"I was about to call you to find out why you had taken it

when I got a call from my agent asking why I'd cut him out, why I'd sold the painting without going via the usual channel and why that gallery. That was the first time I knew something was wrong. My agent was on his way to the gallery to find out how it ended up there when I rang you. I wanted to explain what had happened – it was for us, no one else. You must have got to the gallery before my agent did."

Careen shivered. She knew why that gallery. It was because it was opposite Jill and Gordon's office. The sighting of Michael was no accident either. The whole thing had been orchestrated very carefully.

Ben looked at her intensely. "Careen? There's something more isn't there?"

"The trust, Ben. You're paying for Tony's care. Why didn't you tell me?"

"Tony's alive?" Logan seemed as surprised as she'd been.

"Yes. Tony's alive. He's at the Princeton View Rest Home and Ben here has been paying for his care."

"And you never thought to tell either of us? I thought we were your friends." The expression on Logan's face reflected how she was feeling. Hurt. Disillusioned.

Ben looked confused. "You're not making any sense. I thought Tony was dead. How can I be paying for his care?"

"Tony didn't die. They found him wandering the streets. Brain damaged. He's been in care since. John set up a trust to take care of him. You took it over when John died."

"Careen. When Dad died I took over a lot of trusts. The paperwork was a nightmare. I'm not good at that at the best of times. I signed what the lawyers said to sign. I didn't read most of it." Ben's expression softened as he looked at Careen. "And don't look so incredulous. There is a reason Dad gave you Montage rather than me. I'd never have coped with the paperwork."

"You could've asked me to help."

"We were all grieving. I figured I'd go back and check everything later."

"But you didn't."

"Not my strong suit."

She believed him. It was, well, so Ben.

Logan went to make coffee and Careen retreated to the bathroom to freshen up. As she washed her face she made a decision to tell them everything. Everything apart from the date with Michael. She knew they'd stop her meeting him if she told them. She had to get closer to him. Needed to find out why he was doing this. Jill knew she was meeting him. She had back-up. Ben and Logan didn't need to know yet.

Careen slept well that night. Maybe it was the sleep of exhaustion or maybe just knowing Ben and Logan were there. Feeling stiff in the morning, she rose and stretched. The smell of freshly brewed coffee had her pulling on her silk robe and heading straight for the kitchen.

"Hello, beautiful. Coffee's made." Ben looked tired and Careen wondered how much sleep he'd had last night. "Are you up for a swim?" Ben already had his bathers on and a towel in his hand.

"You brought your bathers?"

"No, nipped out to get some croissants and picked them up. Not much traffic across town at six a.m."

"I was alone?"

"No. Logan stayed until I got back. He said to mention your couch isn't as comfortable as you'd think." Ben was grinning. "Glad I won the toss. So how about a swim?"

"Coffee first." She reached for the cup he was holding out to her. "Thanks." She smiled. It was nice to have someone to get up to.

They had raced for the first twenty laps then settled into a rhythm. Careen pulled herself out of the pool. Fifty laps – not bad. She was a little out of shape but it shouldn't take much to get it back.

Ben was still immersed, hanging onto the edge of the pool and staring up at her.

"What?"

"You are beautiful, you know," he said softly.

She blushed. She quickly turned around to grab her towel to hide the colour she felt rising in her cheeks. She walked towards the bench where she had left her towel. Ben was directly behind her. She could feel his breath stroking the back of her neck. She tensed. Ben's breath; warm and tantalising. Not his. Never his. She could feel the heat from Ben's body, was aware of how close he was. She wanted to lean back against his damp chest, have him wrap his arms around her, hold her. Kiss her. I doubt he's even aware of the effect he has on me. She stepped away before turning around, then wished she hadn't. The look in his eyes was mesmerising. She moved back towards him, a question in her eyes that was answered by the heat in his. He leaned forward, his lips grazed lightly over hers, his hand came up and he gently caressed her cheek.

The slam of the door startled them both and they jumped apart.

"Sorry, was I interrupting something?" The interloper smirked, threw his towel on the bench and strode towards the pool.

The moment shattered, Careen turned to grab her towel and compose herself. Ben had kissed her. It wasn't a real kiss, but it might have been. She shut her eyes briefly, remembering, wanting more. She turned back to him but he was already moving.

"Let's head back up," he said with a rough voice, husky sounding all of a sudden.

Was that a good thing?

"Ben?"

She tried to catch his eye, to make him look at her, but he was avoiding her gaze as he picked up his towel and shirt. Well, if he was going to regret what happened she wasn't going to embarrass herself. She clutched her towel and headed out of the gym.

"I'll just grab the mail while I'm down here." It would give her time to settle, to recalibrate. She kept her back to Ben as she unlocked the mailbox and collected the envelopes. As they rode up in the lift Careen flicked through the mail as a way to avoid looking at Ben.

A moan escaped her lips. "No. No. No. No."

"What's wrong?" Ben was next to her but he seemed so far away.

Not again. I can't take any more.

Then it all went dark.

"Careen. You're awake." Ben was hovering over her.

"Where am I?" She shivered. "I'm freezing." She tried to sit up but Ben pushed her gently back down.

"Slowly, girl. You fainted. You're on your couch upstairs."

"I'm in my wet bathers."

"Um. I didn't think you'd appreciate me removing them." Ben was trying to hold in a smile.

"Yeah, well." Was that all she could think of to say. Not the best come back. Then she remembered. "Did you see the letter?" She tried to sit up again and this time Ben let her. He picked up the towel that had dropped to the floor and wrapped it around her shoulders.

"Yes. Not sure what I'm looking at though and I didn't want to open it without you."

"Not sure I want to open it at all." She shivered again.

"How about you go and have a hot shower and then we'll open it?"

Careen nodded. She wasn't using it as an excuse to delay opening it; she needed the shower to warm up. And though she could justify it any way she liked, deep down she knew what was in the envelope and she wasn't ready to face it yet. If she didn't open it, didn't read the words, it wasn't real. He wouldn't be back. She levered herself up off the couch and, clutching her wet towel like a shield in front of her, headed for the bathroom.

When she surfaced, Ben had a coffee ready for her and she wrapped her hands around the mug as she stood staring out to the water. She was still cold, but she knew it wasn't related to her temperature. Her skin was pink all over from the heat of the shower. She'd dressed in an old pair of jeans and a t-shirt she'd never liked. If this letter was from him and he was back, she would remember this moment, and she doubted she would want to wear these clothes again.

"Are you ready to open it?"

"No."

"It can't be him. Not after all this time." Ben sounded more hopeful than convinced. They both knew who it was from. The envelope was addressed to My Careen, Number One, 1705/85 Beach Street, Port Melbourne. Block letters. Black marker pen. Like all the others. Like the cards she'd received every year for five years after the attack.

"Can you open it?" Careen didn't even turn around, just kept staring out at the bay. Both her hands were wrapped around the mug but it didn't seem to be offering her any warmth.

She heard the tearing as he ripped the envelope. Then an exhale as he started reading.

"It doesn't make sense."

"Is it from him?"

"Same handwriting."

"Jigsaw bits?"

She heard a rustle, assumed he was checking the envelope. "No. Just a note."

"I see."

"Do you want me to read it out?"

"No. I just want it to go away." She caught herself before the sob escaped. "I wish I'd never checked the damn mail."

"Careen." He was beside her now, his arm around her waist, pulling her close. "We'll get through this. We did last time and we will again."

"What if I don't want to? Or can't do it?"

"Of course you can. You're older, wiser and much stronger than you were back then. And you're not alone. You have me and … and we can get Jill onto this."

"I think you need to tell me what it says. You just avoided saying I have Logan." Her voice was cold now, matching the rest of her. She pulled away from Ben. Put her coffee on the coaster and looked straight at him.

Ben read out the note. "Tell the podcast predator to stop screwing around – not everybody is who they seem. And remember, brothers can be troublesome."

"It's not the same." Her voice came out as a whisper. "Why is it not the same?" She wrapped her arms around herself, struggling to contain her fear.

Ben called Jill and relayed what had happened. He had taken a photo of the letter and emailed it across to her. Jill promised to follow up with Sergeant Lawson and would get back to them. Careen grabbed the phone off Ben.

"What does it mean, Jill?"

"I'm not sure. You mentioned yesterday that you think there

might be two people involved. Perhaps this is from the second person."

"But why are they both using the Clown Killer signatures. That doesn't make sense. Is the brother in the note Michael or is it Logan?"

"I'm sorry, Careen, but I don't know the answer to that."

They hung up from Jill and Ben made Careen another cup of coffee. She was seriously going to have to cut down once this was over. Assuming she came out of this alive.

"Are you still with me?"

Careen was staring out the window. She hadn't noticed the view; her focus was internal, at the cold dark feeling that was settling inside.

"He must mean Michael. Logan wouldn't do anything to hurt you."

Careen turned to face Ben, her face pale in the sunlight. "He hasn't yet." She paused to think. "Ben, look at it logically. Who knew John called me 'princess'? Who knew about Tony? Who had a swipe to my apartment? Who can come and go freely at work?" She took a step closer to Ben. "And why specifically mention brothers? What the hell am I meant to think?" Her eyes were full of hurt and Ben pulled her to him, his arms wrapping around her. She snuggled into him, finding the warmth comforting.

"But why? He has nothing to gain and a lot to lose. I don't get it."

She lifted her head to look into his eyes. "Can you talk to him? Find out what this is about?" She felt him tense. Ben and Logan had been friends for as long as she could remember and she knew she was asking a lot of him. She held his gaze. "Please."

He looked at her for a long while; the only sound the gurgling of the coffee machine. "For you," he said finally, and then he pulled her tight to him again, both taking comfort from the other.

TWENTY-NINE

"Lei, what's wrong?"

Lei was sobbing into the phone. "I did not know who else to call. I am sorry."

"Tell me what's happened." Careen hated to hear Lei so upset.

"He found me. He came to Perth."

"Gary?"

"I was going for a walk. He grabbed my arm. Tried to drag me away." Careen could hear the catch in Lei's voice. "I screamed."

"My God." How had he found her?

"Craig was at reception. He saw me. He ran out. He hit Gary. Hard."

"Good."

"Craig called the police. They took Gary away." Lei sniffed, loudly and in a most un-Lei-like manner. "I do not want to stay here anymore. I do not feel safe."

"I don't know what to advise you, Lei. Do you want to come back to Melbourne?"

"No. I am not ready for that. I have been talking with Lena." Careen waited while Lei blew her nose. "I have decided to visit my grandmother in Beijing. She is old and frail and I would like to spend time with her. Gary would never let me."

"I think that sounds like a wonderful idea," said Careen. She could hear some hesitation in Lei's tone. "There is something else, isn't there?"

"I am not sure it is my place to ask, but Lena said I need to."

"Ask away."

"How long will you hold a job for me?"

"Oh, Lei. As long as you need us to. You are worth waiting for." She made the promise before remembering it wasn't her decision. She'd talk to Chris tomorrow; figure something out.

"Hi, Missy, it's Careen."

"Hi, Careen. Chris is in a meeting at the moment. Do you want him to call you back?"

"It's you I actually wanted to speak to."

"Okay." Missy didn't sound as confident as she usually did. "What about?"

"Missy are you in touch with Lei?"

"Um. Yes."

"So you know where she is?"

"In Perth."

"Did you tell anyone? Anyone at all?"

"Her cousin rang last week, said her grandmother was ill and he needed to get in contact with her. I gave him her mobile number." Missy paused. "Is everything all right? Did I do something wrong?"

"Missy, do you know why Lei is in Perth?"

"Yes. She told me." Missy gasped. "I didn't think. It never occurred to me it could have been Gary. He had an Asian accent. I've met Gary. I'm sure it wasn't him on the phone. He said he needed to book a ticket quickly and wanted to know which was the closest international airport. I told him, Careen. I told him she was in Perth."

"Missy, it's important that you listen to me."

"I didn't mean any harm."

"I know you didn't. And Lei is fine, just a little shaken up. Gary was arrested but I'm not sure if they'll hold him. Lei's moving from Perth and I'll leave it up to her if she tells you where she is going, but you need to be careful of anyone asking after Lei – family or not. If you are concerned just ask them to call me or get their number and say you will get Lei to call them back. She needs your help to feel safe."

"I'm sorry, Careen. I'm so sorry. Will Lei forgive me?"

"Lei isn't going to hold it against you."

"Will you?"

"Oh, Missy. You made a mistake. It happens. Lei is okay, that's the main thing. The only reason I called was to make you aware so you know next time."

"Will you tell Chris?"

"Why would I do that?"

"Because of my position. If I can't keep confidential information safe, perhaps I shouldn't have this job."

"Good grief, stop thinking like that. You did what you thought was right at the time. You didn't have a frame of reference for that."

"Thank you," said Missy, sounding uncharacteristically flat.

Careen didn't like to leave her like that.

"And Missy."

"Yes."

"I'm going to be shopping for a holiday wardrobe soon and I'd appreciate your help. That is, if you wouldn't mind."

"Really?"

"Really."

"How cool. I know some great places on Chapel Street. When do you want to go?" And Missy was back to her bouncy self. Careen wished she were that resilient.

THIRTY

Careen was pacing. She had decided to wait at Ben's while he met with Logan at the pub. If it didn't go well, which was very likely, she didn't want to be at home where Logan could find her. She felt safe here. She'd done Ben's dishes, cleaned the kitchen, tidied up the lounge and folded his washing, but had drawn the line at doing his ironing. She didn't even do her own ironing. The problem was this left her with nothing to do, hence the pacing.

She jumped as the door opened and she turned to see Ben. She tried to read his face but there was very little expression. "Well?"

Ben closed the door softly behind him.

"Ben. What happened?" Careen moved towards him.

"Nothing." Ben's voice was bitter. "Absolutely nothing."

"What do you mean, nothing. Didn't you talk to him?"

"Oh, I tried." Ben sank down on the couch and looked up at Careen. "Logan is exhausting. I'm not sure if he was deliberately steering the conversation away or if it's just him. God, it's so hard. I'm doubting my best friend and he's either completely innocent and unaware, or he's a damn good actor."

Careen sat down beside Ben. "What happened?" she asked softly, rubbing the back of her hand across his cheek.

Ben smiled and took her hand. Kissed the knuckles gently, the stubble from his chin grazing her fingers. He reached up and tucked a stray lock of hair behind her ears. Careen held her breath as his hand travelled down and cupped her check and chin. His eyes never left hers. He rubbed his thumb gently over her mouth and she parted her lips in response. His eyes darkened and she saw the shift, from wondering to yearning. He leaned in towards her, a question in his eyes. She smiled. He gently touched his lips to hers. The kiss was like a whisper of a promise. His hand moved to the back of her neck and he gently pulled her to him. She leaned in and bit his top lip playfully, invitingly. His lips moved then from a gentle question to a demand for more. Her heart leapt with joy. She parted her lips and invited him in. Her arms moved of their own accord, circling his neck, caressing, pulling him closer. Their lips parted briefly and she saw a hunger in his eyes that matched hers. That was all she needed to know. He pulled her closer and this time the kiss was harsh and desperate with need. His lips left hers and travelled down, kissing the soft flesh of her neck. She moaned with pleasure and Ben raised his head to stare into her eyes. Their lips met again, this time there was tenderness.

"You have got to be joking." Ben's voice was filled with chagrin. The knock on the door was getting insistent.

Careen pushed Ben up reaching to button up her blouse as she did so. "I don't think he's going away."

"No. I don't suppose he is." Ben cupped her face in his hand and kissed her gently on the lips. "His timing, however, could have been a bit better." He rose, straightening his clothes to hide the obvious effect of kissing Careen. "Coming."

Careen watched him walk towards the door. She couldn't believe he had kissed her. If not for the door ... She smiled to herself.

Ben pulled the door open. "What?"

Ben's neighbour glanced at Ben, then looked over Ben's shoulder with a sly grin.

"Sorry to disturb you. Your girlfriend drive a dark-blue Beemer?"

Girlfriend. She liked that. Ben turned to Careen. "So, girlfriend, do you?" He grinned then continued. "It's hers. What's up?" Careen rose from the couch and walked over to join Ben at the door. Ben put his arm around her automatically pulling her close.

"Got broken into. Alarm's driving me crazy."

In an instant all the warmth was gone. Everything was wrong again.

"No. Not now." Careen found herself shaking. Not now when something finally good was happening. Why did he have to ruin everything? She started off at a run, dashing down the hallway. If he was there, she'd flatten him. With Ben behind her Careen flew down the rickety stairs and into the restaurant. Ben pulled her back as she tried to beat him out the warehouse door. "Wait. He might still be there."

"Isn't that the point?" She pulled away, threw the door open and ran in the street, Ben close behind her.

The car alarm stopped screaming as they scanned the street. The area itself was empty except for a couple standing on the corner. Ben jogged up to them to see if they had seen anything while Careen dejectedly surveyed her car. The driver's side panel had a large dent in it and the window was smashed. A quick glance inside the car showed no damage and after the last few car episodes she had made sure there was nothing worth stealing. Her eyes searched for a note before the total effect of the mess had even settled in. There was a note. The front windscreen wiper had been used to secure it. She reached for it but Ben called her back.

"Don't touch it. Perhaps they can check it for prints."

"You watch way too much *NCIS*." But as she reached for the note she was careful to touch only the corners.

Ben was beside her now and she looked up at him and smiled before she opened the paper. "In this together."

Ben reached down and kissed the top of her head. "In this together."

PAYBACK FOR DAMAGING MY CAR BITCH. NOSY BASTARDS THINK I'M WRITING DOWN MY DETAILS. SCREW THEM AND SCREW YOU. G.

Gary. The police hadn't held him for long; he must be back in Melbourne already. Careen looked up at Ben, he was shaking his head. She'd told him about Gary following her to the airport.

"He doesn't believe in subtlety, does he?"

"Not his thing."

"You need to report him."

"I'll add it to my to-do list.

She wondered at her mild reaction to Gary damaging her car. Her normal reaction would have been anger; she would have rung the police immediately, ensured Gary was charged with wilful damage. However, with the Clown threatening her, a dent in her car seemed trivial. Careen could hear Ben brewing coffee in the kitchen. She smiled to herself. The Clown may have caused chaos but he had brought her Ben. *I wonder what Logan will have to say about this.* The thought came unbidden and unwelcome. She didn't want to think of Logan.

"A penny for them." Ben held out a steaming cup of coffee.

She took the coffee, sipping it slowly.

"Tell me what happened with Logan."

"Last time I tried we got somewhat sidetracked." Ben grinned at the memory. "In fact, Logan thinks you and I have something going on. Suggested I would make a great brother-in-law." He stopped when he saw the disbelief on Careen's face. "I know. Who would have thought?"

"Logan? The Logan who told you 'hands off' all those years ago."

"Actually it surprised me too. And worries me more than I care to admit. Anyhow, that about sums up the entire conversation then one of his friends arrived and I left."

"That was it."

"Sorry. If Mitch hadn't arrived I ..." the expression on Careen's face stopped Ben mid sentence.

"What's wrong?"

"Mitch. Are you sure?" Careen deliberately placed her coffee on the bench and turned back to face Ben. "Mitch. Six-foot, broad shoulders. Mitch the art dealer, by any chance?"

"You're scaring me here. Yes, Mitch is involved in art. I didn't stay long enough to find out in what way." Ben lifted her chin so that she was looking directly at him. "Careen, who is Mitch and what has he done?"

"Saturday. How could I forget?" Careen mumbled to herself.

"Forget what? What is going on?" Ben had put down his coffee and was staring at her.

Careen glanced at her watch. "Because I have a date with Mitch tonight. In about two hours in fact."

Ben spluttered, "You are seeing Mitch?" He suddenly went very still. "You are dating another guy and ..." He stopped, lost for words. "Just before, on the couch. What was that about?" Ben spat the words out. "Have you slept with him?"

"Oh God. No. It's not like that." Careen grabbed Ben's arm as he was turning away. "I think Mitch is Michael," she blurted out.

Ben froze and then slowly turned to face her. "Let me get this straight," he said in an icy voice. "Mitch is a friend of Logan's. You think he is Tony's brother, Michael, and yet you are dating him." He looked at her as if she was a complete idiot, which she probably was.

"It's not like that." She could hear the pleading tone in her voice. "I didn't know Michael knew Logan."

"But you are dating him nonetheless?"

"No. We had coffee and he asked me out. Jill said I shouldn't go. I thought ..."

"You thought you should ignore her and put yourself in danger." Ben was angry now.

"She is going to have someone there. I won't be alone. What else am I meant to do? I need to find out what this is all about," she finished softly.

"So you just thought you would go on a date with the guy who is stalking you. Didn't you think that either Logan or I would be interested in this fact? What else haven't you told me?" There was no tenderness in Ben's voice.

Careen looked up at Ben sadly. "I'm sorry. I've been so confused. I didn't know who to trust."

Ben blanched. "At least I know where I stand."

"No. Not you. I trust you." Careen grabbed Ben's hands, her eyes searching for a little kindness in his.

"Not enough it seems." He pulled his hands away. "So what time is this date of yours?"

Careen turned away so that Ben couldn't see the tears in her eyes. She should've known it was too good to be true. Taking a deep breath she turned to face him again. "Seven p.m. So I had better go and get ready. Don't want to disappoint him." She threw the words at Ben and grabbed her bag from the bench. "I'll see myself out."

She slammed the door behind her and ran down the stairs. Grabbing her car keys out of her bag she stopped short as she reached her damaged car.

"Story of my life. Everything is messed up," she muttered as she put her keys back in her bag and started walking towards the nearest taxi rank.

Careen found herself almost running down the street. She'd hurt Ben, saying she didn't trust him. Between finding out he was paying for Tony's care and then seeing the painting in the gallery – it had all been too much. Then there was his reaction to Michael. It wasn't just the stalking thing. Ben had never seemed the jealous type. Not that she had dated much. Unlike him. He had a constant stream of young arty groupies. And when it came down to it, why had this happened now? There'd been so many opportunities in the past. Was Mel right? Was it Stuart syndrome? Was it all okay now because she wouldn't be running Montage? She needed some time to think things through. Some time alone.

She heard Ben call her name but she was shaking from the argument, confused about what had happened and wasn't ready to face him. She heard Ben call her again and ducked quickly into a bookshop and hid behind a large bookcase. What was she thinking? Her and Ben. She was going overseas soon. If they got together, she'd stay. She'd never realise her dream. She watched Ben pass by and when she felt enough time had passed she peeked out the door. With no sign of him, she quickly turned back the way she had come.

THIRTY-ONE

"Hey, sis." She heard Logan before she saw him. "Fancy bumping into you." Logan squinted at the sign on the shop she'd just left. "You buying books?"

"Ready, mate." A familiar voice asked.

Of course. Logan was with Mitch. Careen composed her face in a smile.

"Mitch. How nice to see you again." Her fists were clenched but the smile held.

"Careen. Hi. Logan didn't say anything about meeting you here."

Careen just stood and stared. Her brain refused to work as she tried to figure out what was happening. What do I do? Logan and Mitch, Michael or whoever the hell he was. Are they in this together?

"Are you okay?" Michael was looking at her oddly. "Logan and I were just heading off. Have to get changed into something a bit more spiffy. I have a date tonight." His smile appeared genuine. In fact he seemed, well, normal.

"Ah 'Tonight's the night...'" Logan, who had obviously had a few beers too many, started serenading them with Rod Stewart's very dated hit song.

"Ugh, has he always sung that badly?" Michael was looking at Careen like a co-conspirator.

"How do you know Logan?" The question was meant to

come out as friendly conversation but she blurted it out as an accusation.

Michael appeared startled at her tone and looked at Logan before answering. "I've known Logan for about six months or so."

"And you just happened to be at the funeral," she said coolly.

Michael glanced sideways at Logan and, seeing no help come from that direction, said, "Logan has been talking about you for a while. He showed me your picture and suggested he set up a date. He tried to get you along to a couple of nights out so we could meet and you never showed."

"Should have come along. Mitch is a nice guy, you know," Logan slurred.

"So you showed up at the funeral." Careen scowled. "Were you a client of Gordon's or not?" She waited for the reply, not realising she was holding her breath. Jill had said they had no record of him.

He grimaced. "That was actually a lie."

"I see. And what else was a lie?"

"The rest is all me. I do work in art. I am having some problems with stolen items. I just hadn't got to the point of bringing someone in. The rest is me. Truly." He reached for her hand and she glanced down, checking for a ring. He pulled his hand away quickly and put it in his pocket but not before she had seen that there was no ring. Was that just a reflex or was he hiding something? "Please believe me."

She looked at his face. He seemed genuine. She glanced at Logan who was looking sheepish but pleased with himself.

"That's all settled then." Logan threw his arm clumsily around Careen. "Let's all go get another drink."

Careen shrugged off Logan's arm. "No, I don't think I will." She turned to Michael. "I have one hell of a headache – probably brought on by all the lies I've been told lately. I'm going home."

"Careen?" His voice sounded concerned.

"Yes."

"I'm sorry. It seemed like a good idea at the time, but it was wrong. Any chance I can make it up to you? Perhaps a drink some other time?" he asked.

"I don't think so. One thing that is important to me is honesty. And there doesn't seem to be a lot of that going around at the moment." The last comment was also aimed at Logan, but judging by his stupor she doubted he would even notice. She turned on her heel and walked away.

Careen walked from Ben's towards Port Melbourne and when she got to the beach she wandered aimlessly, seeking answers in the waves. Her mind was spinning. Logan, Michael and Ben. She had wanted Ben to notice her for ages but now that he had it was so complicated. And the last thing she needed at the moment was more complications. She had to get back on an even keel with Ben because what she needed most was a friend, not a distraction. And he was most certainly distracting.

She pushed her way through the beach gate to her building and was heading towards the lifts when she noticed Ben. He was sitting in the common area on his phone. He hadn't noticed her yet so she took a moment just to watch him. He was obviously agitated, which was unusual for him. He was speaking quickly and taking notes in the notebook he always carried. This also was unusual. This notebook was reserved for quick sketches and was never used for anything else. He must have sensed her watching because he stood up suddenly and ended his conversation.

"Careen. I'm sorry." Ben dropped his phone into his pocket.

"Me too." She reached for him and he enveloped her in a hug. "Friends again?"

"Friends?"

Stepping back she lifted her face to look at him. "Ben, what I need more than anything at the moment is a friend. Anything else is too complicated."

"I see." She saw hurt reflected in his eyes.

"No. Don't pull away from me. There is too much happening and I can't think straight. I don't need any more distractions." She saw by the expression on his face that she had chosen her words poorly. "I didn't mean—"

"It's okay I get your point," he said sadly. "I'll keep my distance."

"That's not what I meant. Oh hell." What a mess. "Ben—"

"It's okay, Careen." He attempted to smile. "Where have you been? I've been worried about you."

"After my tantrum I decided to walk home."

"I know, I followed you. Lost you though. I've been waiting here a while."

"Sorry. I wanted to be alone. To have time to think."

"I should have run faster," he mumbled.

Careen grinned. This was more like her Ben. "Guess who I ran into?"

"Logan?"

"And *Michael*. They were leaving the bar together. Logan was under the weather and Michael was bright-eyed and bushy tailed."

"Speaking of Michael. Don't you have a date with him tonight?"

"Cancelled it."

"I see." Very non-committal.

"Ben, I am more confused than ever. Turns out Michael and Logan have known each other for six months and Logan set it up for Michael and me to meet."

"Over coffee?"

"No, at the funeral I went to. Martin's funeral. Long story."

Careen realised there was a lot that Ben didn't know.

"At a funeral. That's tacky even for Logan."

"Ben, I'm sure Logan is involved. He's friends with Michael."

"Look, while I was waiting I made a few phone calls to a few of my art contacts. Let's head upstairs and I'll fill you in."

Ben was making coffee again and Careen was perched on the bar stool watching. "You will have to teach me the technique one day. I mean, how hard can it be?"

Ben laughed. "You may be able to run circles around all those suits but my culinary skills will always outdo yours."

He placed a steaming hot latte in front of her and stayed standing opposite. "As I said downstairs, I rang around a few people while I waited for you. Michael Fisher is well known, although he does tend to use Mitch rather than Michael when fencing stolen goods. He's been known to go by Mitch Smithson, Mitch Jonesate, Mitch Browner – not very original. He apparently hawks good-quality fakes and the occasional stolen work. They all come with full provenance and certificates of authenticity."

"Ah, sorry about that. It didn't occur to me that the certificate could be a fake." Careen was embarrassed. "I should've known you wouldn't sell it."

"Humph. You can make it up to me one day." His grin was quite saucy and Careen felt herself blush. Laughing at her obvious discomfort, Ben continued. "Michael's been at it a while."

"I know. Jill gave me some background." She filled Ben in on Michael's past exploits.

"The timing fits then if he got out of jail about six months ago."

"Seems to."

"Anyway, after you told me about Tony I paid him a visit.

They let me in because according to their paperwork I am the one who is paying for his care through one of the many trusts Dad set up." His tone was contemptuous. "Tony was in the TV room with other patients. It was obvious that Tony recognised me, his eyes went wide just briefly when I walked in but then he pretended not to know me. He wouldn't talk to me and eventually I was asked to leave."

"And then?"

"What makes you think there is an 'and then'?"

"Ben, you have always liked a mystery. It's not like you to just walk away."

"Good point. So, I go and use my good looks and charm to chat up the nursing staff. Find out what's going on. Tony has a photo of him and his brother Michael on his dresser and the nurse showed it to me. It's definitely your Mitch – a few years younger but just as hard looking."

"He's not my Mitch." Careen scowled at Ben. "But where does Logan fit in? I don't understand what he gets out of this."

"That I need help with. If something happens to you what happens to your Montage shares?"

"You're the other major shareholder and in my will my shares revert to you if anything happens to me. Which means you get it all back – board meetings and all."

"Good grief. No one told me that one."

Careen laughed at the horrified expression on his face and instantly felt guilty for doubting him. He was a major shareholder already, had a steady income and he certainly didn't want the hassle of having to be an active part of the board.

"It was likely part of all those papers you didn't read."

"Point taken."

"Chris has the CEO role and any change to the shareholding would risk this, so I'd say he's in the clear."

"Back to Logan again?"

"Logan doesn't have shares. He has nothing to gain and a lot to lose. He and Chris don't get on and Chris would let him go in a heartbeat if it wasn't for me. If I die, Logan ends up with nothing, no job, no money, no sister. I don't get it."

"What about your personal assets?"

"Logan does get those. But there isn't a lot. Most of the money is tagged to go to charity – the last thing Logan needs is an influx of cash, it would ruin him."

"Does he know?"

"Actually he does. He was poking around one day and he found a copy of my will. He was not amused at all."

"I'll bet."

"So what does he have to gain?"

"No idea. But I think the next step is a chat with Logan." He paused and looked at Careen. "Both of us."

"Somehow I knew that was coming."

They were seated in Careen's apartment, she and Ben on one sofa and Logan on the other. Opposing sides.

"Where are the spotlights?" Logan leaned back, trying to appear casual but it was clear he was nervous.

"Whatever do you mean?" Careen's voice was deceptively silky.

"I feel like I'm in the headmaster's office. If I've been a naughty boy, tell me what I've done."

"What makes you think you've done anything?"

"Careen, Ben calls me, tells me to get my butt up to your apartment for a meeting. Nine a.m. sharp. 'We need to talk' he says. I gather since he sounded serious and you look pissed off that this isn't a 'can I marry your sister' sort of conversation, so I'd like to know what I'm meant to have done wrong so we can get this sorted out and I can go back to bed."

"How do you know Mitch?" Careen asked Logan, her eyes

254

never leaving his face.

"Is that what this is about? Me setting you up on a date and Ben being jealous? Jesus, couldn't we have done this later when my head doesn't hurt."

"Logan just answer the question," Ben interjected.

"Good cop, bad cop. Hmmm. Can't figure out who's the good cop though," he quipped, before catching the expression on Careen's face. "Okay, okay. Mitch. Met him about three months ago. Actually we'd apparently already met at the annual marketing conference about six months before that. I gave him my card and told him to look me up if he was in the neighbourhood."

"Nine months ago – interesting timing given he was locked up at the time." Ben murmured to Careen. He turned to Logan "Do you remember meeting him at the conference?"

"You know what it's like, you mingle, you mix, you drink. Could have. How else would he have got my card? Anyway he remembered that I liked motorbikes and he was in town with a couple of pit passes – was I interested?"

"Convenient." Careen said softly.

"Would you guys quit mumbling?" Logan grumbled. "We went to the track, had a great time and have been mates since." He paused. "So what exactly has this to do with anything in particular?"

"Whose idea was the date?"

"That was mine. You are seriously in need of a love life although ..." Logan stopped and grinned at Ben. "Perhaps not any more."

"Logan." Careen was getting exasperated.

"Definitely the bad cop." He tried for the evil eye but only managed to make himself look so idiotic that Careen had to laugh.

"Why the funeral Logan? That is really tacky."

"But it worked. Or did. I have a vague recollection you dumped him last night. Did I miss something there?"

"Nothing important." Careen sighed, then sat up. "Back to you, Logan. The funeral. Why there?"

"Mitch was keen to meet you. I tried to get you along to a few nights out but you were busy playing spinster executive and then when I found out about the funeral I thought it would be an interesting place to meet up. And it worked. You agreed to go out with him. And then didn't." Logan crossed his eyes as if trying to recall the previous evening. "You guys would be great together. He's a guy who knows how to have fun and he's also serious about his business."

"I'm sure he is," Ben interjected.

"Exactly how much do you know about this Mitch guy?" Careen asked.

"He's an art dealer. Buys and sells paintings – originals only, mainly popular artists, but occasionally promotes an up-and-coming artist. Drives a Jag XF, likes designer clothes and chicks love him – has a dangerous edge about him I've been told."

"Where does he live?"

Logan looked perplexed. "Actually, I've no idea. He's been to my place a few times, even stayed over when I was away with Sam a few weeks ago as he needed a city pad for the night. Never asked where he usually crashed."

"Do you still keep my apartment key in the top kitchen drawer?"

"Creature of habit, that's me. Careen, what is all this about? What is Mitch meant to have done?"

"I'll make the coffee. You start at the beginning." Ben rose and left Careen to fill Logan in.

Logan stood up, pulled Careen off the couch and into an enormous hug. "My God. I'm so sorry, I had no idea".

He pushed her away to arms' length and stared straight at her with a weird look on his face. He then pulled her close again kissing the top of her head. Still holding her tight he glanced over her shoulder at Ben. "So, where to from here?"

"I honestly don't know." Careen's voice was muffled against his chest. "Breathing is getting to be a problem here Logan." She lifted her eyes to meet his. "I love you, Logan, and I'm sorry I doubted you." He pulled her close again. "Breathing, Logan. Breathing." She chuckled as she turned sideways, leaving her head resting on his chest, his arm still loosely around her.

Ben interrupted them. "If you two have finished bonding, we need to figure out what to do next."

THIRTY-TWO

"Careen, darling. How lovely to hear from you," Louise purred.

"I've changed my mind. I will meet with you." Careen kept her voice even as she cringed at the words.

"Why the change of heart? You're not going to talk me out of it you know."

"Are you interested in meeting me or not?"

"Keep your knickers on. I'll be there."

"My office. Three o'clock this afternoon. And bring the diaries."

"Didn't know you still had an office." Louise laughed. "But if that's what you want. Three o'clock. Ciao."

He laughed out loud, but there was no humour in the sound. They didn't get it, did they? Either of them. He knew everything they did, heard everything they said. They were puppets in his play. Soon, very soon, it would be time for the final curtain.

Ben had offered to be with her for the meeting but she needed to do this alone. There was also the fact that she'd written rather a lot about Ben in the diaries and if Louise decided to bring any of that up it could be embarrassing. There was a knock on the door at precisely three p.m.

"Come in."

"Nice of you to have security escort me up. It's almost like you don't trust me."

"Now why would that be?" Careen gestured to the sofa. "Take a seat."

"What, no coffee?"

"No."

Louise laughed as she sat down. "Not a social chit chat then?"

"How's your love life, Louise?" She pointed at Louise's eye, which although she'd tried hard with the makeup, was still swollen and purple. "Looks like things aren't going too well."

"Ah. You're digging into my life because I'm digging into yours." She touched her eye. "This. I ran into a door." She lowered her hand. "I suppose you think you have something on me. Enough to make me stop. Don't get too excited, Careen. No one's found enough dirt on me to date."

"Just asking because your friend Mitch asked me out last week."

After the note in the post box, Jill had done some digging into Louise's life. The "podcast predator" and "screwing around" mentioned in the note made sense when Jill discovered that "Mitch" had been seen with Louise. But she wasn't sure who was feeding who information and wanted to find out.

"You bitch."

"He's the one chasing me, not the other way around."

"And how do you know I haven't got him doing a little research for me?" Careen could see she'd momentarily thrown Louise, but she'd recovered quickly.

"Firstly, your reaction. You didn't know."

"And secondly?"

"Because he's using a different name with you. Mitch Browner."

"And you know him as?"

"Mitch Smithson."

"Really, Brown and Smith?"

"And Jonesate too. Your boyfriend, it appears, lacks imagination."

Louise sat quietly for a moment, smoothed the eyebrow above the black eye, considered her options. "What do you know about him?"

"You want me to fill you in so you can go back to him? Not likely." She opened the file on her lap, pretended to read it. Jill had suggested this tactic when she needed time to think about her next approach. "I take it he's the one feeding you information on me?"

"What makes you say that?"

"And I dare say he dropped off the box of goodies from my personal storage cage." Judging by the expression on Louise's face she was not aware of where the documents had come from but it appeared she had now made the connection – and a decision.

"Who is he really?"

"Michael Fisher. Brother of Tony Fisher."

"No shit?"

Careen had to laugh at the expression. "So you didn't know?"

"No. But it makes a bit more sense now."

"What does?"

"He said he'd help me research you and he seemed to know a lot about you, your history and all the other players. Information I couldn't get my hands on and there was no public record of."

"He's been at it a while. He dated my friend Mel in New York for a while just to get access to info on me." She'd decided to put it out there. If Louise confronted Michael, he'd probably give her everything he had anyway.

"Why's he got it in for you?"

Now she had to make a decision. If she aired Tony's dirty laundry, the fact that he had been stealing for his brother, she would be betraying John, and there would be no way to stop Louise from making it public. She pretended to scan the file again.

"Let's just say your boyfriend played a significant role in Tony's suicide and he decided to shift the blame to me."

"Now I'm intrigued."

"And being used."

"Yes. Well, that's how the game is played."

"Can I have my diaries back?"

"You do know I've copied them." She pulled the three notebooks out of her bag and handed them to Careen.

"I assumed you would."

Careen flicked through the pages, wondering what it would be like to read them again, perhaps it wouldn't be so bad to remember what it was like to be that young naive girl, just for a moment. As she flicked through the last notebook a piece of jigsaw fell out, landed on the floor beside her feet. She couldn't see the picture but the number three was clearly etched on the back.

Careen jerked her feet away, didn't want it touching her. "It's Michael," she whispered. "It's not the Clown. It's been Michael all along."

"What's Michael? Geez, Careen. You're pale as a ghost."

"The jigsaw piece that just fell out. Where did you get it?"

"It was in the diary. I figured it meant something to you. A part of your past."

"You have no idea."

"Then fill me in." Louise grabbed a notebook from her bag, clicked her pen. "All ready to go."

"You really are a piece of work."

"Yeah, yeah."

"Byron Bay."

"What the hell has that got to do with anything?"

"He's out now, you know. They guy who raped you." She hated doing this to anyone. Knew what it was like. But she needed Louise to understand what Michael was doing. She needed to turn Louise against him.

"He did his time." Louise's voice was low and cold.

"And how would you feel if he decided to revisit his old loves? Sit and watch you at a café, follow you down the street, tail your car. Spend time with you regardless of where you were or who you are with. Make sure you know he's there and that you are his for the taking."

Louise was deathly pale. "Why are you doing this?" she said in a squeak.

"Because that is what your boyfriend is doing to me. And you seem to think it's okay. That anything goes in the name of a good story."

"I don't understand."

Careen filled her in. Told Louise about the stalking, the jigsaw pieces, the Clown. Told her about her fear and the nightmares. Told her what it was like to relive it all over again.

"I didn't know, Careen. Honestly I didn't know." Louise was slumped back in the sofa, all her poise and cattiness gone.

"He's down to number three, Louise. When he gets to number one I think he's going to kill me."

"No!" Louise gasped.

"And that will make you an accessory to murder."

Louise grabbed at the side of the sofa. "My God."

"I need your help, Louise. I need to stop him."

THIRTY-THREE

Louise hadn't been much help. It turned out she didn't know much more about Michael than Mel seemed to. She did agree, however, to reconsider reworking some of the episodes in her podcast, but wouldn't make any promises not to include all the latest information; and she insisted that she wanted to be kept in the loop. Careen supposed that was the best she could hope for.

Careen had decided she wanted to see Tony. She needed the confirmation that it was him. Two days later, Logan, Ben and Careen were sitting in a car outside Princeton View Rest Home waiting for Michael to show. Careen wanted to talk to him, face to face.

"Flash joint," Logan quipped. "Must cost a few bob." He turned to Careen. "I feel like I'm on stakeout – *NCIS* – I'll be Anthony DiNozzo, you can be Ziva David and—"

"I'll be Gibbs," Ben finished for Logan. All three of them were avid *NCIS* fans and had recently binge-watched three seasons.

"More like McGee," Logan countered. "This waiting around is a pain. I thought your nurse said Michael always turns up at one p.m. sharp. I hope he doesn't suspect something."

"Why? What have you said to him?" Ben looked worried now.

"Thanks for the vote of confidence. In fact, I've only seen

him once since we hatched the plan and there were so many people at the bar we hardly spoke. He asked after Careen and I said I hadn't seen her for a few days. I asked him if he wanted me to smooth things over with you." He turned to Careen. "And said I would organise a dinner at my place and he could drop by. Said I'd try and tee something up for next week."

"There it is." Ben rolled his eyes.

"There what is?" Logan looked confused.

"The clue where you tell Michael something is up."

"What clue? What are you talking about?"

"You cooking – that's a dead giveaway. No one is likely to believe that for a minute." Ben grinned and Logan punched him.

"Guys. He's here," Careen interrupted.

"Hi, Ben." The nurse stood up, straightening her skirt and blushing furiously.

"Hi, Nicky. You are looking especially pretty today." Nicky's blush deepened and Logan rolled his eyes at Careen. "We're here to catch up with Tony and Michael – we just saw Michael come in. Is it okay if we go through?"

"You know I'm not meant to."

Ben reached up and gently tucked a stray hair behind her ear. "Please, Nicky, we won't be a moment."

Nicky looked torn. "Okay, because it's you. But these guys need to stay here."

"Actually I need them to come with me."

"Ben I can't."

"You go, Ben. We'll wait," Careen interrupted. "Logan, how about we go outside and wait. I saw a nice garden around the back. Okay with you, Ben?"

"What are you …?" Careen grabbed Logan's hand and squeezed it hard. "Ouch. What's up with …?"

"Good idea. See you shortly," Ben quickly interrupted Logan's outburst.

Nicky buzzed Ben through, and Careen and Logan strolled around to the rear of the building.

"What was that all about? We need to be in there," Logan said.

"And we will be, very shortly. Watch and learn, big brother."

They rounded the corner and sure enough Ben was there holding open the access door to the garden. The gardener was obviously on a break, he'd left his tools lying around. They'd got lucky with their timing.

"Very clever." Logan didn't sound impressed. "Where to hotshot?"

"Follow me – let's get this done."

Michael had his back to them as they entered the room, but Tony saw them. His eyes went wide and he started making all sorts of strange noises.

"What's up, mate?" Michael crouched down to Tony's eye level. "What's wrong?"

Tony was now gesturing wildly and Michael finally turned around. "I see." He turned back to Tony. "It's okay, mate. Nothing to worry about." He stood up, turning back to face Ben. "Why here? Why now?"

"It's the only place all five of us could be together," Ben said, taking the lead.

"And upsetting Tony, was that part of your plan? Look at him. Look what you've done." Michael's voice was low and even, not even ruffled. "You want to talk to me, let's go outside." He knelt down so he was at eye level with Tony again. "Hey, mate, just need to talk to these guys. I'll be back shortly." Michael stood up. "Outside. Now."

It appeared Michael also knew about the side door and that it didn't have an alarm. He headed out that way, with the others following. No one spoke but the silence was full of accusation.

"What the fuck do you think you are doing coming in here and upsetting Tony? He has nothing to do with this." Michael turned to them glaring, his fists balled tightly, his eyes flashing.

"To do with what?" Ben replied, his voice even, calm. He was holding Careen's hand and squeezed it to stop her speaking. He shot a look at Logan that very clearly said "silence". They needed answers and Logan or Careen getting fired up was not going to help.

"Very clever, painter boy. Get me to incriminate myself. I'm not that stupid."

"However, it appears you have been caught out so you are not as smart as you seem to think." Calm voice, even tone.

"Stay out of this. It's between me and her."

"The problem with that scenario is, that I am between her and you."

"Big words for a skinny guy."

"A skinny guy who pays for Tony's care, it seems. So I expect a few answers or I will cancel the trust and let's see how you fare taking care of Tony then."

This was a Ben that Careen hadn't seen before.

"You bastard. You owe him that, after all she did. That's his inheritance, not hers. You can't take it away."

Careen couldn't help herself; she stepped forward and poked Michael in the chest with her finger. "It's not his. He forfeited his rights when he stole from John. It tore out his heart. How dare you say he has any claim."

Michael grabbed her hand and pulled her up against him. "Stupid bitch. It was his by birthright. So what if he took a bit early on." His spittle rained on her face.

Careen struggled and Michael let her go, pushing her away

so she stumbled. Ben caught her before she fell.

"By birthright? What the hell is he talking about?" Logan turned to Ben. "What the hell haven't you told us?"

Ben let go of Careen and turned to face his friends. "Tony was convinced he was Dad's son. Dad had a fling with their mother and she told Tony that Dad was his father. Tony grew up with that. Believed it all his life. Started working at Montage to get to know Dad even more. Worked his way up – he was very good. One day he confronted Dad, told him that he knew he was his son. Dad said it was unlikely but he would agree to a DNA test. Tony refused. Said he knew Dad was his father and a test would prove nothing."

"He's your brother?" Logan looked at Ben, shocked.

"No, he's not. Tony's doctor was a friend of Dad's. Dad got him to run a blood test under some premise or other and ran the DNA without Tony's permission."

"Is that legal?"

"Probably not. Anyhow, it came back that Tony was not his son. End of story."

"End of story," Michael spat. "Is that how you see it? No blood-tie therefore you can write him off. Screw him over and throw him to the wolves." Michael gestured towards the home. "You saw what she did to him, her and her meddling ways."

"He stole, she proved it, he tried to kill himself in shame. How do you make that her fault?" Logan was getting fired up now. "If he hadn't stolen the money he would be living the high life now. He stole, his fault, his problem." He took a step towards Michael. "So leave my sister alone."

"You're all so tough, aren't you? Why don't you go in there and tell Tony he got what he deserved, sitting in a wheelchair dribbling for the rest of his life. She drove him to this. Couldn't keep her nose out of things that weren't her business. Couldn't keep her mouth shut. She wanted what Tony had – and she got it." He took a step towards Careen, his face blank, his eyes cold. "Are you happy now? Happy that you made him like this?" He gestured back towards the window of Tony's room. "Happy that you got the money, the hotels? You did this. You schemed and planned, then destroyed my brother. Coldly and deliberately took everything that was his. His inheritance. Arty boy here didn't want it but it was Tony's by rights."

"Tony screwed himself," Ben bit back. "He was the one who stole the money." And then it clicked. Ben stared at Michael. "It was you. You needed the money. Tony was earning a lot, he didn't need to steal, and he had the succession wrapped up. He did it for *you*."

"What the hell are you talking about?" Michael's fists were clenched and his face was like a mask, fixed in hate.

"He stole for you. I have a copy of the court records from your arrest. You were sent down for art fraud – a huge haul. Defence argued you owed a huge amount of money to lenders and they were squeezing. Defence said you only hocked the stolen paintings to fix the debt, as you were scared for your life. Your lawyer argued that you hadn't done it before and wouldn't do it again. Unfortunately, it wasn't the first time you'd been caught – you had forgotten to mention it to your lawyer – and you got sent away. But it was all a lie – Tony was paying off your debts. He stole for you and then he got caught."

"Caught. It was his money. He was going to inherit it all any way. At least he understands family," Michael justified in a low tone.

"Stealing is stealing. And from someone who trusts you like John did with Tony. That's just downright evil." Logan couldn't help himself.

"Don't you call my brother evil!" Michael spat.

"A spade is a spade," Logan quipped, oblivious to the violence brewing.

"Bastard." Michael pulled out a knife, lunged at Logan. "Bastard brother of a thieving bitch."

Logan dodged, the knife slicing the side of his arm. He yelped then threw a punch that glanced off Michael's shoulder. Michael turned and sprang towards Careen, but Logan was on him before he could get too close.

"No one hurts my sister. No one." Logan had Michael around the neck, pulling him backwards. Michael twisted, freed himself and charged at Careen, his knife out. Ben pulled Careen out of the way and kicked hard at Michael's knees. Michael grunted as he fell, the knife spinning away.

"You'll pay for this. All of you will pay."

He dove towards the knife.

"Like hell." Careen picked up the gardener's shovel and hit Michael over the head with it.

"Oh shit."

Ben, Logan and Careen stood next to Michael's prostrate form.

"I didn't kill him, did I?" Careen asked, not sure what she wanted the answer to be.

Michael groaned.

"Sorry, sis. You didn't get that lucky."

"What do we do now?"

"We walk away. He's alive. He's not going to report the attack. Let's just leave." Ben took Careen's hand and started to lead her away.

"Bastard." Logan gave Michael's ribs a solid kick before joining them.

"Wait." Careen walked back towards Michael. Crouched down so he could see her. "What do you want from me?"

"Everything you are and everything you ever hoped to be." Michael turned his head to face her directly. His smile was cold and unsettling, and she blanched at the madness in his eyes. "I got Quentin and I'll get you. Unfortunately, King John died while I was inside so I missed my chance there. But you schemed and plotted and you got everything. I want you to visit Tony and when you do look at him, really look at him. At what you did to him." The hate was tangible and Careen shivered involuntarily. "Yes, you should be scared, because there is nothing you can do to stop me. I have the money and I have the time. And, until I physically harm you, the cops won't do a thing." She took a step back as he levered himself up, a sneer on his face. "And your friend, Mel, she was so helpful. A wild cat in the sack too. Can't say I didn't enjoy that bit of research."

Logan drew back to kick Michael again, but Careen grabbed his arm. "He's not worth it, Logan."

"I'll kill the bastard," Logan hissed.

"Not before the Clown Killer gets that bitch sister of yours."

Careen froze. "You know the Clown Killer?" She heard the catch in her voice.

"We're like this." Michael crossed his fingers to indicate a close friendship. "Only two more pieces to go then ..." Michael sliced his finger across his throat. "Nighty night." Michael's laugh was cold and callous. "It's a long way from over."

"Jesus. What now?" Logan spoke first as they walked back to the car. All of them were quite shaken. "Not sure what happened or what we achieved there."

Ben placed his arm around Careen and pulled her closer. Careen pulled away and turned to him, her face weary, sad.

"Is there anything else you haven't shared with us, Ben? Any other secrets?" She looked straight at him. "You didn't think to mention the long lost brother, the court documents, and the trial. Anything else you might have kept back? Do you happen to know the Clown Killer too?"

"Careen. How can you think that?" Ben looked hurt. "I'm sorry I didn't tell you about Tony thinking he was Dad's son, but I didn't think it was relevant. I thought it was all ancient history. Dad only told me a few weeks before he died." He pleaded with Careen, "He told me that, but he didn't tell me Tony was still alive. I'm still processing all this too. There's so much history and I don't know what's relevant and what's not. I'm not deliberately holding anything back. You have to trust me." His voice shook. He reached for Careen's hand. "You have to believe me."

Careen stopped and stared at Ben, his hand reaching out to her. The Ben she'd been in love with most of her life. Her best friend. She had to believe in him or walk away – and that would be too hard, too lonely.

"I believe you, Ben." She stepped towards him and he pulled her into his arms. She rested her head on his chest and sighed as he kissed the top of her head.

"Okay you two lovebirds. Does anyone want to know how I am? Hurting, perhaps. I was the one that got cut." Careen and Ben continued to hold onto each other, but Careen turned her head towards Logan.

"Sorry, Logan. Are you okay?"

"Fine, thanks for asking." Logan inspected his arm. "It hurts but I don't think it's fatal."

"So where do we go from here? What did we actually learn?" asked Careen.

"We know it's him. We know why. He knows we know and..." Ben paused. "Actually that about sums it up."

"We know at least that he's been impersonating the Clown. That the Clown isn't actually back," Logan added.

"Are you sure? He said he knew the Clown Killer. Perhaps they are both in on this together. Perhaps he's still after me." Careen bit her lip to stop it trembling. "I'm scared, Logan." She let go of Ben and rubbed her arms to stop the chill she was feeling. "Really scared."

"It was Michael playing mind games, Careen. Nothing more." Logan asserted.

"Are you willing to bet my life on that?"

THIRTY-FOUR

"Hey sis. Can you buzz me up?"

"You're early Logan. Wasn't expecting you till half nine."

It had been a quiet ride home from the rest home the day before, each of them lost in their own thoughts. The one thing they'd all agreed on was that they needed to speak with Jill the next morning. They'd arranged to meet her at her office at ten.

"Just let me in."

Logan was not good at mornings but this seemed different. Wrong. She pushed the door release and went to unlock her front door and disable the alarms. She then busied herself making tea. She found the ritual soothing. But it was only Logan. Why did she feel she needed calming? It was the expression on Logan's face on the video screen. There was no impish smile and his posture was rigid. He was here without Ben. Had Michael got to Ben?

She heard the lift ding as it reached her floor. She opened the door. Waited. If it was bad news she didn't want to rush forward to get it. She gripped the doorframe until her knuckles were white. Logan walked out of the lift, saw her and smiled, a weak and watery smile.

"Is it Ben?" She took a deep breath to calm herself, to be ready.

"Ben. No. Ben's fine."

She let her breath out with a whoosh, let go of the doorframe and realised her legs weren't very steady. She stood briefly watching as Logan walked past her. His clothes were crumpled as if he'd just pulled on whatever was handy.

"Just tell me."

"I think you should sit down, Careen."

"That bad?"

"I wish it wasn't." Logan rubbed at his forehead. "Yes. It's bad."

Careen took a seat. "Okay."

"Louise was murdered last night."

Careen's mouth dropped open, her eyes widened. "How?" Her voice was low, breathless.

"She was killed at home. Her throat was slit and her arms placed at her side like she was resting peacefully. Just like the Clown used to leave them." Logan sat down beside her; grabbed her hand and squeezed. "Jill called Ben. He called me. I live closer. I could get here faster. We didn't want you to hear it on the news."

"Why didn't Jill just call me?"

"Careen, a piece of jigsaw was left on her body. It was number two."

Careen squeezed her eyes shut. Focused on the warmth of Logan's hand. She gasped for air.

"Careen, breathe," said Logan, sounding distressed.

She gasped again, got some air. "Was it him?"

"Which him? The Clown or Michael. Christ. I don't know, Careen. I don't know what to think."

Her intercom screeched and Careen almost leapt off the couch.

Logan squeezed her hand. "That'll be Ben. I'm out of my depth, Careen. I don't know what to do. I thought it'd be better if we were both with you."

"You think I'm next?" Careen backed herself further into the sofa. "Does Jill think I'm next? That he's coming for me now?"

Logan stood up and buzzed Ben in. Turned back to Careen. "She's at the office waiting for us now. I think it will be safer there."

Careen hadn't been ready to go when Logan arrived and she needed to get dressed. She pulled on her jeans and grabbed a t-shirt from the neatly aligned stack in her closet. Like that mattered. Everything in its place. Everything structured and tidy. It didn't make her safe. Nothing could make her safe. She threw the t-shirt on the floor and stomped on it. Jumped up and down and rubbed it into the carpet with her feet.

"Everything okay in there?"

Careen looked at the dishevelled t-shirt and sighed. There was no way she would wear it now. She pulled another t-shirt from the pile and slipped it on. If she was going to be killed she was damn well going to look good.

"Yeah. Just having a meltdown. Nothing to worry about."

"I'm coming in."

"Like hell you are. I'm not decent."

"I'll send Ben."

"No!" She pulled the t-shirt on, tied her hair back into a pony tail and slipped on some ballet flats.

"Let's go." She needed to get out of here. Louise was killed at home. She didn't want to be next.

"Do you think we pushed Michael over the edge?" Ben asked.

They were in Jill's office and explaining what had happened yesterday at the rest home.

"I don't know." Jill replied.

"Or was it me?" Careen whispered.

"What do you mean?"

"I met with Louise. Told her about Michael. Told her who

he was. *What* he was. What if she confronted him? What if he killed her because I spoke to her?" Careen's normally confident manner had deserted her. "Did I get her killed?"

"The only person responsible for Louise dying is the person who killed her." Jill's phone rang, interrupting her. "Sorry, I need to take this." Jill strode out the office, her high heels clacking on the wooden floors.

"I like her," Logan announced after she left the office.

"Based on what? You've only just met her." Careen knew he was trying to distract her and appreciated the thought.

"She's a PI. That is so cool. And she's one sexy lady."

"Logan, she is so not your type."

"I have a type?"

"Long legs, blonde hair, short on the grey matter."

"Not nice, sis. Samantha's got a certificate in something from somewhere."

"How lovely for her."

A message pinged on her phone. She ignored it. It pinged again. She didn't get a lot of messages and then usually they were from Ben or Logan. She opened the message. It was a photo of a note. A note written in black marker pen in capital letters. She knew who it was from.

"It's him, Ben." Her voice came out as a whisper. "The person giving me the clues. The one who writes just like him." She grabbed Ben's arm. "Why is he texting me now?"

Does he know that Michael killed Louise? Or maybe it wasn't Michael who killed her. She was holding out the phone, as far away from her as possible, as if by physically distancing herself from the message it wasn't there.

Ben grabbed the phone and read the message.

"It would be better if you shared it with us all," Jill said from the doorway.

"Truant foiled by tight-lipped trio," Ben read aloud.

"Another bloody riddle." Logan hated riddles.

"Any guesses?" Careen was shaking but her voice was steady.

"Another word for truant is mitch, as in mitch off school, skive off." Jill explained.

"Never heard of that one." Logan stood up and moved over to perch on the edge of Jill's desk.

"So Mitch is foiled by tight-lipped trio – who I assume is you three," Jill continued.

"Why tight-lipped?" Logan picked up Jill's paperknife and started twirling it around.

"I would assume that he would prefer us not to mention this message. A subtle threat perhaps." Jill turned to Logan. "Put that down and get off my desk."

"Yes, ma'am." He smiled and winked at Jill.

"Flirting, Logan. Now? Really?" Careen shook her head but she knew he was doing it deliberately, trying to lighten the mood. She could see his heart wasn't in it.

"Ben, you're very quiet. There's something else isn't there?"

"The profile photo." Ben hesitated. "It's a picture of a clown."

Careen didn't move. Didn't make a sound. It was as if she was watching herself from the outside. No emotion. No fear. Just clarity.

"Careen?" She could hear Jill but she was so far away.

"Careen?" Logan was shaking her now.

"Go easy, mate. She looks like she's in shock or something." Ben put his arms around her. "Hey, girl. Come on. Come back to us."

She snuggled into Ben's arms. She was safe here. No one could get to her. She stayed where she was, thinking about all the things that had happened, listing them in her head, categorising them.

She suddenly pulled away from Ben. "I need to reply to that message."

She grabbed the phone and spoke the words as she typed them.

"Why have you been helping me?"

The phone pinged again as the response came in. Careen read it aloud.

"Imitation is not a form of flattery."

She was right. It was him. The Clown was the person sending her the clues. Careen hit reply.

"Did you kill Louise?"

"She was trying to destroy you. You are mine."

Careen typed furiously. *"You left the jigsaw bit. Number two."*

"Jigsaws are not my MO." Came the reply.

"Am I next?" Careen needed to know.

"Ah, my Careen. You'll always be my first. My number one. You have a special place in my heart."

Her sweaty fingers flew over the phone keyboard. *"You didn't answer the question."*

"Are you next? I never said I killed Louise."

"But you did."

"Missing you already."

"Tell me." There was no reply.

"Tell me." She retyped. Still no response.

"No!" Careen screamed. "You can't just leave. You have to answer me."

"He can't hear you, Careen." Ben had pulled her close again. He removed the phone from her hand and passed it to Jill.

"He killed Louise. He admitted it," Careen said in a high-pitched voice. "He killed her." She turned to Jill. "You need to trace the message, the IP, whatever. You need to find him."

Jill quickly scanned the messages. "Actually, he didn't admit to anything." That didn't stop her picking up her mobile. "David. I need your help. Urgently." She gave her colleague a short and concise outline of what had happened and used

Careen's phone to send a copy of the messages to him. Careen could hear David barking orders at the other end. "Let me know," said Jill and she hung up.

"They'll try and trace it, but all he needs is an email address, which he can delete immediately, and access to a phone for the authentication. It's unlikely he'll have used his own phone or email address."

"You're kidding me?" Logan was incredulous. "All this high-tech equipment, surely they can find out where he is. Trace the account or something."

"It's not like on TV Logan."

Jill went to make everyone a cup of tea and handed them out on her return. Logan looked aghast at the herbal concoction she passed to him and Careen had to smile.

"I've had a call back from David," Jill said. "He's liaising with the appropriate division and has been in touch with Sergeant Lawson. Now we wait."

"Careen." Ben was shaking her.

"What?"

"You fell asleep."

She couldn't believe with all that was happening she could sleep. It had, however, been a good sleep. No dreams. No nightmares.

"And you snored too. Really loud," Logan added.

"Glad I haven't got a brother," Jill commented, coming in to her office from the corridor.

"But have you got a boyfriend?" Logan asked her.

"Logan!" Careen chided.

"Any news?" Ben asked Jill.

"It's more complicated than we thought. The police have Michael in custody for Louise's murder."

"But he didn't do it. The Clown did," Careen said, confused.

"Why do they think Michael killed her?"

"They found his fingerprints on the knife that was used."

Careen tried to process this new information. "She was killed in her apartment. Was it a kitchen knife?"

"Yes."

"Michael was sleeping with Louise. His prints are bound to be on the knife."

"Other than his prints the knife is clean."

"The Clown Killer never left a weapon behind."

"I know."

"They must have other evidence."

"As you know, they found a piece of jigsaw with her body. Number two. They traced it back to an online purchase Michael made a few months back. A special order for a clown-face jigsaw. They also found a number of fake IDs, which didn't help his case."

"Surely Michael has an alibi."

"He said he received a call from the Clown Killer. That the Clown Killer told him that he was impressed with the way he'd manipulated you. Apparently, he told Michael he wanted to work with him. Help him finish what he'd started. They set up a meeting in the park after dark to discuss their next move. Michael showed up but the Clown Killer didn't."

"He set him up?" Careen was incredulous. "But why?"

"Because you're his," Logan said. He was perched on Jill's desk again. "That's what he said in the message. 'You are mine.'"

THIRTY-FIVE

She felt as if she'd slept for a week and very nearly had. Either Ben or Logan, or both, had stayed in the spare room and made sure she ate between sleeps. Ben had used this time to go through the paperwork he'd glanced at, signed then filed when his father had passed away. In the papers John had explained why he'd chosen seven years for Careen to remain in the role of CEO. John believed that life should be re-evaluated every seven years to ensure it still had meaning. He had done this all his life and every seven years he had made the decision to continue in his role. John's letter stated, that in passing the inheritance to Careen, he was sure that she would feel bound to stay and would forsake any possibility of choosing her own life. He had therefore dictated that she must leave.

"So it had nothing to do with Tony." Ben explained.

"And everything to do with the fact that John thought I couldn't walk away on my own terms." Careen countered.

"Look Sis. We all know you've got this overdeveloped sense of obligation. You wouldn't leave. You'd battle on in John's memory and for Ben here who relies on the money."

"Relied on. Past tense." Ben corrected Logan.

"Whatever. What John did was the best thing. You can have a life now."

"I was quite happy with my life the way it was, thank you very much."

"Are you sure?" Logan winked at Ben. "Couldn't think of any improvements?"

She spoke with Jill a couple of times and Jill had advised her to listen to her body and rest. She had been through the wringer emotionally and she needed time to recover. Jill didn't believe she was in any danger but she had advised Careen to stay alert regardless.

Logan, who was on Careen duty today, had nipped out to get some groceries and she decided to use the time to Skype Mel. Mel had a right to know what had happened; she'd been part of the whole nightmare that had started twenty years ago. Mel had been quite flat since she'd realised she'd been used to hurt her best friend. Careen could see even Mel's work attire was sombre – grey and black – and she wasn't looking her best either. Video chat had its downsides.

"Michael has been officially charged with Louise's murder. They're sure they have a rock-solid case."

"And the Clown?"

"I don't know, Mel. I really don't know." Careen was still trying to process the fact that the Clown had been the one sending her clues to find Michael and she was sure he'd set up Michael for Louise's murder. She shuddered. What did he want from her? She knew he was a killer, so why did he seem to be protecting her?

"I'm so sorry, Careen. If I'd been with you that night in the car park this never would have started. Then giving Michael all those details. I seem to spend my life messing up yours."

"Hey. None of it is your fault. The car park happened. Michael used you to get to me. If it wasn't for me you'd have never been involved."

"It's not your—"

"Fault. I know that too. Let's just put it away. Forget about him. Forget about the Clown for now. I need my bouncy best mate back not this old sad sack."

"You're right. If I'm miserable, they win, and I'm lousy at miserable. It takes way too much energy." She forced out a laugh. "So what are your travel plans? Are you stopping by on your way to the world?"

"New York's the wrong direction. I'm thinking about Tanzania."

"What happened to Amalfi?"

"Not yet. It's all tied up in the last few months and I'm not ready for that yet."

"Okay, Tanzania it is."

"And only for a short trip. A holiday. I need to start small. It's a group tour. Safety in numbers."

"So spill."

"I'm going on a wilderness safari. Leaving next week." Careen laughed. It felt good. "Imagine me lying in a tent in the Serengeti listening to the snuffling of the warthogs as they push past the tent, the distant roar of lions and the sound of cheeky monkeys scampering over the canvas. Or that's what the brochure promises."

"Very poetic, I must say. But no fun if you're alone in your sleeping bag," Mel chimed in.

Careen blushed. Bowed her head so Mel wouldn't see. "So you have thought about it then?"

"About what?" She stared straight at Mel, all wide-eyed and innocent.

"Taking Ben with you on one of these jaunts, you goose."

Careen blushed again. "Must admit he did show up in one or two of my fantasies. But that's all they are. Fantasies."

"What about you two on the couch. Things got quite steamy as I recall."

"Yes they did, but we're just friends again."

"Why on earth would you do that?" Mel knew Careen had been pining for Ben for years.

"It's complicated."

"I've got all the time in the world."

Perhaps explaining it to Mel would help Careen sort it out in her head.

"Remember when you mentioned Stuart syndrome and I laughed it off. Perhaps you weren't so far off the mark. Ben seemed to relax more and more once I agreed to hand over Montage. Flirted more. Was around more."

"And that was a bad thing because?"

"Because I'm not sure I'm not just in love with the idea of being in love with Ben. I'm not sure he's Mr Right," Careen blurted out.

"Wow. A change of heart there. What brought that on?"

"I've had a lot of screwed-up relationships. Ben has been a constant throughout. He has always been there to pick up the pieces but never quite available. I think I've got used to that. I like having him around. If we get together and I screw it up he won't be there anymore."

"Careen, Ben knows you better than anyone else. The so-called screwed-up relationships were because of ... well, because of that night. Ben knows about that. It means he'll understand."

"And that's the problem. Can't you see it, Mel? He'll *understand*. I don't want understanding from a relationship. I want love, passion, excitement." She blushed then, remembering her and Ben on the couch. Plenty of passion there. "I need time to process everything that's happened. I have to learn to live with the fact that the Clown is still out there. I need to figure out what he wants. If he wanted me dead, I would be by now. I'm not. So what's next? Will he stay in contact? Do I have to be careful not to have a falling out with someone? What if Ben hurts me? Will the Clown hurt him? It's a lot to deal with."

"Blimey, girlfriend. What a lot to process. Any time you need a sounding board you know where I am." She blew Careen a kiss. "that's cos I can't hug you and I seriously want to."

"I'll take it as a hug."

"Good. Now tell me. What did Ben say when you told him?"

"Haven't had that conversation yet."

"Remember to call me when you have. I'd hate to miss the next episode."

THIRTY-SIX

It had been four weeks since Michael was arrested and the Clown had sent Careen the messages. They hadn't been able to secure a trace, and he'd made no contact since. Jill and Gordon, who was back doing desk work and grumbling constantly, were confident that the Clown had gone to ground again, that it was Michael impersonating him that made him surface at all. Careen wasn't so sure. How did he know what was happening in her life if he hadn't been watching? She pushed past her negative thoughts, nervous enough already about her lunch with Ben. She'd mapped out exactly what she was going to say, step by logical step. He'd understand, he'd see it was the right thing.

Ben was sitting at the outside table when she arrived. He'd been painting this morning, blues and purples judging by the look of his hair.

"Happy birthday, gorgeous." He stood up and enveloped her in his arms. She sighed and leant against him, feeling content for the first time in weeks. "So, what's so important you had to drag me away from my painting in the middle of the day? We do have your birthday dinner tonight with Logan and Jill in case you'd forgotten." He let her go, grinned at her, chucked her under the chin, then pulled out her chair with a flourish. "Be seated. I've ordered already. Hope you don't mind. I'm starving. Missed breakfast again."

"No. That's fine. What am I having?"

"Corn fritter stack with eggs and a side of bacon. Lots of sour cream and a touch of salsa."

"Sounds good."

"You're looking nervous. Should I be worried?"

"Ben." She took his hand across the table, looked him straight in the eyes.

"If you're thinking of breaking up with me, it's not happening."

"You do realise we're not actually going out together."

"I suppose that means you can't break up with me then." Ben grinned. "Come on, Careen. Perhaps our timing was a bit off, but you know as well as I do that we're good together."

Careen looked at Ben, the paint streaks in his hair, the crinkles around his mouth from hours spent pursing his lips as he concentrated on getting the colour just right. She saw the love in his hazel eyes. He knew the best of her, the worst of her, and he still wanted her.

"What made you think I was going to break up with you?"

Ben smirked.

"Not that we're in a relationship anyway," she backtracked and Ben laughed.

"Logan called. Said you've been miserable for the last few days, wandering around muttering to yourself. Practising some sort of speech."

"Logan needs to keep his thoughts to himself."

"Never going to happen."

"It's just ..."

"Just what, Careen? You and me. We're right. We both know that. Okay, it's taken me a while to figure it out. I've dated a lot of girls ..."

"You don't say."

"The thing is, none of them lasted because none of them were you."

"Ben."

"No. Let me finish." He stroked his thumb across the top of her hand. "You've always been so ambitious, so in control, so you, that I felt I wasn't quite good enough somehow." He held up his hand to stop her interrupting. "We *are* different. I might be untidy, disorganised and downright scruffy most of the time but I'm creative and I'm ambitious too. I love to paint and I'm lucky that because of you I can. The fact that you were supplying the money made me wary. I'm not the kept man sort of guy."

"But, Ben, it's your inheritance, not mine. It was always your money."

"I didn't earn it, Careen, you did. But now I am too. I'm doing well, it's given me the confidence to go after the only thing I ever wanted other than to paint. You."

Careen could feel the tears welling in her eyes. She smiled softly. "Why didn't you tell me?"

"Embarrassed I suppose. Never too sure how you felt about me."

"Seriously, I would have thought that was obvious to a blind man."

"You're good at hiding your emotions when you want to." He lifted her hand to his lips and kissed her knuckles. "Don't run away now. Let's both take a chance and see where we go from here."

"But what if it doesn't work? What if we can't be friends after?"

"What if it does? Do you want to spend the rest of your life wondering what if? I know I don't."

"Ben, what if you get sick of me? We break up. I'm hurting and the Clown knows. What if he hurts you?"

"You can't shut the world out because of him. That way he wins."

"But I couldn't bear it if he hurt you."

"So, you do care?" Ben grinned and kissed her knuckles again. "I want to be with you, Careen. I'm prepared to take my chances."

And she realised she was too.

Careen smiled as she headed home. Ben had kissed her as they left the café, and if she'd had any concerns about whether they could be more than friends, he had dispelled them. Wow. He'd gone back to his studio to catch the rest of the afternoon light and would pick her up later for her birthday dinner. She was already planning what to throw into an overnight bag. She had a feeling she wouldn't be making it home tonight.

"Happy Birthday, Miss Tamley." Lionel, the relief concierge, smiled as she walked in. "Someone left a card for you."

The glow that she was feeling from lunch with Ben disappeared instantly. She felt her blood run cold and her legs started to buckle; she grabbed the reception desk for support. No. It was meant to be over. He should be gone.

But he obviously wasn't, and if he'd left a card then he'd be watching. She was sure of that. So she took a deep breath, stood up straight and reached for the envelope, ripping open the top. Inside was a postcard and on one side there was a picture of a clown. Only it wasn't an evil clown, it was a smiling happy clown. Was it someone's idea of a joke? She turned it over.

Happy Birthday to my Number One.

Careen gulped down some air, steadied herself, kept reading.

I've never forgotten you — the one that got away. But I think it's time to let you go. You'll always have a special place in my heart.

It was signed simply, "CK". Careen glanced out through the glass doors, spotted a thin man in a dark coat and hat standing across the road watching her. She nodded at him. He saluted her, turned his back and strolled away.

PUZZLE ME DEAD

ACKNOWLEDGEMENTS

Thank you firstly to my husband Vin and son Stephen, who accepted my need to write and allowed me to lock myself away at times and forget about life. They gave me the space to write and dream.

For Dad, Mum, Joanne, Maureen, Brenda, Chris and Alan - my family who have never stopped believing in me.

A special thank you to my sister-in-law Chris Childs, a fellow author, who was never afraid to tell it like it is. To my beta readers Shaun Huntington and Maria Coleman, a big thank you for your feedback. For the members of the writing groups I have had the pleasure of being a part of – thank you for your constant support and honest feedback when I needed it the most.

In writing this book there have been so many people who have helped and supported me along the way – the journey has been frustrating at times but so much fun. To all of you who have been a part of this – thank you.

ABOUT THE AUTHOR

 Kathy Childs was born and raised in Wellington, New Zealand. After numerous careers in New Zealand, the UK and Australia, she founded a boutique hotel and long stay accommodation company based in Melbourne where she now resides. She studied Professional Writing and Editing at Victoria University where the foundations of this novel took shape. Kathy has had considerable success with her short stories. Puzzle Me Dead is her first novel.

www.kathychilds.com